NICK MOHAMMED has been a member of Bradford Magic Circle for eighteen years and in 2012 was made an Associate of the Inner Magic Circle. He is also a rising star in the comedy world, and is increasingly in demand as an actor and comedian. He is Mr Love in *Hank Zipzer* on CBBC and also appeared as Casper in *Absolutely Fabulous: The Movie*, as Tim Grimes in *The Martian* and as Ariyaratna in *Bridget Jones's Baby*.

Follow Nick on Twitter and Tumblr
@NickMohammed
#YoungMagicians

THE YOUNG MAGICIANS

AND THE
THIEVES' ALMANAC

NICK MOHAMMED

PUFFIN

PUFFIN BOOKS

UK | USA | Canada | Ireland | Australia
India | New Zealand | South Africa

Puffin Books is part of the Penguin Random House group of companies
whose addresses can be found at global.penguinrandomhouse.com.

www.penguin.co.uk
www.puffin.co.uk
www.ladybird.co.uk

First published 2017

001

Text copyright © Nick Mohammed, 2017
Illustrations copyright © Glenn Thomas, 2017

The moral right of the author and illustrator has been asserted

Set in 10.5/15.5pt Sabon LT Std
Typeset by Jouve (UK), Milton Keynes
Printed in Great Britain by Clays Ltd, St Ives plc

A CIP catalogue record for this book is available from the British Library

ISBN: 978-0-141-37699-8

All correspondence to:
Puffin Books
Penguin Random House Children's
80 Strand, London WC2R 0RL

MIX
Paper from
responsible sources
FSC www.fsc.org   FSC® C018179

Penguin Random House is committed to a
sustainable future for our business, our readers
and our planet. This book is made from Forest
Stewardship Council® certified paper.

To B, b, F and PD x

1

Euston, we have a problem . . .

The Magic Circle is a weird old place.

Weird and old.

Founded in 1905, the –

BORING!

Yeah, you've made your point!

Don't get me wrong, being weird can often be brilliant. But anyone who regularly fiddles with 52 bits of cardboard for at least four or five hours a day (more on weekends and bank holidays) has got to be the *tiniest* bit *odd*. And any society that bunches those like-minded people together even odder. (And don't even get me started on the card-fiddling stats for a magician over the Christmas holidays!)

I suppose magic and being a magician is just quite . . . *specific*, isn't it?

'What did you do today, magician?'

'Oh, not much – vanished a few doves, cut this lady I don't really know that well in half and made a long balloon into the shape of a poodle – you?'

'Oh, I just ate some lasagne – bye-bye.'

See what I mean?

None of it's real, either; it's all pretend. That's the other odd thing about magic: you can learn it in the same way that you learn the clarinet. It's merely a skill. But the whole point of magic is to make it seem like you *haven't* specially learned any particular skill in the first place. Magic is just meant to *happen* in the moment.

Not true for the clarinet, sadly. At no point when playing the clarinet do you want it to seem like you haven't specially learned the clarinet. Although for some players, despite their best intentions, it *can* still end up sounding like that – OUCH!

Anyway, magic is different from everything else. And I suppose this is one of the many unique things that make it, quite literally, *wonderful*.

Take eleven-year-old Harry, for example. Harry – OH HECK, WRONG BOOK!

Take thirteen-year-old Zack Harrison . . . Zack started learning the clarinet, but ended up preferring practising magic over practising the clarinet when he realized he was far better at wrapping the crusty school instrument in newspaper, bending it in half and then tearing away the paper – not only to show that the clarinet was fully restored but that it had also completely and utterly *vanished*.

Some quick info on Zack: he's a brilliant magician (see above); has a brain that works a bit differently to the rest of us; and can make *a-mazing* beans on toast. Oh, also has a tiny bit of a squint, which means he sees double when he looks to the right without turning his head, but only a trained optician would be able to spot it and so it's definitely not worth dwelling on here . . .

Yes, all right then, come on – so how *do* you vanish a clarinet?

Well, without giving too much away, the truth is . . . you don't! You see, a clarinet actually comes in several parts: the mouthpiece, the barrel, the first joint, the second joint and, finally (yawn, who's still with me?), the bell. So when Zack first covers the clarinet with the newspaper, we assume it's still there because we can see the mouthpiece and the bell poking out at either end. Now, this is where the human brain comes in handy. It makes sense for the brain to assume that the covered-up bit of the clarinet is still there because that's what we expect.

Magicians take advantage of things like this all the time.

In the smae way that we can still eiasly raed this setnecne, our brains often make some amazing decisions without us ever having to consciously think about them.

And so while our brains are busily filling in the clarinet gaps behind Zack's newspaper, the young magician is in fact stealthily removing the barrel, the first and the second joints, and stuffing them down the back of his trousers. (Yes, *that's* how much Zack thinks of the clarinet, Miss Tudor!) So, you

1.

2.

3.

see, sixty per cent of the vanishing clarinet has happened before we've even got any idea that something's up.

I'll let you figure out what Zack does with the remaining forty per cent of clarinet yourself to complete the vanish. Subtlest of tiniest clues: EDIBLE clarinet.

And what of the world-famous Magic Circle? Founded in 1905 – OH NO, NOT AGAIN! Basically it's a club where magicians can hang out. Turn right out of Euston Station, London, go past Sainsbury's, cross the road (zebra crossings, please), turn left on to Stephenson Way and go round the corner, and it's there on the right – you can't miss it. (Well, you *can* actually, but if you get to the Royal Society of Horticulture you've gone too far. Or are completely lost.)

And Euston Station is exactly where we find Zack Harrison right now (1.45 p.m., Monday 22 October – GPS coordinates 51.5284° N, 0.1331° W for the map enthusiasts reading this – SHOUT OUT TO YOU LOT!).

But Zack isn't the only one on his way to the Magic Circle headquarters this afternoon. Yep, that tall boy several metres behind him, clambering up the escalator three steps at a time owing to his terrifically gangly legs, is Jonny Haigh, Zack's best friend.

A few little stats on Jonny too then . . . Tallest boy in his class/his school/the universe – which he likes to remind Zack of *constantly*; has only recently got into magic, partly through Zack but also because his granddad, Ernest, is something of a legend in the Magic Circle. Used to be able to hit all the high notes in *Les Misérables*, but now that his voice has dropped only does this in STRICT privacy.

Behind Jonny? Well – it's not really relevant, but I might as well mention it as I'm here . . . There's a bunch of pigeons kind of just hanging out. Not in a suspicious way, just sort of really chilled and enjoying the train-station vibe. Anyway, let's ignore them for now and get back to talking about *human beings*, shall we?

Ah yes, next is Sophie Yang. Jonny's just accidentally barged past her on the escalator while attempting his world record for the speediest ascent. She's not impressed, if that look is anything to go by. Perhaps she would be if she knew that she and Jonny were about to become great friends. We'll be seeing

Sophie in action very shortly, but all you need to know for now is that she's from the North of England, can name all the lakes in the Lake District in ANY order, and is staggeringly brilliant at a branch of magic known as 'mentalism' (feel free to consult the Glossary at the back of this book, by the way – it's riddled with both necessary and unnecessary information – like 'What Is a Mentalist'). BACK TO BUSINESS . . .

And behind Sophie? Well, the pigeons have just migrated a notch south, which is annoying. Perhaps they could remain where they are just until the end of this chapter – what do you say, make my job a bit easier? Thanks, birds!

Ah yes, so on to our final young magician. He's shyer than the others – hence why he presently has his face hidden behind a well-thumbed edition of *Expert Card Technique*. *Ladies and gentlemen, please welcome, live at Euston Station concourse, with his impeccably neat side parting . . . It's ALEX FINLEY!* Alex is a one of a kind. Doesn't say much, not a huge fan of social interaction, and consequently isn't much of a performer, but, Lordy Lord, you should see what he can do with a deck of cards in his bedroom when the door is closed. When Alex handles a pack, it's like they come *alive*. Not bad for a twelve-year-old who wouldn't say boo to a goose. (Though, to be fair, I'm *ancient* compared to Alex and I've still never said the word 'boo' at – or even close to – a goose. I will of course now make this one of my life's ambitions and keep you posted.)

So that's our four. Our fantastic four. Our glorious gang. Our quality quartet. Our prestigious protagonists. Probably about time we see them in action – yes?

YES!

(Don't worry, I'll be back at various points, whether useful or not. See you soon!)

Zack approached the barriers at Euston Station, reaching into his pocket for his ticket. His hand emerged empty. 'Oh, not again!' he muttered, just loud enough to attract the attention of the nearby guard who looked awfully like a bird of prey with his beaky nose and needlessly long nails.

'Having some trouble finding your ticket, young sir?' the guard announced loudly, as if trying to justify his job. He came over.

Zack's eyes flashed as the man smugly printed off a fresh ticket and wafted it temptingly in his right hand, as if reminding Zack what such a ticket might look like. 'Yeah, I think I might have lost it,' Zack said. 'I'm sure I had it a second ago, but . . .'

The guard closed his eyes and took a deep breath. 'If you don't have a ticket, then I can't let you through the barriers. You have to purchase a new ticket from me, your helpful guard. Plus there will be a fine,' he added with relish, opening his eyes and flexing his nostrils.

'Oh, you're kidding! Really?' protested Zack. 'It must have fallen out of my pocket while I was asleep.'

The guard cocked his head like a duck might when approaching a canal lock, figuring out what best to do.

Zack watched him place the freshly printed ticket in his inner left jacket pocket.

'Is there a problem here?' interrupted the ticket guard's boss, coming over briskly. (Zack could tell the lady was his boss by the way she kept retching every time their eyes met.)

The guard straightened himself up, trying to impress, accidentally pouting in the process.

'Er . . . not at all, Mrs Mann,' he chirped wetly. 'Everything is in hand.'

Mrs Mann looked at the guard as if he'd just admitted he was made of potatoes. 'Just do your job, Frank,' she spewed at him before heading over to a pack of attractive – and clearly lost – male tourists.

Zack waited until she was out of earshot before turning to face the guard again. 'Listen, Frank – do you mind if I call you Frank? – I know I'm *technically* meant to have a ticket, but it's not like I didn't buy one. I've just misplaced it. Is there any way you can let me through . . . just this once?'

Zack gave one of his infamous cheeky grins and ran a hand through his thick hair.

The guard waited, staring at Zack's sparkling teeth for a whole ten seconds before saying, 'If you think grinning at me is going to help you get through these barriers then you're more of a maniac than I am. I've been working at this station for fifteen years; I've never been promoted; I hate my job and life in general. I'm in fact married to Mrs

Mann over there, who's evidently looking for another beau in her life; I've no kids by choice and have a sciatic nerve which gives me chronic back ache pretty much twenty-four/seven. I've never taken a day off and one of my few pleasures is fining my fellow human beings, especially children – so no, I can't *let you through, just this once . . . young sir.*'

Zack sighed, his grin downsizing by about twenty per cent.

'So, what'll it be? Shall we start playing by the rules?'

Zack shifted his weight before showing off his dazzling white teeth once more. 'Oh, absolutely not!' And with that he placed the fresh ticket he'd secretly lifted from Frank's inner left jacket pocket mere moments ago into the machine and waltzed out towards the glorious sunshine – just as an announcement came over the tannoy about how pickpockets operate at this station.

Frank.

Oh, but things were only just starting to go wrong for dear old Frank . . .

Jonny approached the barriers next, immediately attracting the guard's attention, not just because of his remarkable height but because he was also walking with his arms raised – which made him look not only taller but also somewhat insane.

Jonny looked around as he continued towards the barriers, clearly – brazenly – ticketless. He loved train stations; he loved the mix of science, technology and people – in fact, it was one of the many things he loved about living in London: busy bustling places that felt like the start of new adventures, always brimming with life, constantly surprising and – Ouch! Mind where you're going with that wheelie case, lady!

As Jonny approached, Frank's lower jaw began to twitch, excited at the prospect of administering more fines and speaking with authority to minors. But, to his horror, as the boy drew close, without even a whiff of a ticket, the barriers wafted open – as if he was some magnificent superhero.*

Frank felt decidedly queasy. What was going on today? Just as he was thinking of spending a while in the station toilet for some peace and quiet, he spotted a girl heading straight for him, her eyes seemingly glued to a map of London. Frank was resolute ... *Right, I've had enough of kids for one afternoon – this one is getting a fine,* he thought. *I don't care what excuses she has. Even if she has a valid ticket, she's getting a fine. Even if she invented the steam train, this silly little girl is getting a fine!* – which was an odd thing for Frank to think because he knew full well that the steam train had been invented by a man so old he

---

* Sorry to intrude, dear reader, but just to clarify – as much as Jonny would like to think of himself as a superhero, this stunt was pulled off by sewing into the lining of his coat a power magnet which, when he lifted his arms, triggered the barrier's electromagnetic circuit. Along with voiding any credit or debit cards in the immediate vicinity, no doubt – good luck with buying all those casserole ingredients for supper tonight, Frank! As you were ...

was now *dead*. Frank readied himself, beefing up his chest, accidentally pouting again . . .

The girl – Sophie, remember her? – came over, immediately locking eyes with Frank and surprising him by suddenly offering her right hand. Without thinking, Frank held out his own hand in response. But just as he did so, Sophie withdrew hers, quickly taking his wrist with both her hands and moving his arm up towards his forehead.

In performing this odd manoeuvre – successfully confusing the conscious part of Frank's brain – Sophie had achieved everything she wanted: access to his subconscious. (Well, it's something Sophie wanted right at this very moment . . . The rest of the time Frank was free to do with his subconscious as he liked. Such as thinking about ways of punishing ticketless children and destroying Mrs Mann.)

Sophie spoke firmly, not breaking eye contact. 'What is it you're not thinking about?'

Frank's eyes flickered in confusion as she continued her hypnotic induction. 'You were just about to let me through the barriers.'

And then, just like one of those dogs on talent shows that do things their owner says and then get given £250,000, along with a brief appearance on *The Royal Variety Performance*, Frank popped open the barriers like a good little pup.

Sophie made her way out into the sunshine, delighted. She always took an extra-special pride in her first successful hypnotic induction of the day. She consulted her map again. *On to Stephenson Way.*

Frank blinked back to reality. What had just happened? He looked past the barriers, searching for the girl, searching for answers. 'What is happening today?' he said out loud, causing Mrs Mann to look round from her flirty tourists, annoyed at the interruption.

Frank went back to his post, tired. *Just six more hours to go*, he thought depressingly.

Alex approached the barriers next, his head lost in a book almost twice his size. Not that he was particularly bookish; more that this was his way of avoiding eye contact. And if it also meant catching up on how to achieve the perfect pressure fan with a deck of playing cards, then so be it! He had made this journey several times before – often simply to get a break from his parents in Kings Langley, heading straight back home on the next return train – so he knew the station well.

Spotting Alex immediately, Frank inhaled deeply while clenching his buttocks – something (he had read somewhere) that helped focus the mind.

The boy reached into his pocket, bringing out a ticket – beautifully valid, as far as Frank could tell.

Without averting his eyes from the pages of *Expert Card Technique*, Alex fed his ticket into the ticket entry point (as Frank had learned to call it during his training several glaciations ago). The barriers opened smoothly, perfectly, allowing him to pass through.

Alex retrieved the used ticket on the other side.

Frank breathed a sigh of relief, relaxing his bum cheeks. *Finally some normality*, he thought.

But Alex had not yet disposed of his ticket. With the tiniest flick of his wrist, he tossed the ticket into the air, spinning it into a blur. Frank eyeballed it suspiciously as – with the determination of a really angry bee – the blur began to approach.

'No, no, no, you can't reach me from there,' Frank muttered, increasingly concerned. 'Surely not . . .' Closer and closer it came towards him, so fast he could now feel its fan-like breeze on his face. He wanted to blink, he wanted to flinch, but that would be giving in. 'No, stand your ground, Frank, it's all going to be just fine. It's not going to get you on the nose.'

But just as his brain processed that very thought, the ticket nipped him on the nose, forcing Frank to cry out like a tiny baby and causing our gang of pigeons (remember them?!) to fly up naively into the sunlit strewn glass roof of Euston Station, only to come hurtling back down again, instantly regretting the benefits of being indoors.*

---

* Oh, and by the way, we will never hear from Frank again, so I hope you enjoyed his brief appearance. He did eventually get home that evening, casserole ingredients in hand, but ended up rowing with Mrs Mann so loudly that the neighbours called the police. He now faces a huge court hearing for chopping off Mrs Mann's head. And so, yes, it's very unlikely we'll be meeting Frank again unless we happen across him in jail, where – sadly – this story doesn't take us . . . I don't think . . .

2

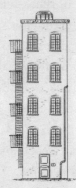

Zack, Jonny and Sophie had arrived outside the Magic Circle headquarters. Staggered, to be precise, at intervals of about ten seconds. But they had made it. They were here! This was the place where a woman was first sawn in half (legally). This was the place where a man named Ali Bongo could appear without anyone batting an eyelid or asking him how to spell it. This was the place where every single piece of literature ever written about magic (including how to turn a handkerchief into an egg) was kept, catalogued and studied. Yes, this was THE Magic Circle: a place of secrets, intrigue and utter wonderment, a place of –

'Is this really it?' asked Sophie.

Jonny and Zack turned round to face the quirky-looking girl, her hair all shaved at the sides. She stared at the rather boring blue door, her eyebrows raised as she shifted her rucksack and put her map away.

'You *do* know what building this is, right?'

Sophie grinned. 'Yes, thank you, *Zack Harrison*, I do know what this building is! This is the world-famous headquarters of the Magic Circle.'

'Did you just read that?' Zack pointed to a small wooden plaque that boasted the society name in bold lettering.

'Ha – might have!' said Sophie, extending her hand. 'Sophie Yang.'

'Zack H–'

'Hang on a minute!' interrupted Jonny, batting his friend's hand away from Sophie's. 'How did you know his name was Zack Harrison?'

Zack gawped at Sophie. 'Yeah, hang on a minute – have we met before?'

'In your dreams, mate!'

'Then how?'

'Well . . . Have either of you read any of Corinda's books on mentalism?' Sophie asked.

Zack and Jonny both shrugged.

'Good, because it's not relevant,' she joked. 'What *is* relevant is that your name is splashed across the back of your rucksack in thick marker pen and I've been staring at it ever since I left Euston Station.'

Zack and Jonny burst out laughing. 'Oh, *now* I feel stupid!' said Zack finally, shaking her hand firmly up and down.

'I take it you're both here for the induction week too . . . Exciting, isn't it?'

Zack threw Jonny a tiny look which – given that Sophie had already demonstrated just how perceptive she was – was easily spotted.

'We are, yes,' answered Jonny immediately. 'Do you know what you might do in your audition at the end of the week?'

'Think so.' Sophie played with what was left of her fringe, moulding the strands into a series of peaks. 'I'll probably do some hypnosis stuff, maybe some mind-reading and then finish with a –'

'Whoa, hang on. Wait a flipping second!' interrupted Jonny, his eyes gleaming. 'You do hypnosis? *Cooooooooooo-oooooooooooooooooooooooooooooooooooooooooooooooooooooool!*'

17

'Sure! What about you?' Sophie looked up at him. 'Got *your* routine sorted?'

'Well, I'm still quite new to it,' explained Jonny, rummaging around in his bag haphazardly and bringing out a set of linking rings, which had somehow miraculously joined together. 'But my granddad has already taught me how to do this!' He held the rings aloft proudly, though secretly at a loss as to how they'd managed to link together *in his bag* . . . There *must* be a gap in them somewhere!

'What about you, Zack?' asked Sophie, her eyes meeting his.

'Oh . . . Well, I'm pretty good at pickpocketing . . . But . . . But I don't know if I'll be allowed to do that . . .' He trailed off, looking uncomfortably over Sophie's shoulder.

Well, if this isn't the behaviour of someone hiding something, she thought, *I don't know what is!*

Alex approached them tentatively, his face peeping over the top of some strange chapter on false deals, his cheeks already beginning to flush as they turned to face him.

'Hi!' Zack smiled at the blond, bespectacled boy. 'You OK?'

Alex's heart began to pound. Why did people always feel the need to talk to him? Couldn't they just leave him alone? He took a deep breath and thought about something unrelated to calm his nerves (sweetcorn, in this instance), just like he'd been advised by the 'doctor' his parents had taken him to see last year.

Deep breaths, Alex . . . Corn on the cob . . . Chicken and sweetcorn soup . . .

'Is . . . is this the Ma–?' Alex began.

'Yes!' the other three chimed like an over-zealous pop group.

'What's your name?' asked Sophie, offering her hand.

Alex stared at the girl's arm, clearly wary. 'I . . . I saw what you did . . . to the guard . . . at the station,' he managed.

Sophie faltered slightly (there's a first time for everything). 'Ah. I see! Well, I promise I'm not going to do that to you.' And she took Alex's hand and gave it the most normal shake in the world. 'Sophie Yang.'

'A-Alex Finley,' he said shyly.

'Well, it's great to meet you, Alex Finley,' said Jonny cheerfully. 'I'm Jonny and this is Zack. Now, Sophie, what *did* you do to the guard?' he added, increasingly captivated by this girl.

'I was just practising!' She held up her hands innocently. 'Just a basic handshake induction – he fell for it beautifully, though!'

'Hey, Alex, don't be nervous,' said Zack, remembering how anxious he'd been the first time he came to the Magic Circle. 'Everyone in this building loves magic, remember.'

'Have you been here before, then?' asked Alex, daring a quick look up at Zack.

'Oh, well, erm . . .' Zack trailed off, sending Sophie's Sherlock radar into a spin again.

'Ooh!' said Jonny quickly, catching Zack's eye and then changing the subject, causing Sophie to raise her eyebrows yet again. 'What are you reading?'

'Erm . . . *Expert Card Technique*,' Alex mumbled, showing them the cover.

'By Hugard and Brau?' Sophie whistled. That was some complicated card magic. 'Wow, you must be pretty good!'

Alex went a shade of dusty pink as Jonny patted him on the head, which wasn't as patronizing as it sounds, more just convenient, given the difference in height. Jonny had never even heard of Hugard and Brau.

'Will you show us something before we go in?' asked Zack, always keen to watch a fellow practitioner of magic at work.

Alex was immediately suspicious, taking a couple of steps back. Surely this was some kind of joke . . . No one ever asked him to show them a trick unless it was a ruse to bash the playing cards out of his hands and all over the school playground. Hell, no one ever even *spoke* to him most of the time. But here were three people he'd just met who seemed excited by the prospect of him showing them something. Three people who – quite possibly – maybe even *liked* him.

He gingerly reached into his pocket, removing a brand-new deck of Bicycle playing cards. Brand new because Alex usually got through approximately one deck per week – more if he'd been practising lots, which was often the case recently. Sometimes he'd overhear his parents complaining about it – not so much because of the cost, but because they would far rather he spent his pocket money on sports magazines or computer games like their friends' 'normal' children did.

20

Alex stretched his fingers, slowly removing the cards from their case, handling them expertly, as if they were an extension of his self. With the cards in his left hand (dealer's grip), he placed his right thumb over the top of the deck, making a *swoosh* as he spread them into a perfect arc (pressure fan).

Sophie, Jonny and Zack gawped. Wow, this guy sure knew his stuff: that was no easy move!

Alex held the beautiful fan of cards towards them, pleased that the flourish had worked out as planned. 'Pick . . . Pick a c–'

But just as Alex most likely went to say the word 'card' he was interrupted by the creaking of the blue door as it slowly, majestically began to open.

They all shifted their eyes to the entrance of the Magic Circle headquarters, wondering what might be the first thing they saw.

A man in top hat and tails, thought Sophie, thinking of the countless pictures she'd seen in books and magazines.

Someone our age, Zack hoped.

Granddad, perhaps, thought Jonny.

Some resident bully, worried Alex, his mind suddenly starting to race as he hastily put his cards away.

No.

It was a lady in her early sixties whose glasses hung on a chain just below her bosom and which bounced about like they were trying to get away.

3

The woman with the bouncy glasses stared at the four down the bridge of her nose, smiling, clapping her hands together enthusiastically. 'Welcome, welcome!' said Cynthia (for that, indeed, was her name). 'Now then, you're our final four. Who have we got?' She brought out a clipboard covered in star stickers and a pen that looked like a magic wand.

'OK, so we've got Zack Harrison ...' she said hastily, ticking him off her list without looking up. 'And you must be Jonny – ah yes, the spitting image of your grandfather, I see. He said you might finally be joining us!'

Sophie looked up at the tall boy. Who *was* this grandfather of his that everyone seemed to be banging on about?

'Which means you must be Alex Finley,' Cynthia carried on breezily. 'Chin up, please. Smiles cost nothing, remember! And *you*, my girl, must be Sophie Yang. How nice to have another lady in our midst. Deanna will be delighted!'

All four smiled and nodded politely, not quite knowing what to make of this lady who – despite the fact she was wearing a baggy jumper with bunnies and top hats on – was undoubtedly good-hearted.

'OK, well, follow me, please – the others have already arrived – very busy today.' Cynthia spun round all of a sudden and disappeared into the darkened entranceway.

Sophie and Jonny grinned at each other as they followed. Zack hung back to let them pass, giving Alex (who was clearly already having second thoughts, judging by the look on his face) a small nudge forward.

Here we go, thought Alex, for this was arguably one of the bravest things he'd ever done.

On the other side of the blue door, Sophie's eyes slowly adjusted to the light. Ahead of them, she could just about make out a long corridor lined with framed, cracked posters, many of which hadn't been dusted in – well – since the music-hall era whence they'd been put up (and whence people still used words like 'whence'). This was what she'd been waiting for: she was finally inside the *actual* Magic Circle.

Zack closed the door behind them, darkening the entranceway further and causing Alex to grab hold of the nearest thing to him (an ornamental death mask of Houdini fixed to a plinth in this instance. Which didn't help).

The wooden floorboards moaned as Cynthia bustled down the corridor calling out after them. 'Our Hall of Fame!' She waved her arms towards several black-and-white photos of men doing horrendous things to women in leotards and sequins but who still beamed regardless. 'Pay attention and you might find yourselves up here one day!'

'Yeah, in about a thousand years!' Zack joked from the back.

Cynthia stopped, momentarily flustered. 'What was that, Zack? Did you say something?'

Zack shook his head innocently, eyes wide. 'No, nothing,' he said. 'I was just . . . I just sneezed.'

Cynthia took a moment before hurrying on; Zack grinned at the others as soon as her back was turned.

Jonny soaked up the heavy, hundred-year-old atmosphere, remembering how his granddad had described the Magic Circle to him when he was very young. He'd not paid much attention back then – preferring to dabble with his chemistry set over his magic set – but this was *exactly* how Jonny had come to picture the place. I mean, it even *smelled* a bit like his granddad!

'Oh, now, do watch out for these as well, please.' Cynthia nudged a mousetrap with her left foot, accidentally setting it off with a clatter. 'Oh Mary Christmas, not again!' she exclaimed. 'Yes, well, so don't do that basically . . .'

Alex kept his eyes firmly on the floor, watching where he stepped. He hadn't expected the Magic Circle to look and feel quite like *this*. This was more like the entrance to some Chamber of Horrors!

Eventually Cynthia came to a stop beside a garish baby-pink door, the paint peeling at the edges.

The others arrived in line behind her, Alex now sandwiched between Jonny and Zack.

'Well, here we are!' said Cynthia. 'This is the Junior Room – I think you're going to feel right at home!' She opened the door and stepped to one side.

Sophie, Jonny, Alex and Zack peered inside. Compared to the cramped corridor, this room was surprisingly large and bright, and had the distinct smell of some rosy air freshener desperately trying (and failing) to mask the smell of something rotting. There were plastic chairs; a few tables covered in green felt; a raised stage area at the front; and – oddly – a few crash mats, which brought with them their own particular whiff.

It all kind of reminded Sophie of the musty church hall where she once attended Brownies. (Just the once because she was never allowed back after hypnotizing Brown Owl into thinking all the other girls were jellyfish.)

In one corner of the room, Alex could see a lad fiddling with some marked playing cards while devouring what can only be described as a giant's giant-sized Mars bar, leaving brown, chocolaty residue on everything he touched. Alex averted his eyes as the boy attempted a grubby double lift, not realizing that pretty much his entire deck was now stuck together and resembled a kind of dirty lasagne.

Sat around another table Jonny spied a group of posh-looking boys with slick hair, big foreheads and too many teeth, like they'd come to a fancy-dress party dressed as businessmen, but these were their actual clothes. All of them were taking it in turns to present the contents of their shiny briefcases rammed full of expensive shop-bought tricks.

Sitting by one of the other tables, Sophie watched a girl who looked as if she had been reluctantly entered into a beauty pageant. *Deanna*, thought Sophie, remembering what Cynthia had said earlier. *I wonder what she's like?*

Deanna suddenly began prancing about as tinny RnB screeched out of her unnecessarily bling phone. As far as Sophie could tell, Deanna was trying to vanish a handkerchief using a thumb tip – along with blatantly trying to get everyone's attention – but the trick was totally overshadowed by the constant and exuberant 'dance' moves that Deanna had chosen to perform (including two lots of the splits, some body-popping and five forward rolls in the direction of the posh boys who – to their credit – paid her no attention whatsoever).

The music came to an abrupt end as Deanna attempted to bend right back into a crab. Sadly, despite her great efforts and not quite having the core strength, she collapsed in a mangled, crabby, panting heap and instantly burst into tears. Immediately her mother* crashed over, showering

---

* At least, Sophie assumed this lady was Deanna's mother ... She looked like a slightly stretched, melted and then re-formed version of Deanna and was dressed exactly the same (though, perhaps rather optimistically, in the same-sized clothing too), so Sophie figured – even without employing her Sherlock Holmes-style powers of deduction – that this was a pretty reasonable guess.

26

Deanna with false praise about how astounded she was by the trick (although, if truth be told, the handkerchief had only vanished because Deanna's mother was now sitting on it).

At the far end of the room, alone, on the raised stage area, stood a serious-looking figure, his face obscured by a theatrical gothic mask, dressed all in black and holding a single red rose.

Zack stared as this young magician slowly and deliberately unfurled his fingers from the stem of the rose and withdrew his hand. The rose remained there, motionless, hanging in the air, completely unsupported. It was brilliant, beautiful magic. Zack looked for the thread but couldn't see it.

All of a sudden Zack became aware that this masked magician was now looking at him, causing him to step back into the dim corridor involuntarily, treading on Jonny's long toes in the process. Without averting his sinister gaze, the conjuror set fire to the base of the rose. It flared up in a flash of white light before vanishing completely. The young magician removed his mask, revealing a large face, still eyeballing Zack.

Henry.

'Well, come on then – we haven't got all day!' Cynthia bustled into the room, pushing the four newcomers forward into plain sight. 'I think that's finally everyone here.'

Slowly all the other faces turned towards Zack, Jonny, Alex and Sophie.

Alex could hear his heart beating in his ears as the eyes of the room bore into him. At least it was Zack, Jonny and Sophie he'd bumped into outside the blue door, he thought reassuringly. If it had been any of these others, he would have turned and got the train straight back to Kings Langley.

It was Deanna who broke Alex's train of thought. 'A girl!' she screamed, pointing a reddened finger at Sophie and starting to whack her mother in the chest. 'You told me I was the only girl magician in the whole *world*!'

Quick as a flash, Deanna's mother wrestled her daughter to the ground, eventually opting to sit on her back as the best way of calming her down. 'Don't worry, love,' she said to Sophie as the four shuffled past her towards a table at the back of the room. 'She'll get tired of struggling in a bit!'

That's encouraging! thought Sophie.

Zack watched out of the corner of his eye as Henry continued to glower at him. This really was turning out to be some welcome!

'So then, greetings, everyone, and welcome to this Magic Circle induction week – your gateway to becoming a successful, professional magician,' began Cynthia, moving towards the stage. 'I see you've already formed your own little groups, but it's important that we *all* get to know each other so that we can share our ideas, so I'll be mixing things up a bit throughout the week.'

Jonny looked over at Zack, grimacing, and Alex gulped.

'No prizes for guessing who Deanna might get paired up with!' Sophie whispered in Jonny's ear with a sizeable wince.

'Now, as you know from your information packs,' Cynthia continued, 'on Thursday evening there will be an audition in front of the Magic Circle Council to determine whether you can be fully enrolled as a young magician and have access to this room. Of course, full membership – along with access to the Magic Circle library, entry to the annual convention, the stage competitions, the lecture hall and the dealer demonstrations – is not permitted until you reach eighteen.'*

Zack, Jonny, Sophie and Alex looked at each other, all thinking the same ... *So what – apart from this smelly room – do we have access to?*

'Anyhow –' Cynthia's eyes lingered on Zack for a split second – 'as some of you may know, Henry and Deanna were the first juniors to be successfully inducted last spring, and they will help guide you through the process this week, should any of you require particular assistance.'

Oh, wow, thought Sophie. So that girl was technically her *tutor*?

Just at that moment, a man with a face the colour of a glass of neat blackcurrant squash came rushing into the

---

* Do feel free to wander into the Appendices at the back for more information on the Magic Circle hierarchy – I BET YOU CAN'T WAIT!

room, breathless and bleeding sweat into his smart dark-blue suit (possibly only *dark* blue because of the sweat). He had large dimples in his cheeks even though he wasn't smiling.

'What the hell was all that racket?' shouted the man, making a pretty sizeable racket himself, his eyes darting about the room like a distressed schoolboy.

'Oh, nothing ... Nothing to worry about, darling,' said Cynthia soothingly, going over to him. 'Deanna was just having another one of her ... moments.'

'*Sorry!*' Deanna's mother mouthed exaggeratedly, as underneath her daughter tried to resist the urge to slip into a coma from the sheer weight of her mother pressing down on her spinal column.

The man looked at Deanna, squashed into the grubby floorboards, a wide grin suddenly taking over his face, like it was Christmas Day and he'd just been served an immense roast dinner with all the trimmings.

'Oh well, one down at least!' he said.

Jonny looked at Zack, Sophie and Alex. *Who* is *this guy?*

'So, everyone,' announced Cynthia. 'May I introduce to you the president of the Magic Circle – and my husband, no less – Mr President Edmund Pickle!'

The four watched as the gaggle of posh boys burst into spontaneous sycophantic applause. *Oh, give us a break!*

'I see we've got several new faces.' President Pickle sighed, casting his eyes about the room, pretending it was massive and that he was struggling to make out everyone in it.

Cynthia smiled through pursed lips, giving the impression that she didn't really mean it. 'Yes, yes, just a handful more.' She gave her husband a pleading look.

He angled his body towards her, seemingly oblivious to the fact that everyone could still hear him clearly. 'We haven't got room for any more, dear . . . I mean, Henry's a good lad, but it's bad enough already with Deanna as well. They should all just come back when they're of age.'

Cynthia looked at the man she'd been married to for several centuries (or at least that's how it seemed sometimes). This wasn't a conversation for now.

'Well . . . *fine*! Carry on, carry on, then!' President Pickle said eventually, taking a seat at the side of the room and checking his pocket watch.

'Right, let's find out a little bit more about you all, shall we?' said Cynthia. 'Zack Harrison? Please stand up.'

Zack tentatively got to his feet. 'Oh dear, not the pickpocket again!' shouted President Pickle, encouraging a giggle out of a clearly tickled Henry. 'I thought we'd got rid of you last time!'

Zack's face flushed with anger as everyone in the room, including Sophie, Alex and Jonny, turned to look at him.

So that's *what he was hiding earlier*, thought Sophie.

But before Zack could even begin to explain, President Pickle was on his feet and striding towards the front, politely yet firmly nudging his wife out of the way.

'And please let this serve as a warning to you all,' sang the man sanctimoniously. 'We treat theft here very, very seriously.' He looked over at his wife for endorsement.

'Well, yes, of course we do,' floundered Cynthia. 'Not that we know for definite that it was Zack – or indeed *anyone* – who stole your gavel, Edmund,' she added under her breath.

'I didn't *steal* anything!' Zack was trying to control his anger, embarrassed at being outed so publicly. 'I don't even know what a gavel *is*!'

'Of course you do, young lad – it's one of these!' President Pickle brandished a small wooden hammer from inside his jacket – the type used by a judge in a courtroom. 'I'd get used to the sound of this, if I were you!' He punctuated his remark with a swift blow to a nearby table, causing it to splinter and splatter, and prompting an ear-wincing pop to bounce off the sweaty walls.

Cynthia elbowed her husband in the pancreas and he emitted a little post-lunch burp. 'Please, Edmund,' she insisted. 'Let's just give him another chance. He's a brilliant young magician.'

President Pickle grumbled something inaudible, rolled his eyes and sloped back to his seat. Hardly a resounding 'yes' but technically not an outright 'no' . . .

Jonny could feel Zack humming with anger, like a kettle about to boil. Instinctively he placed a hand on his best friend's shoulder; this wasn't the time for another flurry of fireworks! Of course, Jonny knew all about Zack's previous dismissal from the Magic Circle several months ago. It had been all he'd talked about back then; he was so infuriated and embarrassed by the whole affair.

Zack had the technical ability to steal, of course. He was already famous for his spontaneous nimble-fingered demonstrations on the school bus. But that wasn't the point; it didn't make him some common thief. *I mean, what would Zack want with a gavel anyway?* thought Jonny. No, he was pretty sure Zack had been framed, and they were both itching to find out why.

But getting all worked up in front of the president of the Magic Circle on the first day of his return wasn't going to do Zack any favours. Nor would it impress Sophie and Alex, who were obviously hoping they hadn't completely misjudged their new friend.

'Let's move on, shall we?' said Cynthia, interrupting Zack's spiralling thoughts and gesturing for him to sit down. 'OK . . . Jonathan Haigh?'

Once again the room turned towards the back.

'Oh, my!' remarked President Pickle, craning his neck. 'Is this Ernest's grandson? Stand up, lad!'

Jonny stood obediently, as Henry tried to look unimpressed by the boy's height but found it difficult because, well, Jonny had the stature of an above-average brontosaurus.

'Spitting image, isn't he?' Cynthia remarked to her husband.

'He certainly is!' said President Pickle, acting almost star-struck. 'Come over here, lad.'

Jonny shrugged at his friends and walked slowly to the front. President Pickle came towards him, a wide grin spread over his face like thick icing. 'Always nice to see magic being kept in the family!' he said, shaking his hand furiously.

'I assume some of you have already come across the work of Ernest Haigh,' Cynthia addressed the room again by way of an explanation.

Sophie sat back on her plastic seat, the penny dropping. Wow. Ernest Haigh's writing was some of the best, most forward-thinking work on magic out there. And this friendly giraffe-boy was his grandson!

'I bet you probably read everything of his cover to cover when you were still a baby!' exclaimed President Pickle, clearly in his element.

Jonny felt somewhat bemused by all this attention. He had anticipated a few people making the connection between him and Ernest, but he'd not counted on it being anything particularly special. His granddad was just like any other granddad, surely. Well, apart from the fact that he not only gave you toffees on your birthday, but also then caused them to levitate, vanish or burst into flames with a snap of his fingers (though thankfully always *before* you'd eaten them). But then couldn't *lots* of grandparents do that?

'Well, actually . . . I've not read any of his books.' Jonny peeled his palm away from President Pickle's clammy hand. 'In fact, we've only recently been back in touch. I got into magic mainly because of Zack!'

Zack couldn't help flushing with pride as a startled hush fell across the room. *Good old Jonny*, he thought; he really couldn't have hoped for a more loyal best friend. Who better to ease him back into the stuffy Magic Circle?

'Surely you're joking?' managed President Pickle, looking for some reassurance, like he couldn't bear the idea that a grandchild of the great Ernest Haigh could be anything but a perfect student of magic.

Jonny made a strange creaking sound in the back of his throat, which he saved for times when he didn't know what to say but wanted to avoid complete and utter silence.

'He's joking!' announced President Pickle to the room, making up his mind and clapping Jonny on the (lower) back (which was as far as the president could reach).

'Oh, you really had us going there!' he said, wiping tears from his eyes. 'Fantastic stuff!'

Cynthia motioned for Jonny to sit down again, partly because she wanted to get on, but also because she wasn't entirely convinced that Jonny *was* joking and feared for her husband's weak heart should he hear any further news to the contrary.

Zack watched as Henry gave Jonny an acknowledging nod as he passed by, which Jonny either didn't see or chose to ignore, causing Henry to narrow his eyes suspiciously. *What is it with him?* thought Zack, remembering how Henry had tried to befriend him, almost forcefully, on his first day at the Magic Circle.

Sophie leaned across the table towards Jonny. 'Just so you know,' she said quietly, 'I actually *have* read all your grand-dad's books from cover to cover. And they're *a-mazing*!'

'Sophie, do you want to just stand up and give everyone a wave?' said Cynthia, keen to play down the arrival of another girl.

Sophie looked over at Deanna, now seated on her mum's lap plaiting their hair together, her face blotchy and damp with tears. Slowly, like she was trying to avoid a particularly cranky rattlesnake, Sophie got to her feet.

Cynthia held up Sophie's application form, searching for her glasses with her spare hand, forgetting that they were always permanently hanging near her waist, held by the chain of garish beads so that she would never lose them (or the beads). 'Can I just check . . . ?' she began, popping on her glasses and frowning. 'It says here that you practise hypnosis.'

Sophie nodded.

President Pickle started to squirm in his seat, wincing theatrically.

'Is that correct?' Cynthia questioned.

All eyes were now on Sophie, the posh troupe shaking their heads at her disapprovingly; Alex, Zack and Jonny excited.

'Well, I don't *just* do hypnosis,' Sophie answered honestly. 'There are plenty of other areas of magic I'm interested in too.'

'And from the *North*, it seems,' mumbled President Pickle quietly, gliding his wife out of her central spot once again. Breathing deeply, he looked down at Sophie. 'Society rules very clearly state that hypnosis is not strictly recognized as

36

a performance art within magic and certainly shouldn't be performed by . . . a *little girl*!' he added with extra relish.

Jonny stifled a laugh as Sophie gawped at the man.

Had the president of the Magic Circle – someone Sophie had dreamed of impressing – *really* just said that? She looked across at Zack for moral support, but he just shook his head, almost as if to apologize on behalf of the club. Even Alex couldn't quite believe what President Pickle had said.

Sensing (i.e. reacting to another prod from Cynthia) that he had perhaps overstepped the mark, the president began to backtrack. 'What I meant was . . . Perhaps you and Deanna could form a double act? Get you girlies in a little team together!'

Deanna's mother started nodding enthusiastically as she continued to bounce her daughter up and down on her lap.

Deanna made a low rumbling noise, sounding a bit like a trapped demon.

'Yes, well, that's certainly something we can try out tomorrow, if you like,' said Cynthia diplomatically. 'Anyway, it's nice to have another representative of the female species in the room, isn't it!'

President Pickle gave her a slight shake of the head, causing her to visibly deflate. She gave Sophie a sad smile.

'Alex Finley?' she eventually called out as Sophie sat back down, perplexed.

Zack smiled up encouragingly as the boy tried to get to his feet, holding on to the table in front of him for support.

'Now, I see you've only put down "cards" as your particular area of interest,' Cynthia said, consulting the form.

Alex tried to say 'yes', but what came out was mostly just the sound of air catching at the back of his dry throat.

'Oh, well, Henry is a wizard with cards,' said President Pickle, taking over loudly once again. 'Perhaps he could teach you some self-working tricks.'

Henry nodded adoringly at President Pickle, like an eager spaniel, then turned to face Alex, his smile morphing into a poisonous sneer.

Someone doesn't like the idea of competition, thought Zack, excited by the prospect of Alex outshining Henry with his fancy flourishes and perfect card-handling.

'Well, don't forget,' continued Cynthia, 'the rules state that you must show knowledge in at least *three* different areas of magic if you're to pass your audition at the end of the week, OK?'

Alex sat down shakily. He must have missed that rule on the application form. All he knew was cards!

'Well, that's enough introductions for now,' Cynthia concluded, removing her glasses and letting them swing on their beady trapeze. 'So, these next few days are all about perfecting the routines you'll be presenting to Council at the end of the week.'

President Pickle nodded solemnly at the mention of 'Council', like it was some holy word.

'Anyway, I think that's us all wrapped up nicely here. Please don't stray from this room of course – and I look forward to seeing you all tomorrow for the first official workshop, when we'll be getting some assistance from actual real-life members of the Magic Circle, OK? Exciting!'

Sophie raised her hand, confused. 'So ... is that *it* for today? Are we not going to be learning any magic?'

'Oh well, you're more than welcome to stay in this room and play with the others,' Cynthia offered kindly, not quite getting Sophie's point. 'I'm sure Deanna's mother has plenty of squash and biscuits for snacks.'

Deanna's mother nodded, beaming – it was her favourite thing in the world to hand out snacks!

'Oh yes,' agreed President Pickle. 'And no doubt Henry will be able to lend a hand. Even though he's not of age yet, Council have already earmarked him as one to watch – so, you know, some of you could learn a lot!' He stared at Zack.

Henry breathed in deeply, closing his eyes, basking in the glory of the commendation.

'Although I suspect Ernest's grandson here will be able to give you a run for your money!' President Pickle added jovially, clearly piercing Henry's ego, causing him to look like a chided, blinded hyena.

'Right, well, we'll leave you all to get to know each other,' said Cynthia, hurrying her husband out of the room and closing the door behind them.

Alex listened as the muffled sound of a blatant domestic echoed down the corridor, reminding him for a fleeting moment of home.

The four of them looked around the room at the somewhat bleak offerings. *So this is what we're dealing with*, thought Sophie:

A demonically possessed little girl dressed in Lycra with a mum the size of a sperm whale (whose pastimes included handing out snacks).

A pack of rich teenagers who would no doubt tire of magic as soon as they found a more expensive hobby.

A spherical kid going around the room introducing himself as Max and who seemed to prefer confectionery to conjuring.

And a rather strange boy called Henry who clearly knew a thing or two about technique but evidently had something else going on inside that oddly large head of his.

Was this really the best the Magic Circle had to offer young magicians? Where were the people who were *really* into magic?

She turned to the other three, and they looked at each other, sharing the same thought.

Zack frowned. 'I swear I *never* stole a thing – despite what President Pickle says.'

Sophie looked at him sternly. 'Well, of course you didn't steal anything!'

Zack looked back at her, his big brown eyes shining. 'What? You *believe* me?' He couldn't hide his surprise.

'Well, it's your word against President Pickle's,' answered Sophie. 'And given the man's clearly a total idiot, then by a process of elimination you come out on top.'

Even though Sophie had used cold hard logic to make up her mind, Zack felt grateful for her support. No one *ever* believed him. Perhaps things weren't so bad after all. 'I'll take that!' he said, giving Sophie a mini fist-bump. 'Hey, why don't I give you lot the tour?' he said, the glint returning to his eye.

Alex shifted in his seat nervously. 'But . . . but the lady said we couldn't leave this room.'

'Yeah!' exclaimed Zack. 'But that didn't stop me last time, did it?'

His friends giggled conspiratorially.

Whether it was this that alerted Henry, or he was planning on coming over anyway, they didn't know, but they were nonetheless saddened to see the boy's insect-like frame approaching them. There was something about him that none of them could quite put their finger on . . . It wasn't just the odd way he moved, or the sinister air, but something behind the eyes . . . Like there was something inside him, bursting to get out. And, judging by the increasing smell, at least a hefty portion of this was *gas*.

'You all right?' said Jonny, standing up (and conveniently placing his head and nose above the boy's obnoxious smell; the other three were not so lucky!).

'I'm fantastic, thank you.'

Zack, Sophie and Alex looked at each other, trying not to act too surprised by the boy's husky high voice, like puberty was deliberately toying with his vocal cords.

'And so you're Ernest's grandson?' Henry stood closer than Jonny would have liked, but still only reached his shoulder.

'Yep, that's right,' Jonny said bluntly, not liking the idea of his granddad and this boy being on first-name terms.

Henry looked down at the other three, a caterpillar smile squirming between his chin and his nose, not quite making up its mind, finally settling into a sort of wiggly grimace.

'You know what?' he said. 'It's not always *what* you know round here, but *who* you know.' He looked down at Zack, then shot a look of pity at Sophie and Alex, before gazing back up at Jonny. 'You're more than welcome to come and sit with me if you'd prefer.'

Whatever response Henry was expecting, it definitely *wasn't* for Jonny to simply burst out laughing, which was arguably even more humiliating than a straightforward 'no'.

Henry waited, stony faced, for Jonny to finish, then looked at the three others beside him. 'Well, you won't learn much from common thieves.' He locked eyes with Zack. 'Nice to see you again, by the way. I was so upset when you were – how to best put it? – *unfairly dismissed*!'

Zack's ears began to glow; much like the time he forgot it was non-uniform day, and was secretly given classmate Hayley's (fitted, girls') jeans (at her behest), only to be outed loudly in the playground by her coven of girly friends (all with names ending in 'y' – Kayley, Kirsty, Carly). EMBARRASSING! But, for some reason, this swipe from Henry cut deeper.

'Suit yourselves if you don't want to join me,' said Henry.

The four shuffled out from behind their table, and Zack led the others towards the door, inching past Henry and trying to navigate through the haze of odour, which was reminiscent of off ham.

Alex tried not to show that he was holding his breath. But, just as he hoped he was out of reach, Henry grabbed him roughly, spinning him round.

'There isn't anyone here better at cards than me, you know.'

Alex nodded, shaking with fear.

'Just remember that. You might want to choose your friends more carefully.' Henry planted a greasy hand on Alex's head and patted it. 'You tiny little boy!'

And with that Henry turned theatrically and made for the stage again.

Or at least that was where he would have ended up had he not tripped over Deanna, who was now flat on the floor, mid sit-up regime (with her mother spotting), trying to get her energy levels back up. The boy fell head over heels, a bunch of soggy rose petals cascading from his pockets as he missed one of the crash mats by half an inch.

Henry roared as Alex quickly closed the door behind him, filtering out the noise such that only the higher frequencies of Deanna's high-pitched incessant squealing successfully penetrated the wood.

'So then,' said Zack, turning to his new friends, 'welcome to the Magic Circle!'

4

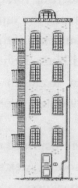

The four stood breathing deeply, soaking up the relative damp of the dim corridor, a welcome relief compared to the rank warmth and stench of the Junior Room.

'What *is* it with that Henry boy?' asked Sophie, wrinkling her nose.

'No idea,' said Zack. 'But he tried to slime up to me the first time I was here too – best keep away, I figured. Anyway, let the unofficial tour begin!'

Zack suddenly whipped round and dashed deeper into the murky corridor. 'Follow me!' he shouted, his voice stirring up the dust and annoying a nearby rat who was taking a well-earned doze.

Jonny smiled at Sophie. 'Ladies first!' he said, extending his arm along the corridor, bowing like an old-fashioned gent.

'Oh, please!' said Sophie, laughing deeply. She took off into the dark after Zack, fearless.

44

Alex stared down the passage as if it was some endless abyss. 'I'll be right behind you,' Jonny reassured him.

Alex gulped as he set off, the muffled sounds of Zack and Sophie's footsteps bouncing off the walls, disorientating him. *Keep going*, he told himself, shuddering as he passed a poster of a Victorian magician dressed as a clown, casually decapitating a woman. *None of this is creepy in the slightest!*

As he sped up, the sleep-deprived rat skittered alongside him, doing nothing to soothe Alex's growing unease. On and on, deeper into the darkness . . . Alex could feel a cold globule of sweat beginning to form at the base of his neck, a trickle away from dousing his back.

Past the poster of David Copperfield grinning and – more importantly – *flying*. Past the life-size cut-out of Paul Daniels grinning and . . . holding a metal cup and some crocheted balls. Past a glittery costume stapled haphazardly to a mannequin labelled SIEGFRIED, with a muddy, bloodied paw-print on the front (don't ask!). Past the painting of a man in overalls simply entitled: ALF RATTLEBAG, PATRON SAINT OF STAGEHANDS, 1892–1923. Past the –

Suddenly, a hand.

It was Zack, a firm but fair grip now on Alex's shoulder, bringing him to a halt. Alex quickly moved off to one side as the rat swanned on past him – pleased to have won the race. Sophie shuddered at its size as she watched it scurry off into the distance.

ALF RATTLEBAG

Jonny caught up with the rest of them, panting a little. 'Now, Zack,' he said. 'Not wishing to sound like a party-pooper, but shouldn't we be a little quieter?'

'Not really.' Zack flashed a grin. 'No one comes down here during the day. Well, no one's *meant* to at least!'

'Why?' asked Sophie, peeling at a bit of crusty wallpaper coming away from the wall and accidentally removing a rather large chunk of plaster.

Zack pointed to a sign above their heads which had been recently touched up:

NO CHILDREN ALLOWED

UNLESS ACCOMPANIED BY A MEMBER OF COUNCIL ☺

Alex mouthed the words as his eyes drifted down towards what appeared to be another giant poster partially covered by a deep red curtain – the kind of curtain that looked quite refined from a distance but up close was bobbled and grubby (and up even closer was *riddled* with mites and STANK). 'Wh-what's behind there?' he asked gingerly, hoping that this was an elaborate fire exit and he'd soon be outside in the open again, away from the rats, creepy clowns and Paul Daniels's balls.

'Yes,' said Jonny. 'What's so special about this poster that it needs a snazzy red curtain?'

Pausing dramatically, Zack looked at each of them in turn. 'This, my friends, is the Grand Theatre of the Magic Circle!' He slowly parted the rouge curtain to reveal a framed portrait of a theatre entrance.

'Oh, wow! I've read about this!' said Sophie.

Jonny looked at the painting inquisitively, amazed by how real it looked.

'But did you read about *this* bit?' said Zack, casually placing his hand on what should have been canvas but which now seemed to just . . . melt away.

'No! You're kidding!' said Jonny. Alex let out a faint gasp, while Sophie's mouth fell open in surprise.

It was the perfect optical illusion: disguised to just look like a poster of the entrance to the theatre, this actually *was* the entrance to the theatre!

Jonny grinned, loving the way the light bounced off the golden frame, confusing his brain, hiding the depth and making the three-dimensional space behind it appear well and truly 2D. Even from his high altitude (often a real issue for magicians when Jonny was watching their performance!), the illusion was flawless.

Zack revelled in the reveal, enjoying the look of surprise on the others' faces – like the moment when a previously burned bank note appears inside a lemon, or a signed playing card turns up stuck to the ceiling.

Slowly the four stepped through the frame . . .

It was the *sound* of the place that struck Sophie first. A dizzying, deep-seated silence – like the silence of

somewhere that hasn't always been silent. Or the kind of silence that comes after something extremely loud which causes you to readjust your ears. *Or like the beautifully deafening silence of a heavy snowfall*, thought Sophie, picturing some wintry scene back up in the hills at home. Soft, cushioning, expansive silence.

Jonny sniffed loudly, before sneezing even more loudly and sending up a load of dust. 'Sorry!'

Zack smiled. It had been a few months since he'd last set foot in the place and – despite his anger about his unfair dismissal – it was good to be back.

Jonny pictured himself on the wide stage, looking out over the crowds, the rusting chandelier hanging on what looked like nothing more than a thin wire, cocking its head in anticipation of what new magical delights might be coming up next . . .

Alex looked at the seating, stacked steeply and disappearing way up towards the ceiling, marvelling at the dizzying height. He strained his neck back further and further until Zack had to steady him to prevent him from falling over.

They stared at the dimly lit arch above the stage, wondering what this place must have been like when magic flourished in Victorian times, everyone holding their breath as suave illusionist Maskelyne bamboozled them with his devilish trickery, or waiting for Houdini to emerge from his cabinet, finally free of a series of metal bindings – dishevelled but heroic. The audience getting to their feet, elated, desperate for more.

But not so much any more, Sophie thought sadly. Oh, to have witnessed such feats! To create that much stir using little more than an angled mirror, a hidden thread or a secret move . . . To produce something out of nothing in a way not even physics could explain. And to hear the crowd go *wild*!

'I can't believe this place actually exists,' she said, awestruck.

'Beautiful, isn't it?' Zack walked down towards the stage, running his hand over the seats.

Jonny picked up a moth-eaten programme lying in the stalls and studied the front cover, wiping away the grime, squinting in the weak light. All of a sudden he cried out, filling the auditorium with its first large sound since Robert Harbin dislocated a lady's middle so that she stood zig-zagged (but still – outwardly – obscenely happy!).

Instinctively, Alex moved closer to Zack.

'Everything all right?' said Sophie, concerned that they might be heard.

'Absolutely fine!' replied Jonny, waving the programme in the air. 'It's Granddad!'

The other three went over to look. Jonny might as well have been gazing into a mirror, so clear was the likeness between him and his grandfather, a smiling young magician standing with his hand outstretched – fire blazing from his palm.

'You know what I love about your granddad?' said Sophie.

'That he's as good-looking as me?' quipped Jonny, making his eyebrows dance.

'Oh no, definitely not that!'

'That he's not dead yet?' said Zack, causing Jonny to laugh out loud, filling the auditorium once more, the chandelier welcoming the long overdue reverberation.

'No!' said Sophie, shooting Zack a disapproving look. 'That he was doing fire from palms in the *1960s*. I mean, the man was so ahead of his time. He was . . . *is* incredible.'

Jonny nodded, his cheeks flushing with pride. Despite the things Zack had told him, he'd never fully appreciated just how much of an impact the man had made on the world of magic. To him, he was just – well – Granddad.

'Do you see lots of him?' asked Sophie, taking the programme and examining it.

'Yes and no,' Jonny answered. 'I think him and my dad fell out over something a few years ago, and we didn't really see him, but since Zack got me into magic we've actually seen each other quite a bit.'

'Well, you're very lucky to be related to someone like him, Jonathan Haigh.' Sophie was clearly a little star-struck. 'The closest I come to having a famous relative is my mum's great-aunt, who was friends with the last person to be hanged in the UK . . . apparently.'

'Oh, how *delightful*!' joked Jonny. 'We should get them together! Granddad's certainly old enough!'

It was Alex who heard it first, his ears trained from years of listening out for strange sounds in the night: a faint sound of breathing coming from somewhere high up in the flies, like a giant slowly psyching himself up.

The others caught the look on his face and then gradually fell silent as it grew louder . . .

Ahhhhhhhhhhhh. Ahhhhhhhhhhhh. Ahhhhhhhhhhhh. Ahhhhhhhhhhhh.

'Sorry, but . . . what actually *is* that?' said Jonny, looking towards Zack, hoping there was a perfectly rational explanation behind the sinister sound.

'I think we might have woken someone up,' said Zack, almost to himself, his heart beginning to pound.

'What?' asked Sophie, concerned. 'What do you mean by that?'

The breathing began to bounce off the walls, moving stage right, then stage left, as if it were alive, in stereo, surrounding them like a ghostly gas. The four turned their heads wildly, trying to keep track.

'*Alf,*' whispered Zack.

At that moment the house lights began to flicker and a deep wailing noise filled the theatre, the sound passing through each of them, jiggling their bones – causing them to feel sick. All four turned instinctively and ran back towards the entrance.

The wailing continued as they sprinted for the curtained doorway, the elongated vowels now broken up by consonants . . .

'*Noooooooooooo! Children! Aaaaallllllllllllowed!*' the voice howled. '*Stayyyy awaaay from heeeeerrre!*'

Sophie's mind began to race even quicker than her feet. This was the stuff of nightmares, sure, but she wondered whether it was perhaps a little over the top, like someone was trying just a bit too hard to ward them off. Still, it was effective. After all, here they were, running for their lives!

She approached the curtain, briefly daring to look back for a clue as to where the voice was coming from. Her eyes scanned the theatre from top to bottom.

Nothing.

But . . .

Was that movement at the back of the theatre? She stopped running, letting the others go ahead, and squinted upwards. The flash of a face, the glint of an eye in the quivering light, a spark of recognition, then . . . nothing.

No, it must be her mind playing tricks. Sophie knew how easily the brain could be fooled, especially when pumped full of adrenalin – she'd read about it in psychology textbooks. Still, in the dead of night that didn't stop her from confusing the noise of the household boiler with the ravings of an intruder. Or the shadows cast by cold moonlight with the clutching, clawed tentacles of some murderous banshee. Or the – NOT HELPING, SOPHIE!

Sophie turned round again, startled to see the others now running back towards her. 'Oh, what now?' she cried out, fifty-six per cent alarmed, forty-four per cent bemused. The boys reached her, their breathing loud, Alex visibly shaking.

'Cynthia and President Pickle are coming down the corridor!' gasped Zack.

'What's going on?' hissed Sophie.

'And who the hell is *Alf*?' asked Jonny.

'Not now!' Zack dragged them all down row F of the stalls towards a small green door at the other side of the auditorium – the four having to do that slightly awkward sideways-walk thing you do when you're squeezing past someone already sitting down in the theatre. 'We're not supposed to be in here, remember!'

He hastily led them through the door like an overenthusiastic usher, closing it just as Cynthia and President Pickle came into the theatre. Immediately, as if on cue, the wailing stopped – the married couple's petty bickering now the only sound.

The four of them looked at each other as they huddled together on a small landing above a winding wooden staircase.

Safe, thought Alex, finally allowing himself to breathe.

Well, for now . . . !

5

Alex clutched the sides of his head as the sound of squabbling grew louder – not just because Cynthia and Pickle were getting angrier but because . . .

'Oh, you're kidding! Don't tell me *they're* heading this way as well!' said Jonny.

This really wasn't great, thought Zack. For him at least. The others might get away with saying they were lost, but Zack would probably face immediate expulsion. And no more second chances this time. No more dreams of becoming president of the Magic Circle.

But what if he jeopardized the others' chances of membership too? Well, that was it; they *couldn't* get caught – not yet, at least! He owed it to his new friends.

Sophie edged towards the top of the staircase, looking at the others as she gripped the banister.

'We're going to have to . . .' she said calmly.

The boys moved next to her quickly. Cynthia and President Pickle were almost upon them, the sound of their argument starting to peak.

'Yes, but not the *stairs*,' whispered Jonny, placing his hand over Sophie's. 'We'll be heard.'

For a second she didn't know what he was getting at, and then – as if this wasn't what a spiral staircase was ultimately designed for – she knew. 'Oh, you've got to be kidding, mate!'

Jonny swung his leg round so that he was straddling the rickety banister rail, looking at the others. 'We're going to *have* to . . . mate!' he said, mimicking Sophie's northern accent, his eyes shining – and then, with a faint swish, shot down into the depths turning and turning, vanishing into the void.

Sophie looked at Zack and Alex, impressed but conscious of time.

Zack understood that this was the only way they could get away quickly enough, but he felt bad for Alex, who was evidently terrified at the prospect of descending the ageing staircase banister-style!

'Why don't you go between us?' whispered Sophie, helping Alex up and placing him facing backwards on the banister, so quickly that he didn't have time to object – a bit like when a doctor asks if you're ready for a needle injection but the needle's already halfway into your arm.

Sophie clambered on behind Alex so that she faced his back; Zack followed suit in front, so the smaller boy was squished between the two of them – oddly close for people who'd only just met, but then this was a pretty odd situation!

'*Now!*' whispered Sophie as she saw the door handle begin to turn.

Zack pushed off with all his might. Not that he needed to; the staircase dropped so steeply that plain old gravity was more than enough.

Sophie's mind quickly turned to how this spiral-bound journey might end. The wood of the staircase, the rusting nails, the cold stone walls – none of these spoke of a soft landing. And, she thought, Alex would be falling on top of her (not *too* bad, she concluded) – though there was Zack on top of that, of course! Hmm, yes, this was going to be a problem, wasn't it?

Zack was thinking the same thing. He thought about calling out to Sophie, but, on glancing up, could now see that Cynthia and President Pickle were about to descend the staircase (on foot, thank the Lord!) and feared that any noise might give the game away.

Alex too was in his own particular pickle – the pickle sandwiched between Zack and Sophie! He counted himself lucky not to be in Sophie's position, but he didn't like the idea of being the buffer between her and Zack – like a little airbag. He'd pop!

Of course, Sophie thought as the world spun around faster and faster, there was the slim chance that Jonny was already lying on the floor waiting ... in which case, yes, there would be some cushioning – if you counted skin and bones as cushioning.

Oh, why had she agreed to this?

Zack tried to slow down, but they were travelling at such speed now; the friction made his palms burn – and there was no way he wanted his palms to end up like Ernest Haigh's on the front cover of that old programme!

Down and down they went, into the depths of the Magic Circle. He had never ventured down here before.

Surely they were nearing the bottom now, thought Sophie, almost instinctively turning her wrist to look at her watch.

No, too dangerous!

She steadied herself, trying to keep her balance, but . . .

Could it be that . . . ?

No, surely not.

Could it be . . . that they were slowing *down*?

Alex could feel it on his windswept cheeks too, something less dramatic about their angle of descent. Either that or he was so dizzy he'd completely lost all his senses.

Sophie turned, half expecting to see solid ground come crashing up towards her, but instead saw Jonny's grinning face as she slowly approached.

The three of them breathed a sigh of relief as they came to a satisfying stop in front of Jonny, who stood there like he was the official finishing post.

'What took you so long?' he whispered.

They clambered off the banister on to the dimly lit landing area, their legs feeling like they belonged to someone else (someone who'd spent at least a year on an EXTREME fairground ride).

'Lucky we didn't keep going!' said Zack as he peered over the edge, spotting a second staircase winding further down into the depths just ahead of where they'd stopped.

'What . . . now?' exhaled Alex, aware that – despite their rather breathtaking speed of descent – Cynthia and President Pickle were still only a few minutes behind them.

'A door – look!' Jonny spied a stout cupboard built into the stone wall, half camouflaged against the grime. He prised open the door and the four peered inside. Save for a few rotting silk handkerchiefs, some feathers, old copies of the society magazine, swords, a dozen top hats, rabbit bones and a billion woodlice, it was completely empty.

Oh, perfect! thought Alex.

They squeezed inside, trying not to touch the sides, which, on inspection, seemed to be teeming with spiders' eggs, freshly hatched baby spiders and several spider mums and dads prepared to do anything to protect their young.

Jonny's long arms reached out for the doors, closing them just as President Pickle and Cynthia emerged from the staircase, still arguing – typically, thankfully, blissfully unaware of everything that had just happened.

The cupboard darkened inside as Alex wondered whether being unable to see the spiders was in fact a good thing or whether it actually made things even more TERRIFYING.

'As soon as it's clear, we'll head straight back upstairs,' whispered Zack, chiding himself once again for leading them all into this – he could feel Alex trembling beside him. But then again, wasn't this everything Zack had wanted? A group of friends to join him on his adventures in the dark, forbidden recesses of the Magic Circle? If Cynthia and President Pickle would just walk on by, perhaps they'd be OK ...

Sophie let her eyes adjust to the light, surprised that she could still make out a fair bit, albeit slightly obscured by Jonny's huge, though now substantially squashed, frame.

She felt something move across her back and shuddered, trying not to panic – for if there was one thing worse than someone panicking, it was someone panicking inside a confined space. Almost immediately she felt it again. Slowly turning round, Sophie was surprised to see a small shaft of light coming from the back of the cupboard. She reached towards it, her hand now feeling the cool current of air that had rippled the back of her T-shirt. Why was there a light coming from the back of a cupboard? she wondered, edging over towards it.

All of a sudden she heard President Pickle's booming voice! But not from where she'd feared . . .

And then it dawned on her . . . A bit like a fake playing card, this cupboard was double-sided and had two openings – the one they'd come through, and the one she was now peeping through at the back. Sophie studied the ominous cave-like room, squirming with greying adults who were all beginning to sit round a large creaking and cracked wooden table.

It had to be, thought Sophie: *the council chamber*. The last place four kiddie-winkles should be hiding!

And worse still – the Council was now in full session.

6

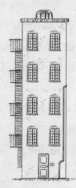

Mr President Edmund Pickle banged his shiny new gavel down loudly, calling the room to order. It was an intense, pernickety and stressful sound – completely unnecessary in such a small space.

From inside the cupboard, Sophie prodded Zack, Jonny and Alex in turn.

'Ow!'

'Sophie, watch where you're prodding!'

'Spiders!'

Through the thick gloomy air she silently beckoned the boys towards the thin crack in the door. They shunted forward.

'Oh, wow!' whispered Zack as he looked through the gap and saw the sea of white hair.

'I didn't think Council met during the day,' whispered Sophie, recalling the wealth of useless facts in the induction pack. 'I wonder what's going on.'

'We should probably leave while the coast is clear,' said Zack quietly.

Sophie and Jonny stared at him.

'Yeah . . . So we *could* do that . . . *or* we could spy on the Council of the Magic Circle. What do you think, Sophie?' said Jonny.

'Ooh, I don't know!' Sophie rubbed her pointy chin, pretending to think about it.

Zack smiled, his teeth shining like tiny beacons on a dark night.

The room appeared to have been carved into the crust of the earth itself, noted Zack – who hadn't ever ventured this far, certainly not this deep, even on his most protracted of earlier adventures – this was like a candlelit cave that wouldn't feel out of place in a scary movie were it not for the Tupperware box of biscuits lying slap bang in the centre of the long wooden table, just out of everyone's reach, it seemed. Zack's stomach let out a warning growl, as if to say, *You really-really-really shouldn't be spying on Council, Zack Harrison!* OH WELL!

Alex watched wide-eyed as President Pickle, Cynthia and a spindly old man who looked dangerously close to death, took their seats at the top end of the table. The room fell silent, save for the noise of the spindly man bouncing up and down on his seat, trying to jiggle it forward closer to the table, like he was connected to some sort of mad machine.

Cynthia and President Pickle stared at him. 'Ready, Bill?' asked Cynthia quietly.

Bill nodded sharply – and let out a burp.

Jonny smothered his mouth, fearful of laughing out loud inside the darkened cupboard as he watched Cynthia close her eyes and wait for the tangy pong to disperse.

'Right!' said President Pickle. 'Let's get things under way, shall we? Bill, do you want to go through your report?'

Bill didn't flinch, but remained facing forward – motionless, his eyes glazed.

'Bill?' President Pickle repeated, a note of worry creeping into his voice, hoping the man hadn't actually died in his seat. That would be annoying – all those stairs to climb to get the body out!

Cynthia gently shook Bill's arm, causing him to wake with a start.

'Ah, there we go!' President Pickle beamed, clearly not put off by the fact that one of his esteemed colleagues could fall asleep on the job so quickly. 'Bill Dungworth, our treasurer, ladies and gentlemen!' He brought his fist to his mouth and made a sound a bit like a trumpet announcing royalty as Bill began to rise.

The four spies looked at each other (as best they could), trying not to laugh: so *this* was the guy President Pickle had put in charge of the society finances ... OH, GREAT!

Bill took just as long to stand as he did to sit down, mumbling grumpily about how he wished he'd never sat down in the first place, leaning heavily on the ornate giant green safe at his side as he heaved himself up.

Clearing his throat, he began to turn his notes round and round, trying to make sense of them.

'OK,' he said in a gargling voice. 'Thank you for attending this *emergency* general meeting.' He took a deep, wheezy breath before continuing. 'I've been going through the society accounts, and this year we've sadly turned in a net deficit of . . .'

The Council waited to hear exactly how bad their financial situation was.

Bill rotated the paper, trying to find the right figure. 'Fifty-one thousand pounds.'

Gasps filled the room.

Inside the cupboard the four backed away slightly. Had they really just heard right?

65

Sophie watched as two of the councillors – who had evidently just returned from a children's birthday party and were still in their 'Oriental' make-up – looked at one another, biting their lower (bright green) lips in concern.

'That's Steve and Jane,' whispered Zack. 'Nice couple, but completely mad!'

'Bill, are you sure that figure is ... correct?' offered Cynthia kindly from her spot in the council chamber. For this wouldn't have been the first time Bill had got his numbers muddled up – like when he once celebrated Christmas on the twelfth day of the twenty-fifth month.

'No, yes – sorry, that's wrong.' Bill planted a finger on the paper, almost piercing it with his long, yellowing nail.

President Pickle let out a dramatic '*Phew!*' – pretending to mop his brow with the back of his hand.

'A net deficit of ... fifty-*two* thousand pounds.'

The room (and – unbeknownst to the Council – the cupboard's inhabitants) fell into a shocked silence once again as Bill sat down, pleased, job done.

President Pickle stood, statesman-like, banging his gavel despite already having everyone's full attention. 'Mr Treasurer, do we have any idea why our finances are looking so bad?'

Bill was loath to stand up again, but did so anyway, making everyone wait. Again.

'No,' he eventually said, sitting back down, hoping – he thought – for the last time today, if not his life.

'Right ...' President Pickle was still searching for an answer. 'Well, I'm sure we're due a windfall soon!' He looked at his wife. 'Do we know of anyone who might be, you know, on their way . . . out?'

Cynthia stood briskly, obviously a trifle disgusted by the suggestion. 'Do I know if there's anyone on the brink of death who may donate a substantial fortune to the society? No, I don't, Edmund. That's to say, there are plenty of old members on the cusp, but none of them are rolling in cash.' She sat back down again.

'Righty ho, then . . .' said President Pickle, chewing the air, not really knowing what else to say. 'I mean, it's just . . . one of those things, I guess, isn't it?' he pronounced feebly.

The Council groaned in agreement, a sonorous, weary, dying sound. Inside the cupboard the four spies were agog. Was this really all the Council of the Magic Circle could say? That it was just 'one of those things'? Surely these were people who could make miracles happen.

From the opposite end of the table, a frail hand rose high into the air.

'Er, yes, Ernest?' said President Pickle.

Jonny shifted forward at the mention of his granddad's name. So Ernest sat on *Council*. Well, that was encouraging!

'Mr President.' Ernest's voice was calm but confident, and sounded much younger than his hand suggested. 'What does this news hold for the future of the society? Is there anything Council can do?'

Cynthia looked down at the table as she felt her husband begin to sweat beside her.

President Pickle could feel his heart pumping loudly inside his damp shirt. Why did Ernest always have to ask these difficult questions? Oh, how different things had looked thirty years ago. Bill had had a brown mullet for one thing and wasn't always asleep (as he was again now), and council meetings were merely a formality. More of an excuse for congratulating themselves on another successful year: magic thriving in the working men's clubs, the society bursting at the seams with wealth and creativity. And now . . . ? Well, President Pickle never liked to dwell on that question too much. It was much easier to focus on how great things were back in the good old days.

A globule of sweat that had begun life on his forehead started to run down the bridge of his nose. 'Well,' he answered tentatively, 'I guess it might mean the society could fold at *some* point, but I'm sure there's a bit more life in her yet!'

'And exactly how many years of life do you think she has in her, Mr President?' There was a slight edge to Ernest's voice now.

'Go, Granddad!' whispered Jonny from inside the cupboard.

Cynthia winced as she saw her husband rubbing his chest – how much his heart must be going through these days. She imagined the blood flow being constricted, pushing its way through his veins like the very last slug of toothpaste out of a crinkled, frazzled tube.

'I'm sure the club will last long enough to see us two through, old man!' pronounced President Pickle, trying to keep things moving along. 'And, like I say, I'm sure a windfall is just round the corner.' His eyes darted towards Bill, who – the four in the cupboard noted – could easily have already snuffed it if it weren't for the slight rustling of his nose hairs indicating a faint breeze of life.

'But what about those just starting out in magic today? My grandson and Zack Harrison . . .' continued Ernest, a clear urgency in his voice now. 'What about *them*?'

The two made-up councillors exchanged nervous looks: no one *ever* questioned the president of the Magic Circle on matters such as this. It just wasn't . . . fitting.*

Jonny squeezed Zack's shoulders, proud of his granddad for standing up for them.

'It's just the way things are headed,' answered President Pickle bleakly. 'We simply have more money going out than there is coming in. Society funds were never going to last forever.'

'Yes,' replied Ernest, licking his lips, 'but if we opened the society up to *younger* members, paying members, that would surely help.'

The question hung in the air like fresh manure. Some of the council members were beginning to fidget awkwardly.

From their claustrophobic closet, the four youngsters watched on with increasing interest. Could the society they'd been looking forward to joining all these years

* See rule 147.25 paragraph 19 of the Magic Circle constitution for Council's full view on this matter.

already be on the point of closure? When would they have their chance to shine? It all just seemed so . . . unfair.

At least there were people like Ernest fighting their corner, Jonny thought proudly. If anyone could help them save the society, it was him.

President Pickle grimaced and drew a sharp intake of breath.

Cynthia lifted her head. She'd tried playing this card with her husband before, but it had always been trumped. Still, it was nice to have someone as respected as Ernest on her side. 'I'd be more than happy to lead on this if you'll let me help,' she said softly. 'Just think how much we'd benefit from adding some young blood into the mix.'

'I'm sure Bill wouldn't object to someone assisting in the Treasury department,' offered Ernest, the tiniest trace of sarcasm in his voice as he looked on at the snoozing prehistoric ornament sitting next to President Pickle.

'And even a small increase in membership would inject some cash into society funds,' added Cynthia, hoping that her husband would see reason. It was an idea she'd mooted before.

President Pickle stiffened, drawing himself up to his full height, exhaling loudly. 'No. Sorry, but children aren't the answer, I'm afraid. According to society rules –'

'But Council can *change* those rules!' cried Ernest, exasperated and steadily rising in his seat, his formidable height even more impressive than his grandson's. 'This is madness!'

The two stood facing each other from opposite ends of the table, President Pickle's head now resembling an entire steaming red cabbage. Oh, how he wished he could expel certain council members! But the magic world would be up in arms. What, you've expelled Ernest Haigh? The first man to make an elephant vanish while surrounded? The first man to fly across the stage and out over the audience? Yes, well, those people didn't have to deal with cross-examination day in, day out, did they? They didn't know how *strange* he'd become – forever rocking the boat at these meetings. Couldn't he just –?

All of a sudden there was a commotion – but not from Ernest or President Pickle.

Zack, Jonny, Sophie and Alex turned back towards the side of the cupboard they had entered through. With a deafening thud, the doors crashed open; all four cried out in alarm and squinted up at the strange angular figure now pushing them against the other door leading to the council chamber.

The whole of Council turned in stunned silence as the dusty cupboard doors began to shake before being forced open, spewing Zack, Jonny, Sophie and Alex out on to the floor.

The four of them looked up as the council members stared at them, bewildered. And then, behind them, emerging smugly from the cupboard, Henry, a mocking grin on his face.

Well, that's it, Zack thought. *We're done for!*

7

'What the fez is going on?' shouted President Pickle loudly, pumped up like a medieval cannon ready to blast.

Henry sidled past the four, squirming to the front, standing on all their toes accidentally-on-purpose as he went past. 'I'm so sorry to interrupt your council meeting, President Pickle,' he whined in his prissy voice, blatantly enjoying all the attention. 'It's just that I caught these *little people* snooping on your meeting and thought you'd like to know.'

'We weren't *snooping*!' protested Sophie. 'We were just . . . lost,' but even as she said it she knew how unlikely it sounded. It was one thing to get lost trying to find your way out, quite another to get lost via a theatre, a spiral staircase and a two-way cupboard.

The others looked at her, grateful that she had at least tried to put up some form of defence.

Zack took a deep breath. He'd been subjected to humiliation in front of Council before. But this time they

72

were all quite simply done for. Spying on Council was one of the worst crimes a member – let alone a *junior* member – could commit! But *he* had led them on this unofficial tour, so it was *he* who must take the flak.

He stepped forward and paused before speaking. 'I'm sorry, Council, but – once again – this is all my fault. It was me who led them down here . . . *Please* don't take it out on them.'

Cynthia moved swiftly round the table, looking very disappointed. 'How many times do you have to be told, Zack Harrison? What was the point of giving you a cooling-off period, just to land right back here?' Her eyes moved from one child to the next, searching for an explanation, before finally returning to Zack.

President Pickle shook his head, looking first at the intruders, then at the seated council members, before finally fixing Ernest with a self-satisfied glare. 'Do you see what happens when we let children in, Ernest?' he said gravely. 'All kinds of nonsense.' He bowed solemnly, clearly expecting some kind of applause (though only receiving a single, dull clap from Steve – and possibly a trump from Bill), before sitting back down.

Ernest coolly looked away from President Pickle, turning to face the four, winking at Jonny, instantly putting them all at ease. He turned back to look at Henry. 'Do you mind me asking what *you* were doing down here as well?' he asked pointedly. 'Eavesdropping on the eavesdroppers?'

'Oh. Erm, I was just . . . erm . . .' Henry began to flounder as everyone looked to him for an answer.

'*Foolish* boy,' said Ernest, cutting him off.

It was a good question, thought Zack – what *was* Henry doing down here?

'I'm sure that Henry was just *doing the right thing* – weren't you, lad?' President Pickle said, keen to gloss over this technicality and pull focus back on to the others.

Henry nodded his head wildly, overplaying his innocence, looking like an expensive malfunctioning toy.

Ernest turned back to Jonny and his friends. 'Perhaps you were all just trying to get into the library . . .' he suggested meaningfully. 'Surely we shouldn't punish our youngsters for wanting to learn from the great magicians of the past.' He looked around at Council and saw nods of approval.

Nice move, Ernest!

'Please do not speak on behalf of the guilty,' interrupted President Pickle, thwacking his gavel once again, causing all those present – including himself – to jump violently.

Cynthia sighed. Oh, how she wished she'd never bought the dreaded thing for him in the first place, now permanently attached to President Pickle's arm. 'I'm just going to take the car out of the garage, sweetheart.' *BANG!* 'Do you mind preparing a charcuterie board for elevenses?' *BANG!* 'I may need to go to the toilet again.' *BANG!* 'Night-night!' *BANG!* . . .

President Pickle gave the four a patronizing look. 'Yes, of course they should study the Greats of magic . . . But access to the library is only granted once they're *of age*.'

Ernest rolled his eyes and shook his head.

'Anyway, we haven't got all day,' the president said hurriedly. 'We must determine a suitable punishment!' he added with relish.

The youngsters looked at each other uneasily. Had their time at the Magic Circle already come to an end? Like a magician who – after a great build-up – produces only a bunch of feathers and the remains of a dove as the finale to a flamboyant routine.

'Gosh, we haven't had to administer a punishment to a *group* in quite a while!' said President Pickle, clearly enjoying himself. He brought out a large tome entitled *Magic Circle Constitution*, slamming it down dramatically.

'No!' protested Zack, half to himself, half to the room. 'This is all *my* doing. Why can't you just punish *me*?'

'Zack, it was my idea to head down the stairs, mate,' said Jonny, unwilling to let his friend take sole responsibility.

But the president wasn't listening; his nose now buried in the yellowed, well-thumbed pages of this, his go-to bible.

'Is it true?' said Sophie, her voice suddenly ringing out around a chamber that hadn't heard a young female voice in . . . well, ever.

'Silence in the council chamber!' shouted President Pickle, his face still buried in the constitution.

'But is it true that the society is on the verge of collapse?' Sophie persisted.

Cynthia willed her to shut up, worried that she was only going to make matters worse. But there was no stopping this one, it seemed; she suddenly felt a rush of admiration.

'Well, I don't know how much you heard from your cubby hole back there,' replied President Pickle, looking down his nose at her like he was facing a target. 'But I can assure you that you are positively mistaken. The society and its members are absolutely fine, thank you very much. Which is more than I can say for you lot! Now then . . .'

President Pickle flicked to the centre of the tome, running his finger down the edge, licking his forefingers theatrically. 'Hmm . . .' he mumbled, enjoying the weight of his position, re-digesting these rules and sub-clauses one by one, reminding himself why he agreed with them so much. 'Right, OK, so I'm afraaaaid . . .' he said eventually, raising his eyes to look at the four. 'That . . .' He paused, playing up the suspense like a game-show host – 'the constitution states – providing Council is in agreement – that the punishment for eavesdropping on a council meeting is . . . immediate and *permanent* exclusion from the club. Sorry.'

They all looked at each other, aghast. 'Permanent?' whispered Sophie.

'What?' shouted Zack. 'Why can't you just exclude *me*?' His face started to flush. This was just like the last time. Why did this man have to be so *unfair*?

'I *am* excluding you,' answered the president, turning to face him. 'Plus these three other scallywags as well! Providing Council are in agreement, which I suspect they are. One rotten apple and all that.'

'But Zack's not rotten!' countered Jonny.

Alex nodded weakly. He hadn't enjoyed their descent into the depths of the Magic Circle, nor their short stay inside the two-way cupboard with its spidery contents, but this was the most fun he had ever got up to in his entire life. And there was something older-brotherly about Zack. He was worth standing up for.

'Well, that's just the way it is, sadly.' President Pickle closed the tome with a dull thud, dust shooting out all around him. 'Let's put it to a vote, shall we?'

Cynthia moved back over to her place at the head of the table as Council stood (for, in accordance with rule 8.9, clause 1.1, all members must stand when voting). She frowned at Zack disappointedly, her look a blatant mix of: *I tried, I failed, I did warn you.*

Zack couldn't believe it. First the (false) accusation of theft and now the prospect of bringing down his friends with him! How could he have been so irresponsible?

Almost like she could read his mind, Sophie grabbed his hand and looked into his eyes. 'We all agreed to follow you, Zack,' she told him. 'We're all in this together.'

Whether this was another of her confidence tricks or just kindness, Zack didn't know, but whatever it was, it seemed to cool his hot head. He looked at Jonny and Alex, who met his gaze with a reassuring nod. The mood was clear: if Zack went down, they were all happy to go down with him.

Was this even a place they wanted to be a part of anyway? thought Sophie defiantly.

'OK,' said President Pickle. 'All those in favour of the immediate and permanent expulsion of these four minors, please raise your hands.'

Jonny took full advantage of his lofty position to get a bird's-eye view of the vote as about half the hands in the room went up. Zack, Alex and Sophie bobbed and strained to see the outcome of the vote. It was clearly not unanimous: some hands hadn't been raised . . . Perhaps they were in with a chance!

'Right, that's six members in favour, including me.' President Pickle scratched the result on to a pad of paper, clearly unimpressed that Council weren't united on this. 'And all those against?'

Jonny watched as four hands rose into the air: Ernest's first, then Steve's and Jane's – 好! – and lastly, tentatively, Cynthia's.

Her husband gave her a pitying look, the kind he gave her when she forgot to give him extra gravy with his Tuesday evening meal of braised beef and dumplings.

'But only four against, I'm afraid, with no abstentions. So . . . motion carried,' said President Pickle, faking a glum face. 'Right, well, Council have clearly spoken.' He pompously picked up his gavel.

As he did so, Ernest coughed pointedly, both to get the attention of the president and to clear his throat (there was no point in wasting a good cough at his age!). 'Excuse me, Edmund, but I don't believe Bill has cast his vote yet.'

Everyone looked at Bill, who was still deep in REM sleep (and currently dreaming about a kangaroo named Florence Featherstone who made shoes for a living with tools she kept in her pouch).

What is Granddad up to? wondered Jonny.

'In the interest of *abiding by the rules*,' Ernest continued, 'shouldn't we include *his* vote as well? I would hate to see these four young magical minds dismissed purely on a technicality.'

'Well, it's not going to change the result as we've already won by two votes, but for the sake of formality . . . BILL!' President Pickle shook the old man forcefully, causing him to wake with a start and mutter the name 'Florence!'

'Which way are you voting, Bill? For or against?'

Sophie studied the old man; he looked like a cross between a skeleton and a pine cone. If only she could get into his eye line, she could compel him to vote against the motion. Though President Pickle was right (for once!): they were still outvoted.

Bill looked around the room, completely uninterested, not even noticing the youngsters who'd just appeared. Oh, why couldn't he go back to his dream? Florence had almost completed her second pair of Cuban heels – it was exciting stuff! Not like this drivel . . .

'*For*. Or against?' pressed President Pickle, trying to give Bill a not-so-subtle clue.

'Erm . . . against!' said Bill loudly, like he'd properly thought about what was at stake here, but in fact just repeating the last word that had come out of the president's mouth.

'Well, no matter – either way, that settles it!' said President Pickle, slapping Bill on the back so hard that his false teeth moved an inch forward, making him look like a porcelain donkey.

'He's not your gavel, Edmund!' said Cynthia, shoving some paperwork hard into her husband's ribs while Bill adjusted his teeth back into the recesses of his mouth, slobbering.

'Oh, you're all right, aren't you, Bill? You don't mind?' said President Pickle jovially.

But Bill was already fast asleep again, this time dreaming about a giant owl who lived on a vineyard.

'And so, as a formality, shouldn't we all now vote again?' pushed Ernest.

Zack, Jonny, Sophie and Alex looked at Ernest, worried that perhaps the man had finally lost it.

Just let it go, Granddad, thought Jonny. *We've still lost by one vote. This is just dragging things out, surely.*

'Well, if you *must*, Ernest,' said President Pickle. 'Let's do it the other way round, though, shall we? End on a high! All those against?'

Jonny watched as the same four defiant hands rose – at least this confirmed who their friends were, he thought.

Pickle lifted up Bill's cataleptic arm while he snoozed, his head lolling. 'And so, with Bill, that makes a total of . . . *five* against the motion.' He scrawled another note on his pad. 'And all those *for* the motion, please raise your hand.'

He raised his own hand and quickly totted up the numbers, noting them down on his pad. All of a sudden he froze. 'Five?' he whispered. '*Five?!*' He went around the room again, shaking his head in desperation. 'I don't understand!'

The accused stared at each other in excitement. What had just happened?

Jonny looked around the room, trying to see if there was someone he'd missed. No – everyone could be accounted for; no one had abstained.

'And so I believe, Mr President – though do correct me if I'm wrong,' said Ernest graciously, 'that we must have miscounted last time. And so, as there is no majority, the motion is *not* carried and our four youngsters are free to go – perhaps with a warning from Council? Or at least don't get caught next time!' he added, turning to his grandson with a mischievous glint in his eye.

'But how can this be?' said President Pickle, evidently devastated and completely flummoxed, for even though he was the president of the Magic Circle, the last time he'd successfully worked out a trick was when seventy-five-year-old Crazy Colin's magical cabinet had accidentally caught fire during a gala show, revealing its hidden compartment (along with its slowly roasting contents: Colin's assistant/great-granddaughter).

'Right, you lot,' Cynthia said, keen for the youngsters to leave while they could. 'Out!' She grabbed Henry by the arm too, leading him towards the door.

The others followed obediently, not wishing to outstay their welcome. As they left, they glanced at Ernest, Sophie mouthing a quick 'Thank you!', Zack and Jonny giving him a sly thumbs up.*

President Pickle caught Alex by the arm as he passed the table. 'Don't forget – I don't know what you think you overheard, but you're mistaken. Don't go spreading any silly rumours now, will you?'

Alex scurried out of the door, glad to be leaving this oppressive place – and thankfully not back through the way they came.

The council members looked at President Pickle as he slowly picked up his gavel and turned to dozing, dreaming, oblivious Bill.

* OK, go on then, how did Ernest do it?!
    So, on the first round of voting Ernest covertly voted both for *and* against the motion. On the second time round, Ernest chose simply just to vote against the motion, which – along with Bill's well-thought-out choice – made the votes equal. Why bother? Well – apart from to humiliate President Pickle and to vindicate our favoured four – simply for the thrill of creating a bit of a spectacle! That's magic in a nutshell really. All pretty pointless most of the time!

8

Sophie, Zack, Jonny and Alex blinked as they fell out on to Stephenson Way, soaking up the low-angled late-afternoon sunlight and breathing in the dusty, exhaust-fume-filled, sweet London air. Nice!

'So, how did you enjoy your first day at the Magic Circle?' Zack asked casually.

Jonny and Sophie burst out laughing – more through sheer relief than anything else – not quite believing how much had happened since they had first entered the building only hours ago. Even Alex couldn't help smiling.

'Oh, Zack, mate,' sang Jonny. 'I can't believe you were going to take the rap for us – you're so kind!' He smothered his friend in an all-encompassing hug.

'Well, it's pointless us *all* having a black mark against our name, isn't it?' said Zack, trying to free himself.

Sophie smiled as she watched them tussle. 'Yeah, yeah, all right, you two!' she said eventually. 'Putting our undiluted gratitude aside, Zack, I've got two questions. Firstly, what was all that wailing inside the Grand Theatre? And secondly, do you think it's true that the society is on the brink of collapse?'

Jonny let Zack go.

'Let's walk and talk, shall we?' said Zack, heading down the road. 'Just in case we're overheard.'

'OK, come on, then,' said Jonny, turning round to face Zack and walking backwards. 'What on *earth* was all that racket in the theatre? Who's *Alf*?'

'W-was that voice . . . real?' stammered Alex.

'What, none of you have heard of the legend of Alf Rattlebag?' asked Zack.

'Oh, *that* Alf!' said Sophie. 'Oh well, of course. Now it makes perfect sense, thank you, Zack. NOT! Come on, out with it!'

'Well, it's a long story,* but Alf Rattlebag is a ghost said to haunt the Magic Circle premises ever since he died the night the Grand Theatre opened, back in nineteen twenty-something.'

'So, the voice we heard was his ghost?' said Sophie disbelievingly.

'Yep,' answered Zack, like this was all pretty straightforward. 'The unofficial Patron Saint of Stagehands, his poster says. Always there for a magician in need. He was a good guy.'

* See Appendix 2 for this loooooooooooooong story!

84

'So . . . he's a *good* ghost?' asked Alex, trying to gauge exactly how scared he needed to be.

'Well, he certainly didn't sound like it!' said Sophie. 'He also sounded pretty *human*, for a ghost.' She was clearly unconvinced. 'Don't tell me you buy into all that!'

Zack shrugged. Sophie was right, he *didn't* usually buy into the idea of ghosts and things, but this one had just seemed so *real*.

Alex didn't know which he preferred: the idea of a ghost or the idea of a man pretending to be a ghost! Something to ponder about in the middle of the night, he thought with a shudder. And what was it with this Henry? No, the Magic Circle wasn't quite the safe haven Alex had hoped it might be. Though so long as he stayed with these three . . .

They sat down on a bench outside Euston Station as a pack of tourists sprinted past like a herd of gazelles evading a lion.

Jonny picked up a newspaper, tearing it in half as he spoke. 'I don't even think *Granddad* thought things were *that* bad, judging by the look on his face – I can't wait to talk to him about it!'

'Do you think he might be able to give us the lowdown?' asked Zack.

'Maybe . . .'

'Well, either way, it's just so *unfair*!' Sophie raised her voice passionately as she got up and began to pace about. 'Don't the Council care about the future of magic?' She didn't want to believe that such a place could be so out of touch. 'We could help in all kinds of ways – I *know* we could!'

'But that's not the point,' said Zack as he watched Jonny tear the newspaper in half again. 'It doesn't matter whether we'd run it better than them. President Pickle obviously thinks the society was set up by a particular generation *for* a particular generation, and that's that. He'd rather it died with them than see it handed over to a bunch of *kids*! And if that means the end of the Magic Circle, then so be it!'

Jonny continued to rip the paper into increasingly small pieces. With a flourish, he pulled his hands apart, and at once the newspaper was whole again, fluttering in the breeze. He smiled proudly – he was finally getting the hang of it! *Granddad will be so pleased*, he thought.

A nearby tourist stared at Jonny and the newspaper, unsure of what she'd just witnessed, and then took a picture of what she'd been reliably informed by Frank* was Big Ben, but was actually Pret.

'Nicely done!' said Sophie, glad to be reminded that there was still a lot of fun to be found in conjuring.

'No way! How on *earth* ...?' Zack was staring at the front page of the newspaper, a puzzled look on his face.

'Oh wowsers, don't tell me you don't know how it's done!' said Jonny, hoping he'd managed to stupefy his best friend – that was *definitely* a sign of progress.

* Remember Frank?

'No, not that – I could see the duplicate as soon as you picked it up,' said Zack, reaching for the paper and extinguishing Jonny's hopes in an instant. 'The headline – look!'

They studied the freshly restored front page of the *Evening Standard*, reading the headline together:

**VAULTS OF BANK OF ENGLAND
BROKEN INTO FOR FIRST TIME EVER!
POLICE BAFFLED!**

Underneath was a picture of a man looking baffled, alongside a caption that read: *Scotland Yard's Detective Inspector Caulfield completely and utterly BAFFLED!*

They continued to read the article . . .

The baffled detective inspector has no idea how thieves managed to enter the Bank of England, but insists that he has everything under control. DI Caulfield was alerted to the news this morning, when Governor of the Bank of England Hugh J'Account phoned Scotland Yard in a panic, apparently also 'completely baffled' as to how thieves had managed to penetrate the vast subterranean vaults and leave undetected with sackfuls of gold. This baffling news comes just days after Hugh J'Account was boasting about how no one has ever broken into the Bank of England vaults before and how it would be impossible for anyone to do so undetected. 'The worry is,' commented DI Caulfield, 'that we have no idea how the thieves accomplished this. And that is obviously our main concern right now. However, I do have absolutely everything under control, despite being quite baffled.'

For more photos of DI Caulfield and Hugh J'Account standing in the empty vault and looking baffled, please turn to page five.

Jonny fumbled his way to page five, and they all stared at the series of black-and-white photos of DI Caulfield and Hugh J'Account in various startled poses, a mixture of fear, confusion and surprise on their faces.

They put down the paper and sat back against the bench, Sophie whistling loudly.

'So how's that one done, then?' said Jonny, perplexed. 'I mean *surely* the Bank of England has CCTV!'

Alex scanned the pictures of the vault more closely, looking at the giant safe door, clearly unscathed and bolted from the inside, immediately triggering the cogs in his conjuring brain. *How, how, how?*

'Apparently the cameras didn't pick up on anything,' answered Sophie, reading the caption beneath a large picture of the vault entrance. 'It's almost like the thieves were –'

Even before she could finish her sentence, Alex felt the word tumble out of his dry mouth: 'Ghosts.'

'Now come on, Alex,' Sophie said, running her fingers through the short spiky hair on the side of her head. 'Why would a ghost want gold?'

Alex pondered for a bit. It sounded like the start of a bad joke you might find screwed up inside a Christmas cracker. Something that a dad might tell and retell for ever and ever and find absolutely *hilarious*. But it was a fair question.

Jonny looked over at Zack, who was now sitting with his head back and eyes half closed. He recognized it as the classic 'I'm Zack Harrison and I've just thought of something' mode.

'Oh, here we go . . . What have you just worked out?' asked Jonny.

Zack chewed on his bottom lip. 'Well, it can't be done,' he said eventually.

'That, my dear friend, I believe, is the whole point!' Jonny looked at Sophie, but she was now staring at Zack too.

'Out with it, Zack!' she commanded. 'What are you thinking?'

'Well, if it can't be done – and clearly it can't – then it must be . . . a trick.'

The others gazed at him in excitement. This word – trick – meant so much to all of them.

It was true: the theft did have all the hallmarks of some great magical stunt, thought Alex.

'And even though I don't quite know how the thieves managed it . . . I *do* know of a book that might be able to shed some light on the matter,' Zack added mysteriously.

'Ooh, what book?' said Jonny, always keen to add to his ever-increasing list of books to read, mostly classic recommendations from his granddad.

'Have you ever heard of *The Thieves' Almanac*?' Zack looked at his friends, pleased to see them instantly taken in by the intriguing title. 'The Magic Circle banned all mention of it years ago, but rumour has it that there's a series of books about how to use magic to commit crimes. Apparently the majority were "lost" in a fire, but one survived and is still around today: *The Thieves' Almanac*.'

'Who's it by?' asked Sophie, eager to know more.

'The writer is anonymous, but people think that a load of different magicians might have contributed. It's always being mentioned on magic forums. Apparently the methods described are some of the most devious ever imagined!' Zack grinned at them.

Oh, how he would love to peep inside the book, even just for a split second! It was bound to be packed full of daring, devilish methods. It was a book magicians dreamed of. Want to know how to prise a prized portrait out of its glass cabinet without setting off the alarm? Then this is the book for you! Want to know how to get into one of the most impenetrable bank vaults in the country completely undetected, without damaging even one of the 800 locking mechanisms that surround the nation's shiniest treasure? Then buy this book now!

Except that this book wasn't for sale. *Fortunately*, some might say. No, this book was most probably just a thing of myth. Maybe . . .

'Are you saying that a magician had a hand in this?' asked Jonny, holding up the newspaper.

'It certainly looks that way,' said Zack. 'But there's one way to find out for sure.'

'OK . . .' said Sophie slowly, starting to like the sound of where this might be going.

'Well, the only copy of *The Thieves' Almanac* is thought to be deep inside the Magic Circle library,' Zack said. 'What if we could lay our hands on it – maybe even take it to this DI Caulfield? That would help shed light on things, right?' He patted the picture of the inspector, so that the man's expression changed from a baffled grimace to a crazed grin, like the Queen's face on a folded bank note.*

'Zack, mate, you do know that if we get caught sneaking around the Magic Circle again, and especially the library, we'll *never* be allowed back in?' said Jonny.

'Well then, let's not get caught this time! That was your granddad's advice, wasn't it?' Zack stood, smiling.

Sophie bit her lip, weighing things up. Zack's taste for adventure was infectious. Yes, she wanted to know more about this notorious book, maybe even peek inside if they managed to find it. But Jonny was right: what if they got caught? President Pickle had made it clear that there would be no second chances. The Magic Circle was a club she'd dreamed of joining since she opened her very first magic book. It was the *only* place where a magician could flourish. Did she really want to jeopardize her future as a magician?

---

* Do happily flick your way towards Appendix 3 for a detailed tutorial on how to do this if you so wish!

But then, if the society was on the verge of collapse anyway, what did they have to lose? Access to some overly warm, stinky room? A lifelong friendship with Deanna? Lectures from the sexist, patronizing president? Ah yes, but what about the society's rich history, its network of magicians, the library people kept talking about, the Grand Theatre . . .

'Let's do it!' she said at last, eyeing the others with a renewed sense of mischief. 'The worst that can happen is that we lose something we never really had in the first place.'

'And the best that can happen,' added Zack, 'is that we show the Magic Circle how things should be done. That we're not just a bunch of pesky kids!'

'I'm loving this!' said Jonny, waggling his fingers at Zack. 'But when? And *how*?'

'And where even *is* the library?' asked Sophie.

'Well, let's not do anything today – not while Council are knocking about the place.' Zack paced back and forth in front of the bench. 'But if it's anything like the last time I was here, there won't be anyone about first thing in the morning. How about we get there early tomorrow, before the second day of the induction week starts?' he suggested.

'And how, my man, do you plan on getting us inside before the doors open?' asked Jonny, eyes sparkling. 'Anyone know how to pick locks?'

Alex nervously raised his hand.

Sophie, Jonny and Zack grinned at him.

'Well I never!' said Jonny. 'It's always the quiet ones, isn't it?'

Alex lowered his hand as if he'd just owned up to making a smell.

'Then that settles it,' concluded Sophie. 'See you all outside the Magic Circle tomorrow morning – seven a.m. sharp!'

'Yep.'

'Seven a.m.'

'Sharp.'

'Brilliant!'

'OK.'

'See . . . see you then.'

'Yes, bye.'

'Can't wait!'

'Safe journey, everyone.'

'Hang on a minute – aren't we all going the same way?'

9

Morning!

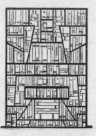

Sophie walked cautiously through the mist along Stephenson Way. A passing commuter appeared out of the air, like a bored zombie, barely noticing her, his eyes glassy from decades of staring at the computer, and now fixed on the screen of his phone beeping mercilessly at him with more reminders and chores, his suit creased in the same way it had been since the mid-nineties, his hair dishevelled from another late night on Excel.

Sophie shivered, pulling her Parka tight as she rounded the corner and approached the blue door of the Magic Circle. She could just make out Alex, Zack and Jonny standing in line, in height order – looking like one of those posters showing the evolution of man – suspended in the foggy air.

'Lovely morning!' said Zack in a hushed voice as she approached.

'Well, hopefully it means we won't be seen,' she said, giving Alex a wave.

'And how was the hotel, darling?' asked Jonny, chomping on a banana, his head quite literally lost in the clouds above. 'Don't they think it's a bit weird you're there all on your own?'

'Well,' said Sophie, a mischievous look in her eye, 'I *may* have used some of my powers of suggestion to get round that!'

'Tell, now!' Jonny loved the sound of this.

'Well, I've hypnotized the staff into believing I'm about forty-five.'

'Jeez, Sophie!' said Zack, laughing out loud. 'Is that even legal? Where do your parents think you're staying?'

'Dad's not around,' said Sophie, casually piercing a carton of orange juice with the straw, 'but my mum thinks I'm on a school trip for the week. It's fine. If she finds out, I'll just hypnotize her until she forgets all about it – I usually test stuff like that out on her anyway.' She popped the straw in her mouth, draining the carton in one.

Jonny and Zack shook their heads. They'd spoken about this formidable new acquaintance of theirs on their way home the day before. She was one of a kind. *Their* kind, Zack figured. Or 'Completely and utterly ace!' as Jonny had put it.

'And how about you, Alex?' asked Sophie. 'Not get much sleep last night?'

He scrunched up his brow. How did she know? How did she know he'd spent most of the night awake, fretting over his locks and picks like he now had something to prove?

'Oh, it's quite obvious if you think about it,' answered Sophie, clearly reading his reaction. 'Bags under the eyes, the creased coat collar suggesting that you had a thirty-minute doze leaning against the window on your way in from Kings Langley, the oil on your fingers – no doubt from some late-night practice with a grubby padlock . . .'

Alex grinned. Despite his nerves, his first day at the Magic Circle had been one of the most exhilarating of his life. And even though he was anxious about what might lie ahead, so long as it was with these three, then he figured it was worth it.

'We should probably get on,' said Zack, glancing at his watch. 'We've got less than two hours before everyone arrives.'

'Good luck, mate!' Jonny said to Alex encouragingly.

'We'll shield you – take your time,' added Zack.

Alex gulped. *Here goes!* He'd learned to pick locks on holiday with his parents after they'd 'accidentally' locked him in his room for a period that happened to coincide with happy hour at the hotel bar. Little did they know that Alex had almost immediately picked the door lock and had spent the evening in the hotel swimming pool.

He pulled out a small thin metal tool shaped a bit like a bone you might find in a chicken, although – unless the chicken had had some kind of major operation or was actually a robotic chicken from the future – it's unlikely you'd find this kind of metallic implement inside a hen carcass. Kneeling down, he carefully inserted one end into the keyhole, slowly rotating it, delicately sussing out the locking mechanism.

Zack, Sophie and Jonny had formed a screen around Alex – a bit like when family members gather round when you've got to get out of your swimming costume on the beach, which kind of works but pretty much always contains a load of embarrassing gaps.

Zack nodded politely as a passer-by raised his head from the morning papers to stare at them, the gent's fingers already grubby with ink from the stocks-and-shares pages, his eyes roaming suspiciously as he spotted the soles of Alex's shoes sticking out under Jonny's lanky frame, making it look like Jonny had four feet.

'It's a condition he has,' Sophie said confidently, clicking her fingers at him.

Suitably confounded, the passer-by passed by into the mist.

'How are you getting on, Alex?' Zack whispered.

Alex had his eyes closed, feeling his way through a series of pins, plugs and levers, searching for the right kind of resistance, listening for a faint click.

Just another three millimetres to the left and . . .

'There!' Alex said softly, feeling a huge gush of relief as it gave way. The lock slid across smoothly, the door opening and sucking in a waft of cool air.

Sophie, Jonny and Zack turned round as Alex looked up at them like a cheeky street urchin.

'Nice work!' said Jonny.

'And so quick as well!' Sophie helped him up.

Alex blushed as he hastily put the tool back in his coat pocket, shying away from the compliments.

'OK then,' said Zack, patting Alex on the back. 'Let's do this. On three, two, one . . .'

They entered quickly, the mist curling in around them, suitably obscuring their business from the growing mass of zombies going about their morning rituals on Stephenson Way, and heaved it shut with a deep, echoing thud.

They were inside!

And alone . . .

Ish!

The four stood in the weak light, absorbing the increasingly familiar surroundings.

Jonny lit a match (he had a torch, but this felt WAY more exciting), the flame sending their silhouettes dancing around the hall.

'Is there anybody with us?' he called out spookily, holding the match under his chin so that his face was in shadow – before removing it promptly when it seemed he might sustain third-degree burns.

As if on cue, a current of cold air extinguished the flickering flame, cooling Jonny's singed chin.

Zack shivered and rubbed his eyes. He wasn't good in the mornings: he often resorted to sleeping in his school uniform and forgoing breakfast just for those extra few minutes in bed. Which meant he always looked somewhat bedraggled and felt RAVENOUS! But this morning he'd been up like a shot, keen to embrace the day; keen to see his three new friends again, keen to solve an impossible crime, keen to play a part in saving this failing society. He'd even managed a breakfast of scrambled eggs, toast, bacon, beans, tomatoes, hash browns, mushrooms, cereal, granola, digestive biscuits, buttered baps, a Petit Filou, cold pizza from the night before, some leftover lamb tagine, hummus, a plastic cheese slice and seven of his five-a-day – all of which took precisely ninety minutes to prepare and one hour to devour (meaning that Zack Harrison had actually been banging around the kitchen since 3.30 a.m. – a personal best). Still, at least he wouldn't get hungry any time soon!

Jonny lit another match, this time placing it on his upturned left palm; it flared up, lighting the entrance hall. 'One of Granddad's!' he said.

Sophie smiled up at him: with his palm held aloft, he was almost indistinguishable from his granddad in the photo they'd seen. 'Right, which way?' she asked.

'My granddad said we were near the library when we were in the council chamber,' Jonny told her.

'Of course!' Sophie was already moving off along the dusky corridor. 'I bet it's down that second set of spiral stairs then – come on!'

The boys hurried after her, hopscotching to avoid the ever-increasing number of mousetraps. Alex was particularly glad to see no sign of yesterday's giant rat, other than an impressive display of his huge droppings – as big a hint as any that he was still knocking about the place eating his body weight in whatever rats ate. Still, no time to dawdle.

They soon reached the pink door of the Junior Room, now bolted shut with four massive padlocks.

'OK,' said Zack. 'We've got just under two hours before we need to be right back here.' He checked his watch.

'Surely that's enough time,' said Jonny, blowing out the dwindling flame on his palm and finally removing the small torch from his rucksack.

'Yes, but we don't know where we're going or what we're looking for!' Sophie reminded him.

How difficult could it be to find a mythical volume amongst the world's biggest collection of magic books? Alex wondered.

They tiptoed further down the corridor, recalling with growing unease the dramatic events in the Grand Theatre the day before.

'OK, so how do we go about this?' Sophie had reached the curtained opening and turned to face the boys, a faint whiff of trepidation in her voice.

She silently parted the red curtain to reveal the 'painting' of the entrance underneath and peered through – destroying the illusion in an instant.

'The stairwell is just the other side of the auditorium,' said Zack, joining her. 'If we make a run for it and stay quiet, hopefully we won't wake . . . whatever it was in there yesterday.'

The others nodded, breathing deeply, readying themselves for a sprint.

'OK, *now*!' said Jonny in his best stage whisper.

They whizzed into the theatre, marvelling at its size once again before quickly getting their bearings. 'This way!' Zack beckoned as he made his way across the stalls towards the small green door.

Sophie took a moment to look around, her eyes darting about in the dim house light, scouring, searching for any signs of life (or afterlife).

Nothing.

'Coming through!' Jonny bounded across the theatre in no more than twelve long strides, reaching the green door first. He opened it carefully, craning his neck round the crusty frame.

Nothing.

Sophie, Zack and Alex joined him in a tangled clump and stood there, panting.

Alex glanced briefly back into the theatre. Was that a . . . ? No. *Nothing!*

'Shall we?' said Jonny, shutting the green door behind them and leaping on to the banister rail.

Sophie and Zack clambered aboard enthusiastically, helping Alex up once more before plunging and twisting down into the depths.

'Don't forget to get off at the next landing!' warned Sophie over the rushing air as soon as she felt herself slowing down.

They came to a stop next to the double-sided cupboard, hopping off one by one, their legs like jelly. 'I think let's keep out of here?' said Zack, tapping the cupboard door and startling a mummy and daddy spider canoodling inside, infuriating them wildly. (Someone – probably some local woodlouse – was going to pay for this later!)

'Right,' said Sophie, dusting herself down. She reached for Jonny's torch and shone it down the second set of stairs that wound off into the distance in a wide spiral. 'This way, I think . . .'

The four crept forward, hugging the outer stone wall, not daring to get too close to the crumbling edge.

No chance of sliding down *this* banister, thought Alex, relieved to see that large parts of it had already crumbled away, which in fact wasn't that relieving in the slightest.

'Or, guys, we could just pop in here,' said Jonny casually, stopping a few steps down and pointing at a wooden door set into the curved wall.

Sophie shone the torch where Jonny was standing. In luxurious writing the word LIBRARY had been carved beautifully into the wood, filled in with striking gold leaf. And then, underneath – as if to deliberately undermine the ornate finish – someone had stuck a large laminated sheet of bright lilac card pedantically listing the opening times and guidelines on how to use the library's loan system. It goes without saying that at 7.20 on a Tuesday morning this library was very much CLOSED thank you.

'So . . . wh-what do you think is all the way down there, then?' said Alex, still peering over the edge of the echoey chasm.

'Oh, I'm sure we'll find out another day!' said Zack playfully as Alex drew back from the gaping gulf.

They all squeezed into the doorway, Jonny scrunching up his head, shoulders, knees and toes,* trying to fit.

'Hmm – we might need your lock-picking skills again, if that's OK, Alex,' said Zack, moving aside to give him some space.

Alex edged his way to the front, turning this way and that – like one of the bits in Tetris – angling round Jonny's jagged frame – and knelt down. He patted the area around the keyhole with his fingers, scrutinizing the lock.

Zack grinned at Sophie and Jonny. Breaking and entering!

Just as Alex was reaching for his tools, the door suddenly wafted open. Alex was up like a shot, backing into the other three. 'That wasn't me!' he shrilled in a small, frightened voice. 'It . . . It must have already been open.'

The others looked at each other. 'Strange . . . it's not locked.' Zack felt the sides of the door, examining the frame. 'Hey, look – someone's been at this before!'

Sophie and Jonny now saw that the area around the lock was covered in scratches. 'Well, whoever did this was pretty clumsy. Not a patch on your handiwork, Alex,' said Sophie, trying to encourage him.

* And eyes and ears and mouth and nose!

Alex's mind was already racing: who could have come trespassing before them?

Alf?

Werewolves . . . ?

That's enough now, Alex!

'Well,' concluded Jonny. 'These marks look like they were made some time ago, so I'm sure whoever did this is long gone.'

'Let's just keep quiet all the same,' said Zack, creeping forward through the doorway.

At once they were surrounded by the sweet, succulent smell of books.* Now, it might seem obvious to say that the library was full of books – but, well, the library was full of books.

However, this was a library unlike any they had ever seen before. It was nothing like his school library, Jonny thought, which – on a good day – might contain a couple of books about the agricultural revolution and an encyclopaedia about growing up (with suitably patronizing 'anatomical' illustrations, including several pop-up bits).

No, this library was absolutely crammed with magic books. Tall books, zigzag-shaped books, books as small as playing cards; illustrated books, theoretical books; books about billiard balls, books about balloon animals, books about illusions, books about other books, books

* Which is only weird if you think about it for too long, so please just keep reading and move on! Or if you're really keen, stop reading right now and give this chapter a big old sniff! And then carry on.

on books on books about other books; books stacked upright, books stacked sideways, upside-down books, books with fancy tassels – a proper hodgepodge of conjuring books; a dry-stone wall of books, all interlocking perfectly, filling every possible space.

Jonny imagined the librarian getting a new book, measuring its dimensions with a protractor and a set square, before locating the perfect spot along a shelf and popping it in.

Sophie looked around in the dim reddish light – used to protect ageing tomes, she remembered from her science lessons.

They were standing on a wrought-iron balcony, overlooking a vast cathedral-like room, the starting point for a network of walkways and steps that all led off into a maze of shelves. Inscribed into the wood at the ends of the shelves were the finest names in magic: *Acer, Ainley, Anneman, Aronson* ... Next shelf: *Berglas, Blackstone, Bongo, Brown* ...

Even though he'd heard rumours that the Magic Circle library was big, Zack was astounded to find such a vast place beneath the streets of central London. It was the size of a football pitch, but on multiple levels. An entire stadium of magic books!

Alex's eyes jumped from one shelf to the other: *Calvert, Cardini, Cooper, Curry* ... *Daniels, Davenport, Dunninger, Dynamo*. He stood, enchanted, soaking up the thick papery air – surely this was reason enough to become a member of the Magic Circle? It was the most beautiful library he had ever seen. Magician or not, who wouldn't want to get lost in this world of work on wizardry?

'So, where do we start?' said Sophie quietly. 'Left, right, up, down, straight ahead – anyone got a preference?' Her eyes flew over the complex of steps, walkways and ladders turning every which way – a proper 3D labyrinth.

Jonny scanned the ceiling. 'There!' he said, pointing to a small arrow almost obscured by the top of shelf *E* (*Eason, Elmsley, Erdnase*); it was attached to a beam by a couple of small chains, embossed with the words RESTRICTED SECTION: THIS WAY!

Well, that's handy!

They raced forward excitedly, trying to keep an eye on the arrow as they rounded corners, retracing their steps whenever they came to a dead end or lost sight of it.

Shelves of books flew by (*Fischbacher, Gellar, Hugard . . .*). Jonny scrambled up a thin ladder, a mound of periodicals (*Ibidem*) piled precariously alongside, arching almost impossibly on to the top of shelf *J* (*Joshua*). The others struggled to keep up – Zack regretting a shortcut between shelves *K* (*Kaps, Kellar, Klok*) and *L* (*Lorayne, Losander, Lovell*), which were so jam-packed he could barely get through.

Some of the names Sophie hadn't even heard of. Knowing there was no time to stop now, she tried to form a mental list. Look at all the stuff she was missing! *Malone, Nixon, Okito, Page . . .* Even an entire shelf dedicated to material by magicians with surnames beginning with *Q!* Who ever heard of a single magician with a surname beginning with *Q?*

Bringing up the rear, Alex glanced over his shoulder at the crisscrossing honeycomb of aisles, platforms and shelves, dizzied by the intricate mosaic of books – how would they ever find their way back? *Oh, who even cares?* he thought, surprising himself; all he needed in life was right here: a mound of magic books and three great friends!

'This way!' called Jonny from up ahead. 'We're nearly there!'

Alex passed shelves bursting with *Rowling*, *Shaxon* and *Thurston*. He slowed to a walking pace past *Uri*, *Vernon*, *Welles* and *Lount* (filed here because Mr Lount once marketed an effect called 'Xray Xtra'). To his right he spotted an autobiography on Ying & Yang (a paperback, rather thin account of Steve and Jane's life, still in its cellophane packaging), before finally coming to a stop alongside shelf *Z* – a rather large manual on false shuffles by Herb Zarrow.

Panting slightly, Alex studied the book, intrigued, slowly reaching out his hand –

'Freeze!' Zack's voice was cushioned by the sea of books.

Alex turned to face him, his hand frozen in mid-air, ready to grasp the book; the hairs on the back of his neck were beginning to prickle. What on earth was it *now*? It wasn't even night-time. Surely scary things didn't happen first thing in the morning. Immediately his mind started to fill with images of hooded figures approaching in the dim red lighting . . .

Sophie and Jonny turned to see where Zack was now looking, his eyes trained on the ceiling way up above where Alex was stood.

Oh wow . . .

Oh Jeez . . .

Oh NO!

Hundreds upon hundreds of tiny threads descended from the ceiling – a web of wires connecting each book in what was surely one of the most intricate and archaic alarm systems ever devised!

'Oh, man, you've got to be kidding . . .' whispered Jonny, unnerved and impressed. 'This must have taken someone *ages*!'

'Well, let's not find out if it works!' said Sophie in a low voice, worried about what each of these million fine tripwires might trigger should a book be removed from its shelf.

Alex moved away from Mr Zarrow's manual on false shuffles and joined the others.

'Let's just take things a bit more slowly from now on,' said Zack.

Ahead of them was a cordoned-off aisle, at the end of which they could make out a dark-green cabinet, its doors shut and – judging by its appearance – locked.

Zack looked at the plaque mounted proudly above the cabinet: RESTRICTED SECTION: YOU ARE HERE!

'But surely this is too easy . . .' Sophie's brow was furrowed. 'If books on false shuffles and balloon animals are alarmed, then why is the restricted section so easily accessible?'

She was right, thought Zack. This stank of misdirection. There had to be more to it than . . . *this*.

'What's that?' said Jonny suddenly, putting a finger to his lips. They all stood there, ears tuned to the creaking, whining sound of . . . What was that?

It sounded to Sophie like the squeak of rusty wheels, made even creepier by the slowness of the pace. This wasn't someone aiming to give them a shock; this was no Alf. This person knew how to build suspense, scaring them gradually, working them up into a fearful frenzy as the sound got louder and louder, closer and closer.

They all looked around frantically, peering into the red haze. There were a billion hiding places, but they couldn't pinpoint where the noise was coming from.

It was Jonny who spotted it first, crying out loudly and then quickly covering his mouth to stop anything else from coming out.

He could make out the form of a strange-looking figure above them, his head hanging low, seated at an oak desk and gliding down from what was fast becoming an inexplicable ceiling full of countless surprises.

The four gawped, bewitched and trembling, as they watched the man and his desk, slowly falling like a ball-bearing travelling through thick treacle. A network of pulleys manoeuvred him into position, depositing him on the floor with a soft thud.

On the desk lay a small nameplate:

LIBRARIAN

'Whoa, what an entrance!' whispered Jonny quietly from in between his fingers.

They all stood there, bunched together like penguins protecting their young, desperately trying to work out what to say.

'Ex-excuse me,' stammered Sophie after about thirty seconds – which is actually rather a long time when you're facing someone who's just floated (yes, that's right, *floated*!) down from the ceiling of a library and who hasn't yet looked up. Awkward!

Suddenly the librarian twitched to life with a series of jagged movements, whirs and clicks. Inch by inch, his head angled up – juddering and stuttering – as he rose from his seat like someone with far too many bones, all of which needed replacing.

They all took a step back in shock as they studied the metal face before them.

'Cool! It's an automaton!' exclaimed Zack, moving forward to get a closer look.

'An automa-what?' asked Jonny, still cautious.

'An *automaton*,' repeated Zack as he studied the librarian closely. 'A robot, basically, but from Victorian times.'

Sophie waved her hand in front of its face, but the unblinking eyes gave nothing away; it looked neither happy nor sad, neither knowledgeable nor confused, neither amiable nor ANNOYED!

'He looks a bit like my old violin teacher!' said Jonny as Alex leaned forward to touch the lank, lifeless hair. He shuddered.

On the desk in front of the librarian was a small silver bell, next to which was another plaque with the words PLEASE RING FOR ATTENTION. Zack looked at the others, raising an eyebrow, his hand hovering.

At nods from the others, he lowered his hand on to the icy metal ringer.

Alex winced at the tinny sound, afraid of what it might summon next. He scanned the ceiling for anything else that might descend from the heavens at the sound of the automaton's bell. Bloodied spikes? An elephant? Milk?!

No.

Not this time anyway.

Instead, a stubby piece of brown paper – the sort that you might receive when visiting a steam-train museum – shot out of the automaton's mouth with a faint *shush*.

Sophie reached forward and removed the slip, then read the text out loud:

'*Quiet please! Only President Pickle and those approved by Council have access to the restricted section of the library and must demonstrate their status by answering the following question.*'

The automaton began to twitch as a second slip – longer than the first – shot out of its mouth. Sophie removed it carefully, like a dentist's assistant.

'*Robert-Houdin is renowned for being 1) an escapologist, 2) an actor, or 3) a magician? Please lift my left thumb if you think the answer is one, my left forefinger if you think the answer is two, or extend my left middle finger for answer three.*'

They looked at one another, thinking hard, as a third piece of paper emerged from the gaping mouth, hanging there like a decaying tongue. Zack pulled this slip free, reading out loud:

'*Trespassers BEWARE! Make a mistake and you'll come to a crushing end!*'

Craning their necks, they looked fearfully up at the ceiling again.

Just above them was now a huge net of books – Tarbell's entire hardback course in magic, to be precise; a series famed for its completeness and accounting for some of the heaviest and largest books on magic ever produced. It hung there monstrously, the net bulging and swaying lightly from side to side.

'Let's get the answer to this correct, then!' said Jonny.

'Was Robert-Houdin *Houdini's* real name?' asked Zack, looking at Sophie. 'If so, then the answer must be number one – escapologist.'

'No, surely that's what they want us to think . . .' Sophie was staring at the slip of paper. 'Anyway, wasn't Houdini's real name Erik Weisz?'

'OK, well then, the answer must be number three,' said Jonny, looking at Alex for confirmation. 'Wasn't Robert-Houdin the magician who could make an orange tree grow live on stage?'

Alex nodded, and Sophie agreed. 'Hmm. Yes . . . he was. That must be it, then. Robert-Houdin was a magician, plain and simple.'

'Sure?' said Zack, reaching towards the librarian cautiously.

Sophie nodded. But then ... Was there something she was missing? It just all seemed a bit too easy. Perhaps it was a bluff.

'OK, so in that case we need to extend his left middle finger,' said Zack uneasily, looking down at the librarian's metallic palm face down on the desk, his fingers curled inwards slightly, his angular knuckle jutting out like an armoured glove.

Just as Zack touched the rusting hand, Sophie yelled, 'Wait!' causing them all to jump. 'It's a trick question! It's answer two – we need to lift his left forefinger.'

The others turned to look at her. 'He was an *actor*? What ... ? Why?' said Jonny.

Sophie beamed at them. 'Don't you remember the famous quote?' They all stared blankly at her. 'In one of his books Robert-Houdin said that a magician is in fact an *actor* playing the *part* of a magician – therefore Robert-Houdin was renowned for being an *actor*. It's answer number two.'

The three boys grinned back at her. She sure was good, was this one!

Sneaky librarian – shame on you!

Zack reached forward and lifted the left forefinger slowly, feeling a slight resistance before the finger gave way with a painful click. At once the automaton sprang to life again, its clockwork heart whirring deep within its chest.

The four moved back a few steps, alarmed to see that the net above simply moved with them, like it was able to track their every step. They raised their arms above their heads, readying themselves for an onslaught of Tarbell – a crash course in magic!

But thankfully no such onslaught came. They were in the clear.

Slowly spluttering, like a car low on petrol, the automaton – along with the desk – rotated a full ninety degrees anticlockwise. The librarian's mechanical arm rose shakily, pointing to the green cabinet, which had now opened up with a definite click. Permission granted!

They walked gingerly down the aisle towards the cabinet as the automaton creaked its way back up into the ceiling, along with the deadly net of books.

Way more interesting than your bog-standard library lending system with its boring stamps, loans and fines, thought Zack. Wires, pulleys, robotic staff and the threat of immediate expulsion and imminent death – now, *that's* what everyone wants from their local library!

The others watched as Zack pulled the cabinet doors open, desperate for their first glimpse of the notorious *Thieves' Almanac*.

Inside, neatly arranged in decreasing order of size, were more books on magic: rare first editions, signed copies of lecture notes, a pamphlet on sexy magic (whatever that was), several books on 'bizarre magick' verging on the paranormal, and then, staring them in the face on the bottom shelf, about a third of the way across – a gaping hole, the width of a book. In its place a red bookmark poked out angrily, shining boastfully in the glaring light.

Sophie removed it slowly, as the others held on to each other, too excited to breathe. Scrawled along it were the words:

The Thieves' Almanac - missing since last April, presumed STOLEN!

And then, on the other side – almost as an afterthought – was the addendum:

Probably by Zack Harrison!

10

Having exited and re-entered the Magic Circle, Sophie, Zack, Jonny and Alex took their seats at the back of the Junior Room at precisely 9.01 a.m. in fevered discussion, their voices intermingling as they spoke over each other excitedly.

'I promise I didn't steal that book!'

'Zack, mate, no one's accusing you of stealing anything, OK? Calm down!'

'I-I found a –'

'So *The Thieves' Almanac* was stolen and now the Bank of England has been broken into ... That can't be a coincidence, can it?' said Sophie, tugging at her short fringe in excitement.

'What was it the librarian said?' Zack tried to focus. 'Only members of *Council* have access to the restricted section.'

'What, you think someone on the Magic Circle *Council* is helping these thieves? They took the book themselves?'

'Maybe. The mastermind behind the bank robbery *must* be a magician, surely!'

'Yes, but . . .'

'I-I found a –'

'Then again, if *we* managed to get past the automaton,' Jonny pointed out, 'anyone who's into magic could. It needn't have been a council member.'

They gazed around the room at the gaggle of juniors filing in: Max sticky with beans and egg; Deanna already sprawled across the floor, seemingly doing as many different versions of the splits as her elastic body would allow; the posh boys dressed up to the nines. Cynthia fiendishly ticking everyone off on her clipboard like a madwoman at bingo.

'OK, maybe not *them*. But who knows?'

'I-I found a –'

'Out with it, Alex!'

'I found *this* on our way out of the library . . .' Alex opened up his clammy palm to reveal a limp red rose petal. 'You . . . You don't think *Henry* could have been down there, do you?'

As if on cue, Henry glided into the room, all in black once more, looking like an exhausted Grim Reaper shrouded in the acrid smell of death (where death = farts). He nodded at the four of them, cursing under his breath as Deanna rolled into his shins.

'Well, listen – we need to find out who stole *The Thieves' Almanac* – and soon,' said Zack, his voice low now that Henry was in earshot. 'Not just because they might be involved in this Bank of England plot – but it will help clear my name. There's no way President Pickle will let me become a member otherwise!' He looked at Henry, now sitting awkwardly on a hard plastic chair, his face deathly white.

'Does he think he's a vampire?' said Jonny, following Zack's gaze.

Steve and Jane suddenly entered noisily, dressed in their Chinese robes again, and covered in thick face paint, throwing sweets into the room like it was the start of the second half at a pantomime.

'We don't usually allow snacks before ten a.m.,' said Deanna's mum, clearly anxious that her position of official snack-giver might be usurped.

'Yes – can you maybe not do that right now, thank you, Steve,' added Cynthia distractedly.

Steve winked at the children in the room like he was in a cartoon, throwing a couple more gummy sweets behind him as he turned to sit down.

'OK, can I have everyone's attention, please?' Cynthia stepped on to the raised area at the front of the room. 'So, welcome to the second day of your induction week. Now, we're extremely lucky to have some *real-life* members of the Magic Circle come and visit us this morning.' She looked at Steve and Jane, who were now blowing up long, colourful balloons. Steve stopped huffing to give everyone another wave, letting go of his balloon in the process so that it flew around the room with a distressed squeal. Jane pretended to reprimand him, before bowing, proving that she was in on it all along – ever the double-act! Zack, Jonny, Sophie and Alex couldn't help but smile.

'Yes, thank you,' continued Cynthia, hastily removing the saggy remains of the balloon from her cleavage and flicking it back at Steve with a twang. 'So, Steve and Jane are here to give us a glimpse into what it takes to become a *professional* magician, which I'm sure most of you will have thought about.'

Sophie nudged Jonny in the ribs.

'Then, as I mentioned yesterday,' continued Cynthia, ignoring the stifled giggle from Jonny, 'we'll be splitting you up into pairs to encourage you to share ideas and skills.'

The four looked at each other uneasily – they'd forgotten about this.

'And Henry is on hand, as ever, for any tips on making the most out of these sessions.'

Henry twisted in his seat to face the room, a smug lopsided sneer slimed all over his face.

'Anyway, without further ado,' said Cynthia, clapping her hands together, 'please welcome Steve and Jane Morris, aka Ying and Yang!'

The room watched in near silence as Steve and Jane, in full traditional Chinese dress (or – more correctly – what they had *interpreted* as full traditional Chinese dress), barged their way on to the stage, both looking like they were about to explode they were so full of things ready to 'appear'.

Even Alex couldn't help but smirk at the objects 'hidden' about the duo – almost as if they didn't care whether people saw where the silk scarves, flowers, umbrellas and balloons were about to appear from, like this type of magic was just a fun, easy puzzle!*

Steve paced back and forth, his right fist clenched over his midriff like he was holding a microphone and this was a primetime Saturday night TV show. He blathered on mindlessly, telling a string of dreadful jokes, giggling at his own punchlines, making constant digs at Jane, clearly loving the attention, in a world of his own.

'I went to the doctor's the other day . . . Knock-knock . . . The problem with my wife is . . . Who wants a balloon?' and so on and so on.

Sophie turned to face the others, gobsmacked. Was this really what it took to become a professional magician nowadays? How did they still get bookings?

Zack leaned over, whispering, 'If this isn't reason enough for the Magic Circle to be taken over by younger people, I don't know what is!'

Sophie nudged him, spotting Cynthia giving them another teacherly look from the front.

'These two *were* on our side at the council meeting, though,' reasoned Jonny.

Fair point. Ish, thought Zack.

Steve and Jane might be completely BONKERS, and their magic was dire, thought Sophie, but they were clearly

---

* I'm sure you don't need this hint, but just in case: traditional Chinese robes are rather large and have exceptionally wide sleeves!

great advocates of the society and loved the idea of children being part of it.

Steve continued pattering away, though now in a rather generic 'foreign' accent, apparently playing the part of some ancient Oriental wizard, as he bounced around the room producing a mass of bottles, thimbles, coins and hankies handing them to Jane – who appeared to be playing the part of a sort of 'accepting peasant' – all to a CD that Steve had borrowed from his local Indian restaurant and would hand back tonight over an overly spiced, celebratory lamb jalfrezi.

As a finale, Jane lifted up her robes to reveal that Steve had actually stolen her dress, leaving her in just a pale nightie. Quite what the narrative was meant to be, no one really knew, but at least the act was over!

Cynthia looked around, encouraging everyone to applaud, though even *she* was weirded out by what they'd just seen. Oh, how she wished some of the more acclaimed members of the Magic Circle would come and perform for the juniors. Oh well. She was grateful for Steve and Jane's enthusiastic contribution all the same.

'Well!' she said, still trying to look elated at what had just happened over the past few minutes. 'First of all, does anybody have any questions they'd like to ask these exceptional Magic Circle members? They were once young magicians just like you, remember ... Not that there was a junior clubroom back in their day, but still ...'

The four friends could think of a thousand questions, all of which were rather rude, had rude implications or were wholly irrelevant (and rude).

Henry's hand slithered up. 'What's it like being on Council?' he asked Steve in his odd voice.

Steve twinkled at the boy, clearly delighted by the question. He mopped his forehead with his sleeve, puffing like a Chinese dragon. 'Well, it's an honour to serve on Council. No doubt you saw how much fun we were having in the chamber yesterday!' he added indiscreetly.

Cynthia gave him a tight-lipped pointed look: if he didn't shut up, everyone would be wanting a peek inside the Council's chamber. And then what would she say to her husband? All her work on the junior arm of the organization would be for nothing!

'Yes, well, we're not here to talk about council matters,' she said hastily. 'Does anyone have anything else to ask?' She strained her neck, looking around the room, desperate. 'Well . . .' said Cynthia, glossing over the one-hundred-per-cent lack of interest. 'I'm sure they all just want to hear about your act and your lifetime of experience one-on-one,' she concluded weakly.

'Erm . . . I've got a question!' said Sophie, suddenly raising her hand.

'Oh good – well done, Sophie!' said Cynthia, looking relieved as Deanna gave her new nemesis a billion evils from the seat in front.

Jonny, Alex and Zack stared at Sophie. What was she up to?

'It's not so much about your act, but I just wondered whether, in your lifetime of performing magic,' she said, 'and as members of the Magic Circle Council, you have ever come across *The Thieves' Almanac*.'

Wow – this was not part of their plan!

The room fell deathly quiet; the adults all turned to look at Sophie, a mixture of fear and embarrassment on their faces, as if she'd just asked a question about devil worshipping or where babies come from.

Henry began to squirm in his seat – so this wasn't the first time he'd heard about the book, Zack noted. Perhaps he and his rose petals *had* been in the library before them.

For the first time in fifty-odd years Steve didn't have a decent comeback. He looked over at Cynthia, who was clearly dismayed. What was it with these new children? First eavesdropping on a council meeting, and now this! Didn't they know not to ask questions about that reckless book? Couldn't they just ease off for once?

From the back of the room the fruity voice of President Pickle sounded, like a horn announcing his arrival.

Oh great – of *all* people to appear out of thin air . . . *What perfect timing*, thought Cynthia, briefly closing her eyes and wishing it would all just go away! 'Edmund, we were just –'

'Any mention of *The Thieves' Almanac* on society premises is strictly forbidden,' President Pickle interrupted authoritatively, stomping to the front of the room like a prize bull. 'Unless, that is, you have any information as to its whereabouts,' he added, scrutinizing Zack.

Sophie chewed her lip, wondering whether she should continue. She took a deep breath. 'I just wondered whether you thought the book might have been used to help someone . . . break into the Bank of England.'

The question hung in the air like an unwanted guest. Henry was blatantly attentive now, poised like a spider pretending he was dead, but alert and ready. Zack studied him. From the moment Zack had first set foot in the Magic Circle, Henry had acted strangely – trying just a bit too hard to be his friend.

'My dear little girl!' sang President Pickle, his creamy cheesy grin swirling around the lower part of his face as he swivelled on his hips to address the entire room. 'I don't know where you dream up these preposterous ideas! Next you'll be saying *I've* got something to do with the affair!'

Well, that had *crossed my mind*, thought Sophie.

President Pickle eyed her for an uncomfortable amount of time, fiddling with the presidential chain around his neck.

'It's an interesting thought,' came the calm voice of Ernest Haigh.

The four friends turned in their seats, delighted to see someone who was on their side.

Henry scowled at him, evidently remembering his humiliation of the day before.

Ernest came forward, patting his grandson on the shoulder as he passed. 'Well, *I* think it's a perfectly reasonable question, Sophie,' he said, winking mischievously at her. 'If *I* was looking to break into a secure bank vault and leave without a trace, I'd be sure to study *The Thieves' Almanac* first – it's bound to contain some *very* useful information. Or so rumour has it.'

So they were on the right lines, thought Zack, pleased – his instincts had been correct!

'Ernest, *please*!' murmured Cynthia. 'Don't encourage them!'

'What *is* this book everyone keeps on about?' asked one of the toff brigade – not used to being left out, his bouffant hair bouncing up and down obnoxiously.

'You might as well tell them,' said Ernest plainly. 'You know what happens when you keep these youngsters in the dark. They just go and find out for themselves!' His eyes sparkled. 'And we wouldn't want that to happen again, would we?'

Jonny stared at his granddad. Did he already know about their early-morning escapade? He was certainly acting like he knew more than he was letting on.

Cynthia looked from Ernest to her husband and sighed. 'Can you either tell them about this dreaded book or just let me get on with this meeting? Unless you're here to teach them some magic . . . ?' she added, suddenly hopeful.

President Pickle suppressed a wheezy laugh. 'Oh, Lord, no! I'm just here to keep an eye on . . . everyone.' He gave the four friends a weasel-like grin, then turned to address the room. 'Listen, this whole Bank of England business –

nothing to worry about, OK? I'm sure the proper authorities have everything under control.'

Yeah, right, thought Zack.

'Given the nature of the crime, Scotland Yard will no doubt come and seek our counsel at *some* point, but I will deal with them myself. Now, why don't you just carry on with whatever it was you were doing?' President Pickle continued. 'Unless Steve and Jane are about to perform again, in which case I'm off!' He laughed loudly at his own joke, clapping Steve on the back of the head with a hard *thwack* and waggling the back of his hand in a dismissive gesture towards Jane.

'OK, well, let's get on then,' said Cynthia. 'Pair up, please, and then I'd like you to teach one another an original trick from start to finish . . . Ernest, are you staying?'

Ernest gave her a kind smile. 'As much as I'd love to, dear lady, I was actually on my way to the *library*,' he said, looking pointedly at Jonny and the others. He headed for the door. 'Of course,' he murmured as he passed them, 'if I *do* happen across *The Thieves' Almanac* while I'm there, I'll be sure to contact the proper authorities!' He gave Jonny a wink as he pulled a long dark handkerchief out of his top pocket. With a flick of the wrist he transformed it into a solid cane, his eyes flashing at Cynthia. 'How about that!' he said, before limping out of the room and shutting the door.

As the others started to get into pairs, the four friends grinned at each other.

'I didn't know Granddad needed a cane,' said Jonny thoughtfully. But then, how well did he *really* know the man at all? Following the longstanding dispute between Jonny's father and Ernest, the two of them had been kept apart for most of Jonny's life. (Granny Haigh had passed away before Jonny was born.) In fact, it was only because of Jonny's interest in magic that his parents had allowed him more contact time with the mysterious man – yet even then they suspected that his interest in magic was merely a ruse; an excuse for Jonny to satisfy his curiosity about Ernest. Perhaps this had been true at first, but Jonny had now well and truly caught the magic bug.

'You OK?' asked Zack, seeing that his friend was lost in thought.

'Oh, fine and dandy!' said Jonny. 'We should get into pairs.'

Sophie looked up to see that Deanna was now heading towards her, tense and bubbling with fury, clearly in a defiant strop. 'Why don't you want to be in a double act with me?' she said through pursed lips, clearly raging underneath.

'I'm sorry?'

'She's asking if you'd like to be partners,' clarified Deanna's mum, with a big smile.

'Oh, erm, I think I might go with Jonny, if that's OK … Or Zack … Or Alex,' added Sophie, feeling Deanna start to vibrate in front of her.

'You sure?' quizzed Deanna's mum. 'You were all she could talk about last night.'

'It's all right – *I'll* be Alex's partner.'

They all turned to see that Henry was now standing beside Alex, grinning.

Oh, please, no – anyone but you, thought Alex.

Just then Cynthia wandered over, her husband behind her. 'Actually I think it might be a good idea to split you four up,' she said, though Sophie suspected this idea had come more from that daft dawdling husband of hers, now gurning stupidly in the background.

'Zack, perhaps you and I could pair up?' said President Pickle, quickly sidling up to him like he was on a treadmill.

Zack could smell the president's stale cologne. *Oh well, that's just perfect*, he thought, giving him a polite nod.

'Yes, great idea. Sophie, why don't you join Deanna? Alex, Henry should be able to show you some lovely card magic. And, Jonny, have you met Max . . . ?'

It was a long old morning as Cynthia, Steve and Jane circulated, offering advice, while the young magicians showed each other their favourite tricks.

Alex – without doubt – had the worst of it. Henry, on the other hand, seemed positively delighted by the whole affair as he lorded it over Alex like some kind of military official who'd just been presented with a fresh slave. Alex looked up at the sinuous magician forlornly, as Henry manoeuvred him into a corner of the room. 'What are you and your little gang up to? And what do you know about *The Thieves' Almanac*?' he demanded.

So Henry *had* heard of the book.

Alex shook his head. 'P-please! I don't ... *We* don't know anything about it!'

Zack looked up, sensing that his friend was in trouble. But just as he was about to go to his aid, President Pickle blocked his way. 'Now now, no need to worry. I'm sure the delicate lad will be just fine! Probably do him some good to have a break from *you*!' He grinned.

'What's that supposed to mean?' said Zack.

'Don't take that tone with me. Remember who you're talking to, young lad!' snapped President Pickle in a darker tone. 'I'd just like us to have a little chat, that's all!'

Meanwhile, in the centre of the room, Sophie sat shell-shocked as Deanna performed *at* her, showering her in glitter and bubbles, not really doing anything – and certainly not sharing anything magic – just aggressively showing off. Sophie smiled, not wishing to antagonize her. Plus, she'd just had an idea about what 'technique' of her own she'd like to share with the girl!

Steve and Jane watched from a distance, trying to think of something positive to say.

All of a sudden Deanna stopped mid-flow in an amazing feat of deceleration, snarling at her dazed audience like a defensive chimpanzee. 'Why aren't any of you applauding?'

'Oh, it's because everyone is enjoying it so much!' Her mother nudged Steve and Jane, and then gave Sophie a shake.

'Yes, that's right ... I was saving my applause for the very end,' added Jane wimpishly.

Like a rattlesnake attacking its prey, Deanna launched herself at her mother, beating her repeatedly with a garish fairy wand, causing it to light up and churn out bleepy music like an inappropriate soundtrack to the fight. Steve and Jane watched the real-life Punch and Judy Show with increasing concern as Deanna's mum went full pelt trying to take charge of her child, crashing her to the floor like a member of the riot police squad, smothering her completely. Fifteen–love!

'Are you four all right after yesterday?' asked Jane, turning to Sophie with a sympathetic look. 'President Pickle can be such a *bully* sometimes,' she added quietly.

'If truth be told,' muttered Steve conspiratorially, 'there's a growing number of members – even those who sit on Council – who'd happily let youngsters in. It's just that President Pickle is so influential.'

Interesting, thought Sophie. So they weren't alone!

'But you didn't hear that from me!' Steve winked. He tapped his nose theatrically, causing two chocolate coins to drop out of his nostrils which he pressed into Sophie's palm.

Sophie smiled, both touched and disgusted – how long had those coins been in there?

In another corner of the room, Jonny was faring much better teaching Max his hydrostatic glass routine, which – with the help of surface tension – allowed you to turn a glass of liquid completely upside-down without losing its contents! Max grinned widely, his cheeks visibly inflating, as Jonny held the glass over his head, hoping he'd got the technique right and wasn't about to drench the boy with Deanna's mum's overly strong orange fruit cordial. Jonny continued by placing matchsticks in the glass of inverted liquid, which dutifully floated up towards the base, 'proving' that there was nothing covering the mouth. He finished by clicking his fingers, instantly turning the orange juice into a long orange handkerchief that dribbled out on to Max's head, muffling his glorious shrieks of delight.

Meanwhile Zack was still sitting facing the president of the Magic Circle, their eyes locked territorially.

'I know it was you who took that book,' said President Pickle eventually. 'And as soon as I have proof, I'll have you and your partners in crime out of here quicker than Houdini and Bess could perform Metamorphosis* – understand?'

So it was *President Pickle* who had scrawled Zack's name on that bookmark. Zack could feel his earlobes begin to pulse hotly. *Don't rise to it*, he told himself, wishing that Jonny was there to distract him. *That's exactly what he wants*.

He cleared his throat. 'I know I might look a bit different to the others around here,' he said coolly, 'but I swear I've never laid eyes on that book. Nor did I take your *gavel*, or whatever it's called.'

---

* An illusion whereby Houdini – bound and sealed inside a packing crate – escaped and switched places with his wife, Bess, on top of the crate, quicker than the audience could say 'Metamorphosis'!

'Well, your girly girlfriend over there certainly seemed to know a lot about it – perhaps *she's* the culprit?' he said, with a wry, unsettling smile.

'Leave her out of it, just leave everyone else out of it!' shouted Zack, causing Steve and Jane to look up as Deanna stared into Sophie's eyes, falling deeper and deeper into a trance (naughty Sophie!).

'Temper, temper. I was only putting it out there as a suggestion!' chided President Pickle mockingly, though clearly trying to goad Zack into giving something away.

Could this all be a bluff? Zack wondered. Perhaps President Pickle had taken the book himself, and was now in need of a scapegoat?

'Everything all right over here?' asked Cynthia, keen to avoid any more trouble.

'Yes, dear – the boy was just teaching me a trick, that's all,' lied President Pickle irritably, pulling his collar away from his neck, which bulged over like one of those pink dangly things turkeys have.*

'I'm so glad that we've all moved on after yesterday's little . . . tiff,' said Cynthia as she headed off to the next pair.

Hmm, not quite, thought Zack.

'Go on, hurry up then – let's see a trick,' sighed President Pickle, rolling his eyes at Zack like tricks were just for fools

---

* While we're here, I'm reliably informed that this is actually referred to as a *wattle*. Not to be confused with the *snood*, which extends from the turkey's *beak*, rather than its *neck*. Everybody clear on that? Yes? Good! Because it's not important! As you were . . .

and that the president of the Magic Circle shouldn't have to endure such things, 'before we all broil to death!'

Zack was not in the mood for performing. Still, what better way to get his own back? He proceeded to bamboozle the living daylights out of the president with a series of impeccable coin vanishes. President Pickle tried to keep up as coins leaped from one hand to the other, passed through his shoe and on to his head, jumped into his pockets and reappeared under his watch. To end, Zack transformed the 10p pieces into shiny bronze pennies.

It was a majestic display of dexterity, and soon the whole room had turned to watch, amazed by his lightness of touch. Jonny and Max were on their feet, starting the applause. Even Deanna gawped – though perhaps, Sophie thought, this was because she was now in a semi-permanent state of deep trance.

President Pickle frowned, not knowing what to say, trying to look like he'd followed Zack's every move. 'Hmm ... Yes ... No,' he said after a while. 'Not bad. Though Council won't like not knowing how something works,' he concluded, patting Zack on the head.

Wasn't that the whole point *of magic?* thought Jonny, shrugging.

'Well,' said President Pickle, standing suddenly and addressing the room like a king. 'It's been lovely to see what you all get up to, but that's enough chit-chat for now!' He was aware of the grumbly feeling in his tummy, and rubbed it fondly, priming it for lunch. 'Let's give these youngsters a chance to learn a few things for *themselves*, shall we?' He raised his eyebrows at his wife. 'That's how it was in our day, after all. None of this mollycoddling!'

Cynthia shot him a look.

'And good luck, of course,' he continued. 'Remember, it's all about making a *good first impression* in front of Council.' He sneered at Zack. 'Right, I think it's time for my . . .'

The four friends watched as he jogged out of the room clumsily, bashing into a chair, salivating, in clear desperate need of his all-day-breakfast panini.

'Yes, OK, good,' said Cynthia, clapping her hands. 'Perhaps that's enough magic for one morning. Let's show our appreciation to Steve and Jane, shall we?'

The pair left the room, bowing as if they'd just played the London Palladium. 'Thank you – thank you so much, you've been wonderful. Goodnight!' Just as the door swung shut behind them, Steve's arm shot back in with a final spray of sweets.

You can tell a lot by how someone leaves a room, thought Sophie as she watched Deanna begin to wake up, disturbed by the shower of fruit salads.

'Right, well, I hope you've all learned something new today.' Cynthia smiled at them. 'So this afternoon – like tomorrow – will be reserved for private practice. You can do that here in your pairs, or at home if you'd prefer.'

The four friends looked at each other – no prizes for guessing which option they'd be going for!

'And just to remind you – you'll be expected to perform at least three different types of magic in front of Council, so it can't just be all cards. OK, Alex?'

Alex didn't care if he had to perform three *million* different types of magic, just so long as he could be back with his friends.

Henry's sixty-fifth high-frequency trump of the day whinnied gracelessly out from his backside as he turned to Alex. 'I look forward to seeing you again very soon,' he hissed.

Alex seized the moment to wriggle out from his corner, darting over to Zack.

'Now,' continued Cynthia, 'if anyone leaving can do so quietly,' she said, lowering her voice. 'Just so we don't disturb De–'

But dear darling Deanna was already sitting bolt upright, like a cobra ready to strike. Sophie smiled at her innocently.

'HOW. LONG. HAVE I BEEN ASLEEP?!' she screamed, pacing the room, chewing noisily on a fruit salad and rounding on her mother once more. Deanna's mum rolled up her sleeves and put her hair into a bun, like she did when baking a truck load of fresh brownies. She crouched low to the ground, readying herself.

Zack, Sophie, Jonny and Alex hastily regrouped. 'Let's get out of here!'

11

The four of them headed back towards Euston Station in a daze.

'Well, one thing's for certain,' said Zack, blinking in the sunshine. 'Henry's *certainly* heard of *The Thieves' Almanac* – did you see the way he reacted when you mentioned it?'

'Stroke of genius bringing it up in front of everyone,' said Jonny, flinging an arm round Sophie, who promptly shrugged it off.

'What about President Pickle, Zack? Did he give anything away?'

'Not really. Though it did make me think . . . What if *he* was the one who took *The Thieves' Almanac*?'

'So you think he might just be *pretending* to be an idiot?' asked Sophie, unconvinced. Did President Pickle really have it in him to keep up the act while he secretly canoodled with criminals?

'Well, he *is* the president of the Magic Circle,' said Zack.

'I wonder why he hates kids so much?' Jonny mused.

'He doesn't seem to mind Henry. Speaking of which, are you OK?' Zack stopped and turned to face Alex, who took a deep breath and nodded.

'And did Henry give anything away?'

'Ju-just that he's got his eye on us . . . I think,' stammered Alex.

A rumble of thunder sounded in the distance and they all looked nervously over their shoulders, like this was some pivotal moment in a horror movie, half expecting to see a bedraggled Henry appear behind them. But instead . . . Sainsbury's!

They shook their heads, grinning. That was quite enough overactive imagination for one day! Zack yawned, his early morning start beginning to catch up with him.

'So, where do you want to meet tomorrow then, sleepyhead?' asked Jonny as Alex spun his return train ticket in the air and caught it with his other hand.*

'How about we meet at my tree house?' Jonny suggested.

Sophie stopped in her tracks. 'You've got a *tree house*?' she said, trying to weigh up whether this was either ultra impressive or wonderfully childish.

'I sure do!' he said proudly. 'Green Park, sixty-fifth horse chestnut on the left – please don't forget to wipe your feet! Completely illegal, of course, but has one hell of a view!'

---

* Oh, Frrrrrank! Wakey wakey! NB: Some of you may be wondering why Frank is back at work after decapitating his boss/wife. The truth is, there just wasn't enough evidence to convict. Er, WHAT?

'Well, that sounds ... perfect,' said Sophie. 'Beats my hotel room view any day!'

'And it's not somewhere Henry or anyone else can easily pry either,' added Zack, rubbing Alex's shoulder reassuringly.

'Exactly.' Jonny nodded.

And so the quartet went their separate ways, intermingling with the usual mix of tourists and business people who had no clue that beneath their feet was a magical reference library run by an automaton, which contained a book called *The Thieves' Almanac* that had – ironically – been stolen and perhaps used to help break into the Bank of England, just five stops down the Northern line from Euston, Bank branch.

And BREATHE!

That night, the four young magicians drifted in and out of odd dreams like a teacher with chronic diarrhoea might wander in and out of lessons.

On arriving back home, Alex had taken himself straight off to his bedroom – much to the delight of his parents, who were having the Conways round again for another gazillion flagons of red wine and a mince-based meal. He had slept awkwardly once again, his sleep interrupted by a series of nightmares in which he was being pursued by a hideously deformed adult version of Henry, hurling cards at him like daggers. Not even the spluttering sound of Mrs Conway violently throwing up in the bathroom woke him – although the sound *did* become part of his dream at one point, as Henry spat poison into Alex's eyes like a dilophosaurus. *Rrrretch!*

Jonny had decided to pay his granddad a surprise visit, hoping to impress the others with some inside information. But although he was sure that one of the upstairs curtains had twitched, Ernest didn't seem to be in.

Jonny slowly plodded back home while Googling the various ways in which one might break into the Bank of England. But the search just triggered a whole load of new questions, along with – Jonny suspected – a whole load of alarms at MI5. He quickly tried to dilute his search history with less incriminating queries like 'pomegranate recipes for one?' before tucking himself up into his long bed, his feet still poking out of the ends like periscopes.

Sophie had arrived at her hotel and hastily bounded up the stairs to her room, the lift having been out of order since the Cold War. There was something magical about leaving a room untidy and returning to find it spotless, the bed freshly made, everything back where it should be. Oh, if only it could be like this when she got back from school and opened the door to her bedroom at home, she thought as she sank on to the marshmallow-soft bed and closed her eyes. But there was no time for relaxing just yet; her mind was still awash with a whole fuzz of bizarre questions. Who had taken *The Thieves' Almanac* from the library? she asked herself. And when? Whose was the face she'd seen high up in the Grand Theatre? And what was Henry hiding? Would the society fold, or would it receive the windfall President Pickle kept alluding to? Was everything linked to the Bank of England break-in or was that simply a coincidence? And was the president of the Magic Circle himself connected to the criminals? How convenient that Scotland Yard should seek advice from the very person they suspected of having a hand in the crime! Or was this all some ingenious ruse? Sophie wondered. A test of their ability to solve the inexplicable – a labyrinthine route to membership of one of the most baffling organizations on the planet?

She dimmed the lights and sat cross-legged on her bed, her go-to meditative pose for times like this when her head was spinning. Perhaps she was going about this the wrong way. A bit like when the automaton had challenged them about Robert-Houdin's true profession, it seemed like they were missing something ... Something or someone that was staring them in the face. As a way of re-imagining the whole dilemma, she tried to think of the person who was the least likely to be in collusion with the thieves. Steve? Deanna's mum? Both ideas were laughable. But then who? And why did she care so much? Well, she knew the answer to that at least. All Sophie had ever wanted was to become a member of the Magic Circle. 'Oh yes,' her mum would say on one of her more lucid days. 'That's what you need to do, join t'Magic Circle down London.' The mere name conjured up images of a brilliant secret society, an enclave of eclectics, somewhere Sophie could truly feel at home. She even had dreams about magic – old tricks given a new gloss using unlikely methods and subtle psychological twists. It was what made her bound out of bed in the morning, getting through the school day so that she could spend the afternoon at the library, scouring books and the internet, reading and learning, honing her craft. But was the reality now that she'd set foot inside the Magic Circle? Well, they do say, *Never meet your heroes* . . .

No, the Magic Circle was not *at all* what Sophie had expected. But that didn't mean things couldn't change, did it? She heard the toll of President Pickle's voice reverberating inside her head like a death knell: 'Well, yes, but it wasn't like that in our day. There's no point in change for the sake of change. *Blah, blah, blah, yawn, yawn, yawn!*'

She closed her eyes and began to drift off . . .

She was in the council chamber, beside the spidery cupboard. In front of her sat the silent council members, dressed in dark robes, faces hidden. A chilling fog crept over the floor, covering her toes. She shivered. At the end of the table were President Pickle (with bull's horns) Cynthia (still with clipboard and pen in hand) and Bill (a skeleton in a floral dressing gown). In one swift move, President Pickle picked up his bloodied gavel and waved it around like a conductor. Instantly the Council started arguing loudly, and shouted at Sophie, pointing, mocking her for being a girl. The nearest cloaked figure slowly turned to face her. It was Ernest. She

searched for a kind smile, some words of reassurance, but none came. Instead, he lifted up a long bony finger and put it to his lips. His eyes pleaded with her, and then . . .

She was in the library, the noise of the council chamber fading away. The mechanical librarian was gesturing at the restricted section. She stared at the cabinet as it shot towards her, the doors falling open. Sophie felt her pulse quicken as she scanned the titles inside, knowing that she wouldn't find the one they were after. But there, where she expected to see a space, was in fact . . . a book!

She reached out and prised free the brown volume, feeling its weight and breathing in its smell. Slowly she turned it over. Three words had been etched into the leathery cover: The Thieves' Almanac. Sophie looked up at the librarian, who stared back at her stonily. Surely he wouldn't mind if she took a quick peek? She hastily flicked through the book, turning page after heavy page. Don't wake up! Don't wake up! She didn't have time to stop and study the anatomical drawings, the endless diagrams of intricate mechanisms, locks, picks, dangerous contraptions and ill-looking instruments, glossaries of strange terms, chemical formulas, appendices upon appendices, a book within a book . . . All at once – as if it had a mind of its own – the tome fell open at the start of a new chapter. Sophie's eyes widened as she read the heading: 'How to Break into a Bank Vault'. This was it . . . As she started to turn the page, her heart pounded. Don't wake up, Sophie! Please don't wake up!

All at once – a hand on her shoulder, turning her round, shaking her. Sophie looked into the ghostly eyes of . . . Alf! He smiled at her knowingly – as if she was his now.

Sophie let out a shrieking cry as she blinked awake, still in her meditative pose. Oh hell, why did she always have to wake up at the critical moment! She was going to have to work on this!

Zack too had set about solving the Bank of England puzzle, desperately searching the small collection of magic books in his bedroom for clues and inspiration. Flicking through the well-worn pages of his first ever magic book on theatrical pickpocketing, he remembered with fondness the first time he'd managed to steal a satsuma from his mum's pocket without her knowing. This, however, was a markedly different challenge.

He lay on his bed, staring up at the ceiling, covered in glow-in-the-dark star stickers, making it look like there was no ceiling in place at all. *How, how, how?* he thought. *How do you break into the Bank of England without being seen?*

How?

How?

HOW?

Oh!

And then, with a jolt that almost made him fall out of bed, he knew the answer.

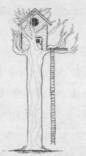

12

The next morning Alex woke up very early – partly because he was keen to see his friends again, but also because he'd been asleep since four o'clock the previous afternoon.

He showered and brushed his teeth – careful to avoid the patch of bile that Mrs Conway had left behind. Looking at himself in the mirror, he realized that something was different. Sure, he was the same boy who was known to jump at the sound of someone opening a packet of crisps, but Alex felt a new sense of confidence rising within him.

Before this week Alex hadn't really had anyone he could even call an acquaintance, let alone a friend – apart from a boy named Ben Beeston who, after tolerating him when they were very young, had quickly fallen in with the cool crowd at school and now teased Alex along with the rest of his pack.

But Jonny, Sophie and Zack? Well, of course there was always the worry that perhaps even *they* might turn out to be like Ben Beeston. That one day Zack might stop performing whatever trick he was in the midst of showing them and solidly smack Alex around the chops just because ... Well, just *because*. But thankfully he didn't think Zack, Jonny and Sophie were like that.

Alex turned left out of Green Park Tube, taking the Buckingham Gate exit, and started the somewhat odd sport of counting trees. It was a bright autumn morning, cool and crisp, the kind that carried the faint promise of Christmas. Alex counted slowly as he walked along the tree-lined path ... *thirty-four, thirty-five, thirty-six* ... He'd been to Green Park a couple of times – once on a school trip, and once with his mother, who was using it as a shortcut to get to some amusement arcade or other close to Piccadilly Circus. *Fifty-nine, sixty, sixty-one* ... Alex looked up into the branches above for clues. Eventually he stopped beside the sixty-fifth tree. He looked up, confused – mainly because this was more of a sapling than a tree; an infant only an inch or so taller than Alex. And so unless it was some elaborate illusion (quite possibly!), then this definitely wasn't right.

It wasn't long before Alex realized his mistake: the sixty-fifth *horse chestnut*! Ah!

He went back to the start of the path and began the even odder sport of counting *horse chestnuts*! On several occasions Alex questioned his expertise, getting up close to the bark (flaky greyish-green), examining the leaves (compound, palmate, with five to seven leaflets) – until he realized that, at this time of year, underneath each and every horse chestnut lay a pile of fresh conkers. Ah yes, much easier to spot! Alex continued past the sapling, giving it a polite nod of recognition, trying not to lose count.

Fifty-eight, fifty-nine, sixty . . .

He was now in a small glade, his eyes drifting up the trunk of the sixty-fifth horse chestnut on the left. It was an extraordinary specimen, presumably hundreds of years old, its thick trunk engulfing the wrought-iron railings that hugged the edge of the path, bending them like soft chocolate.* Alex craned his neck back – he couldn't even see the top!

Alex stood back, rocking on his feet, making sure no one was watching, before running towards the tree at full pelt. Quite what the small lad was hoping to achieve was unclear as he leaped at the trunk, grappling around the sides, trying (and failing) to fit his arms around the wide girth, stumbling over the buttress roots. He sank to the ground, breathless. Hmm, that was never going to work! For a second Alex worried with a shudder that this was all an elaborate hoax; that perhaps the others were watching him through a set of binoculars, laughing. Ben Beeston all over again . . .

'Alex!'

He looked up as a small rope ladder unravelled from somewhere high up above. *Ah yes*, he thought with a huge rush of relief. *This is more like it!*

* I'm thinking Curly Wurly, by the way.

149

He put his foot on the first rung, testing it. For a few seconds he just stood there, swaying slightly in the breeze, the tip of his nose grazing the bark. A little dog waddled over, wagging its tail. *Oh no.* 'Shoo!' said Alex quietly, shaking about on the ladder, desperately hoping that this sixty-fifth horse chestnut on the left wasn't the canine's favourite morning wee spot.

'Katie! Katie!' shouted an elderly lady nearby. The dog sniffed the air before running off again.

Phew!

Alex steadied himself and began to climb. Bit by bit he ascended the tree, not daring to look down, not daring to look up, simply concentrating on the next rung. Slowly but surely he rose into the branches above Green Park.

He could now hear words of encouragement coming from above. 'Come on, Alex. Not far now, mate!'

Mate! He had *mates*! Well, that was enough to make *anyone* climb a little faster. He kept going, higher and higher.

At last Alex felt a strong hand grasping his, hoisting him on to a firm wooden ledge. He looked up into the confident, beaming face of Jonny Haigh.

'So, Alex . . .' Jonny's long legs dangled off the edge like fleshy stalactites. 'What do you think of my tree house?'

Alex looked around, clinging on, slightly dizzied by how high up they were. He was sitting on a small platform made of thick floorboards nailed securely to the main trunk. Ahead was a little hut-like den cradled by almost

horizontal branches that resembled a welcoming upturned hand; it was brilliantly woven into the fabric of the tree, perfectly hidden from view.

Peering round the tiny doorway, Zack and Sophie grinned at him. 'Breakfast?' Zack brandished a slightly burnt sausage on the end of a fork.

Jonny helped Alex into the den. It was actually a lot bigger than it looked from outside, with several posters tacked to the walls, a small shelf of books ranging from chemistry to conjuring (and back again), a stout bench, a couple of bags of birdseed and, in one corner, a camping stove – that Zack was currently tending like he was the daddy at a family barbecue, filling the room with delicious smells.

'And the *pièce de résistance*, of course!' Jonny unhooked two latches on either side of the south-facing wall and pushed up the ceiling above. Sophie and Alex took a few steps back as the ceiling, along with the top portion of the wall, rose smoothly and glided back over their heads so that sunlight streamed through the gap, filling the room with damp mulchy air. 'I told you it had one hell of a view!'

Sophie and Alex crept forward, their eyes shining, peering through what surely had to be nature's finest window out over Green Park and Buckingham Palace, where the standard was flying proudly in the soft morning breeze.

'All right, all right, we've seen it all before, Jonny – enough showing off!' said Zack as he heated a pan of beans. 'Doesn't anyone want to know how the thieves broke into the Bank of England?'

Sophie, Jonny and Alex looked at him excitedly.

'No way – you haven't worked it out ... have you?' asked Jonny. 'I couldn't find *anything* on Google.'

Zack grinned as he hastily spooned out four platefuls of sausage and beans. 'OK,' he said, his mouth already full. 'Bear with me on this one ... Who can tell me how many electronic locks protect the Bank of England vault?'

'Ooh!' said Jonny, blinking fast and pretending to do the maths. 'About 571,' he said in a computer voice, remembering the fact from his extensive online research.

'Correct!' said Zack, whacking him on the back. 'And when are these locks deactivated?'

'If ... If there's a power cut?' asked Alex tentatively, blowing on his beans.

'Ah, but, Alex, you're forgetting – the Bank of England has backup generators,' said Zack. 'They even have a backup generator for their backup generator!'

'Zack ...' Sophie was growing impatient. 'This is all very entertaining, but –'

'OK, OK! My point is, the only time these locks *aren't* activated is when the bank vault is empty and there's nothing that needs protecting. Like immediately after a break-in – agreed? I mean, what would be the point in keeping the place locked then?'

Sophie, Jonny and Alex looked at each other. Where was Zack going with this?

'But how do you break into the vault in the first place?' asked Sophie.

'Well,' said Zack, 'you don't.'

'What?' Jonny sighed, disappointed.

'No. It's completely obvious when you think about it. As with any good trick, the simplest, boldest solution is usually the right one. Take the linking rings. *Surely* there must be a gap in one of those rings ... Or David Copperfield flying. *Surely* he must be on wires ... Or the Bank of England. *Surely* there's no way inside. And all those things are absolutely correct. There *is* no way of breaking into the Bank of England. Not without being seen, at least.'

'Zack, Zack, Zack!' said Jonny, utterly confused now. 'Slow down. What on earth are you going on about?'

'St Margaret's Lothbury,'* said Zack unblinkingly, as if this was the answer to everything.

'Right, o-kaaaay.' Jonny turned to the others. 'I think he's finally lost it.'

'The . . . the church next to the Bank of England?' said Alex, suddenly piping up.

'Exactly!' said Zack, grinning. 'It wasn't the real bank vault that was broken into.'

'Oh God, I think I know where you're heading with this!' said Sophie, clapping her hands together and causing a bean to trampoline off into Green Park, way, way below.

'St Margaret's Lothbury,' repeated Zack, lowering his voice for no real reason apart from to add more drama. 'Its catacombs are the perfect place to construct a replica of an *already-broken-into* Bank of England.'

'But,' Jonny began, 'surely anyone working at the Bank of England would notice their vault was suddenly in a different place!'

'Yeah, sure,' said Zack. 'But what if someone managed to access the Bank of England's lift system so that, rather than taking them down to their real vault, it moved diagonally down to the *replica* vault beneath St Margaret's next door . . . Can you see where I'm heading?'

* Do check out this wonderful place if you ever get a chance – it's positively pious!

'And so when that Hugh guy from the Bank of England travels down this lift,' Sophie said, the words tumbling out of her mouth excitedly, 'and sees that the vault is completely empty, he a) panics, and b) deactivates the electronic locks to the *real* Bank of England vault so that DI Caulfield and his crew can come and see how this seemingly impossible raid was achieved . . . Leaving the real vault *unlocked*!'

'Exactly!' Zack put down his knife and fork and wiped his mouth, showing the others his haphazardly drawn sketches – now soggy with ketchup. They were so enraptured they hadn't eaten a thing, while Zack had already managed to wolf down a full plate alongside his rather lengthy explanation.

'I mean, how did you even come up with all this?' whispered Jonny.

'Well, it's just a theory,' said Zack, helping himself to seconds. 'It works . . . theoretically!'

'Well, it's as good a solution as any.' Sophie studied the diagrams as she munched on a buttered bap.

'Yes.' Zack was pleased to find that his three friends approved. 'But if I'm right, it means that the real vault is sitting there, unlocked, right now, while Scotland Yard faff about in the wrong place!'

'Won't . . . Won't the thieves have already come back for the gold?' asked Alex.

'I suspect they're waiting for the police to leave the area first,' said Zack. 'But I bet they won't wait long. That's what I'd do anyway: I'd take the gold from right under their noses!'

REAL BANK

DIAGONAL
ELEVATOR

REPLICA
VAULT

'Are you *sure* you didn't steal *The Thieves' Almanac*?' asked Sophie, nudging him.

Zack smiled, feeling strangely flattered. His solution to this problem was indeed cunning enough to have come from the pages of *The Thieves' Almanac*.

'Wh-what should we do?' asked Alex as a blackbird landed on a nearby branch, eyeing his leftovers greedily.

'We should go and see this DI Caulfield,' said Jonny, tearing down the *Evening Standard* article that he had chosen to stick next to a poster of chemist Marie Curie, who was now looking at them all rather coyly.

'I was hoping you'd say that,' said Zack, clearing away the plates.

'Gosh, imagine how gobsmacked President Pickle will be when he learns that we've helped Scotland Yard!' said Jonny.

'Well, come on, then!' Sophie was already halfway out of the door. 'We haven't got a second to lose!'

13

It was just a short walk to get from Green Park to Scotland Yard, located just south of St James's Park Underground. Its infamous triangular sign rotated rather boringly in the morning light, neither impressive nor foreboding.

Surely they could try a bit harder than that? thought Jonny as he watched the sign rotate at the same slow speed as the plate inside a microwave. Wasn't this meant to be one of the most daring and enlightened institutions in the world?

The most troublesome part of their journey had been for all four of them to descend from the tree house unnoticed as the park filled up with its regular morning brigade of Londoners, park wardens, dawdlers and drug dealers. Fortunately Katie the dog had come bounding over again, this time chasing a Canada goose, driving it pretty potty, and serving as a distraction while the four of them clambered down, ready for another day's mischief.

Sophie looked across at the boys as they headed over the granite concourse towards the entrance to Scotland Yard. She began to slow down. 'Right, you three.' She tried not to sound nervous as they approached the revolving glass doors. 'Time for a quick crash-course demonstration in hypnotic induction!'

'Oh, I've been itching to see what this looks like!' said Jonny, biting his lip.

They entered the revolving door one at a time, emerging into the foyer like eggs plopping out of a hen's bum.*

Inside, Zack could sense the quiet hum of power. Perhaps the plain sign outside was just a piece of well-placed misdirection – *What we do is perfectly ordinary – nothing to see here!* – though the building housed more unsolvable mysteries and deceptive ploys than you might expect to find in your standard magic show.

Behind the wide reception desk was a huge glass wall, rising up several storeys high so that they could see into the offices – it was like looking at the cross-section of an ants' nest, alive with movement as the workers carted files, typed up reports and gave presentations ... just like real ants would do if they had the technology.

Sophie looked at the main doors, where two armed brutes stood peering through their visors menacingly, searching for reasons to open fire.

---

* I'm informed that it's not strictly the hen's *bum* where eggs come from, but it's fine to refer to it as such here. Just NEVER anywhere else!

'What exactly are you going to do?' Zack asked her as they approached the severe-looking woman behind the reception desk.

'I'm going to try good old-fashioned northern charm first,' she said with a grin. 'And then, if that doesn't work, I might have to resort to more . . . subtle measures.'

'Wicked!' said Jonny and Zack in unison, like they used to five years ago when this word was all the rage and could be used as a response to pretty much anything.

Sophie walked confidently over to the desk as Jonny, Zack and Alex flanked her, like a strange form of backup. The woman sat typing, hawk-eyed, before hitting the ENTER key loudly and looking up. If she was surprised to see the faces of three* children staring back at her then she hid it well, though Sophie detected the tiniest quiver in her eye movement, a sure tell that something was awry.

'Can you not put your hands on my desk, please?' the woman barked, removing Sophie's arms with a firm, muscular hand. 'And what's *that*?' she added, pointing at Alex's hair. 'Get it off my desk now! Unless you've got DNA evidence that proves Jack the Ripper's true identity, get out or I'm calling security.' The receptionist glanced at the guards, who flexed their fingers, ready for action.

Sophie fixed her eyes on her. 'We're here to see Detective Inspector Caulfield – it's a matter of national security.'

* Alex was too short for her to see.

160

For a second Zack thought that Sophie already had the woman entranced, such were her bulgy glassy eyes, but it was more that this strapping woman couldn't believe that a bunch of kids had the audacity to walk in like this and take her for a fool. 'Girl – you've got less than five seconds before I press my button. Do you know what happens when I press my button?' she asked, bringing out a large red button and pushing up her sleeves.

'*Wednesday*, I think,' answered Sophie, moving her right hand across the woman's field of vision. 'The day after your birthday, remember? It's always sunny on your birthday.'

Jonny looked down at Zack and Alex. Did this stuff actually work? he wondered.

But the woman now suddenly looked a little . . . hazy, her eyes unfocused.

Sophie carried on darting her hand in the air, like a conductor without a baton. 'You were just telling us about your birthday party and how we need to see DI Caulfield. It's very urgent, you said. He told us to let you through.' She continued to join up meaningless words and sentences, confusing the woman still further.

All of a sudden the receptionist started to move out from behind her desk.

Jeez, thought Zack, *this is actually working!*

Jonny was simply gobsmacked.

As the woman approached them, the two guards closed in, suspicious (rightly so!) of her strange entourage. 'DI Caulfield has asked to see them. Let them through,' she said.

The guards looked at one another. This was all very questionable, but they didn't want to challenge the authority of a woman who had once chucked her revolving chair over thirty metres in the air purely because she'd found an unwanted slice of tomato in her egg sandwich – and she'd already asked them once.

'Let them through,' mumbled the guard on the left (which was the only way to tell the difference between the two ... Well, apart from the fact that the one on the left had lost the nail on his big toe on a stag do). The guard on the right – complete with a full set of toenails – dutifully obeyed, holding his security card to the scanner, which beeped until the doors slid apart with a *swish*.

Jonny, Zack and Alex smiled at them innocently as Sophie led her friends through, eyes still fixed on the receptionist.

'Thanks so much,' she said politely.

And the other three watched, amazed, as the woman shuffled vacantly back to her desk.

The induction would wear off soon, thought Sophie, and when that happened, no one should be within a fifty-mile radius of the woman ...

The doors swished shut behind them.

They were inside Scotland Yard ...

She had done it!

They headed cautiously down the glass corridor, peering through the windows as the ant workers scurried from room to room.

'Sophie ... Did that really just happen? I don't know what to say,' said Jonny.

'Well then, don't say anything!' She picked up the pace, trying to appear confident.

Alex caught the reflection of one of the guards, still watching them ominously from the doorway behind, the gun round his waist scraping noiselessly against the glass. The boy quivered, moving closer to the others as they headed towards a bank of shining lifts.

The doors before them parted automatically and the four filed in, instantly overwhelmed by the sheer number of buttons on display labelling the various departments and sub-departments. Who knew that Scotland Yard had a boutique hair salon? Yep.

'Can anyone see one labelled DI Caulfield?' said Jonny, half to himself though clearly just loud enough to activate the inbuilt voice recognition. '*DI Caulfield's office*,' the automatic voice announced in a surprisingly upbeat American accent. Immediately the doors swished shut and propelled the four youngsters up through the centre of Scotland Yard.

Well, that wasn't so difficult!

Zack, Sophie and Alex grinned at Jonny, who shrugged. If only everything in life were that easy. Breakfast – ready! £1,000 – here you go!

'Are you ready, Zack?' asked Sophie. 'Your turn now.'

He nodded as the lift began to slow, giving him that slightly queasy feeling in his stomach – though perhaps this was just nerves.

'*You have reached the twenty-third floor,*' the voice chimed pleasantly. '*DI Caulfield's office. Have a great day now – and remember: don't have nightmares!*'

Sophie stifled a laugh as the doors opened. *I bet that doesn't get annoying, day in, day out!*

They stared into the bright room before them. A penthouse of gigantic proportions, basking in the morning light, decked out like a show home. In the centre a man sat at a desk, his entire body hidden by a huge computer screen. Zack looked around. Instead of paintings, several projectors presented a montage of images that changed and flickered

like an installation at a museum – myriad photos and headlines charting DI Caulfield's successes. In each and every photo he was smiling smugly.

Zack looked at the others. Jeez, *this* guy!

The images finally stopped on the *Evening Standard* photo – now all too familiar: DI Caulfield outside the Bank of England looking utterly baffled (and a trifle jowly). The detective inspector whined from behind his screen as he pushed himself back on his revolving chair, spinning in frustration.

'Hi!' hollered Zack.

The man was out of his seat like a shot, cursing, patting down his hair and reaching towards his holster – grappling for a weapon that wasn't there – before deciding (since he was facing four unarmed children) to make his fingers into a gun, waving it in their direction haphazardly.

'Whoa!' said Zack, putting his hands in the air. 'Don't shoot!'

'Wait a second!' The inspector was clearly not used to being caught out this early in the morning – annoyed that someone should see him before he'd had a chance to properly do his hair and cover any unsightly blemishes with his secret stash of fancy foundation. 'Who the hell are you? And how did you get through security?'

'Well, actually, they just let us in,' Sophie answered simply – which was oddly, completely true.

'What do you want? You can't be in here,' said the inspector, lowering his 'gun' and reaching for his chair.

Zack approached the desk and took a deep breath. 'OK, so ... I ... *We* ... We think we know how the thieves managed to break into the Bank of England.'

For a while DI Caulfield just blinked, before emitting a loud croaking sound, somewhere between an incredulous laugh and a nasty throat infection. 'Sorry, but what makes you think that a bunch of kids are *cleverer* than us here at Scotland Yard?' The detective went to sit down on his revolving chair, missing the seat completely and falling flat on the floor, bum first, beneath the desk. He immediately tried to style it out, pretending it was a joke but failing hugely.

'All right, all right, sit down,' he said curtly – clearly embarrassed and at a loss for words – gesturing towards a brilliant white sofa, still in its plastic covering. They took a seat, Zack perching on the exposed arm. 'No – not on the arm, for heaven's sake!' DI Caulfield rushed over with some antibacterial wipes. 'I got this from Italy!'

He sat down on a black armchair in front of them. 'Right, hurry up then,' the detective said finally, tossing the wipes into a bin designed for sanitary towels. 'You've got exactly one minute to explain why you're here before I call security. And just don't *touch* anything, OK?'

Alex, Jonny and Sophie looked at Zack, who was still standing, not daring to move, in case he upset the feng shui or this guy's feelings any further.

'Well,' Zack said, 'it might take a bit more than a *minute* to explain, but I reckon you'll want to hear us out.'

Zack repeated what he'd said up in Jonny's tree house earlier that morning, unfolding the grubby set of diagrams and keeping it simple so that the inspector could keep up.

The other three listened attentively, proud of their friend.

DI Caulfield sat on the edge of his seat, not speaking, occasionally sweeping back his slick hair and rubbing his chin, trying not to get too distracted by the muddy shoes on his carpet.

'And, in a nutshell, *that's* how we think they did it,' finished Zack, handing over the diagrams.

The inspector studied them carefully, avoiding the ketchup stains like they were bloody fingerprints requiring forensic examination. 'So you're saying the gold hasn't actually been stolen and we're just looking in the wrong vault?' he queried, getting to his feet and pacing to and fro.

'Well, it's what we *hope* is the case,' said Zack. 'But I doubt the thieves will hang around for long . . . Or at least *I* wouldn't, if I were them!'

DI Caulfield gave him a suspicious look. 'Sorry – who did you say you were again?' he asked irritably, still trying to make sense of everything. *Could* these children be right? Surely not – surely it was all way too elaborate, he thought.

'Well, my name's Zack,' said Zack. 'Over there is Jonny, Sophie and Alex, and we're –'

'Magicians,' Sophie interrupted proudly, standing up.

DI Caulfield stared at her like he'd never heard the word before. 'Aren't you a little young to be magicians?'

'Yes, well, we're . . . *the Young Magicians*!' said Sophie like this was the name of some well-known emergency service or the title of a much-lauded book.

The other three looked at her, pleased with how easily the name had rolled off her tongue.

'You're the *what*?' asked the inspector, smirking slightly. 'So, are you in the Magic Circle, then?'

'No, we can't join until we're of age,' Jonny told him.

'Well, isn't there some adult I can speak to instead? This isn't the Famous Five!'

'Four.'

'I was including myself.'

'No,' said Sophie, raising her voice. 'We're the Young Magicians. And if you insist on patronizing us any further, then we're just going to have to tell the whole world how *little children* managed to get past security at Scotland Yard!'

'Plus, I *did* take a sneaky photo of you falling off your chair!' admitted Jonny, flashing the man a grin and taking another stealthy pic as he spoke. He rotated the camera to look at the screen. 'Oooooooh dear –' he winced – 'I don't think you're going to like this one either, mate, your cheeks look really look quite . . . chubby!'

'Oh HELL, not again!' DI Caulfield wiped his brow with a beautifully manicured hand.

Conscious that he wasn't really doing much to help, Alex suddenly stood up, removed his muddy shoe and held it threateningly over the exposed arm of the fancy sofa.

DI Caulfield reacted like he'd been stung by a hornet the size of a Fiat Bravo. 'No, no, no, not on the sofa! Please!'

The others looked at Alex as a blob of Green Park mud landed with a plop, sullying the brilliant white arm, probably forever.

'OK, OK, fine!' said the inspector eventually. 'Let me look into it. Just move the shoe away from the sofa. And not a word of this to anyone, do you understand?'

'Oh, we wouldn't dream of it, Inspector,' said Zack, following the others towards the lift, Alex moving a little strangely with only one shoe on.

'Do you have a business card?' enquired Jonny politely. 'Just in case we need to contact you again.'

'No, I don't!' snapped DI Caulfield, but not before Zack had dextrously swiped one from the man's top pocket, spinning it over to Jonny.

'Great,' said Jonny, scrutinizing the card and wrinkling his nose. 'I'll send you the photos.'

'Out!' screamed the inspector, his good features creasing and contorting further, causing him to look like a distressed gargoyle.

'*You have selected "way out"*,' the computer voice announced as they entered the lift. '*Doors closing.*'

The four watched briefly as DI Caulfield sighed heavily and sank back on to his gorgeous white sofa, his bum remarkably missing the plump cushions and causing him to fall flat on the floor once again, his roar diminuendoing to nothing as the Young Magicians shot back down into the bowels of Scotland Yard, feeling slightly weightless.

'Well, that all seemed to go rather well!' said Jonny cheerily.

14

They headed back over the granite concourse with a mixture of disbelief and pride. Had they really just bypassed security at Scotland Yard and told one of the country's leading investigators how to do his job? Had Alex really held one of his size-six shoes over the man's sofa to get him to do their bidding? Yes. Yes, they jolly well had!

'Well, I'd say the Young Magicians' first mission was a humungous success, wouldn't you?' sang Jonny, raising Sophie's hand in the air.

She dragged her arm back down again. 'But what do we do now?'

'I guess we just wait for the evening papers,' said Zack. 'If DI Caulfield takes our advice, then he'll act today.'

'Well, in that case,' said Sophie, always practical, 'we've got our auditions to think about. How about we use the time to teach Alex some magic that doesn't involve cards? What do you say, Alex?'

He nodded, pleased. He knew about as much about non-card magic as the armed guard on the left with the missing toenail knew about finger knitting. But with more pressing things to attend to – namely saving the nation's gold from falling into the hands of a bunch of cunning crooks – Alex hadn't wanted to bother his friends with his worries.

'Great idea!' exclaimed Jonny, reaching into his pocket and bringing out a rather grubby metal fork. 'I can teach you how to do *this* if you like!' He began to rub the end of the fork furiously between his thumb and forefinger, willing it to bend. The others stared at the piece of cutlery.

After thirty seconds of straining and huffing, Jonny gave up. 'I think this might be the wrong fork . . . As in, I think this might be a *real* fork,' he clarified.

'OK, so maybe don't do *that* tomorrow, Alex,' joked Zack.

The others laughed as Jonny took the fork in both hands and bent it the good old-fashioned way, popping it into a nearby bin that smelled of Henry.

'Promise I can still be one of the Young Magicians, though?' he said as he caught up with them.

None of them noticed the passer-by who narrowed his eyes at them and quickly followed . . .

15

It was a fun, lazy rest of the day. Well, lazy in comparison to dashing about subterranean libraries or evading top security at Scotland Yard. And it felt good to be away from the Magic Circle.

They spent the hours wandering between parks and cafés, Jonny spending all his pocket money on a spicy bean-burger the size of a jet engine, which – similar to a jet engine – was really rather hot and would no doubt end in significant gas propulsion out of one end at some point fairly soon.

Finding a quiet spot in Hyde Park, Sophie, Jonny and Zack took it in turns to show Alex several basic but bamboozling effects with ropes, coins, cups and dice, only pausing briefly to go and check the afternoon headlines scrolling across the adverts at Piccadilly Circus.

No . . . nothing about a foiled bank plot – not yet at least.

Alex couldn't have hoped for better tutors. Each contributed something different: Jonny – a master of patter, presentation and posture (charming, fresh and bold); Zack – technical dexterity, originality and misdirection (quick, different, beguiling); Sophie – psychology, body language and eye contact (nuanced, natural and focused).

'Don't forget to project, Alex – and smiiiiile, remember!'

'Just watch your angle when you're performing that muscle pass, Alex.'

'Everything about your posture and attitude should suggest where the coin *isn't* – that's the real secret to this effect.'

A jogger watched with interest as Alex successfully cut and restored rope, stacked dice one on top of the other in a flash, and produced coins out of thin air.

Sophie, Zack and Jonny were pleased to see their new friend performing the routines with growing confidence and dexterity. Surely he could get through the audition now. Not that this should be a mantra for life, but if Steve and Jane could do it . . .

Alex repaid the favour by teaching the others some of his favourite and most complex card effects, confounding them with his sleight of hand and passionate explanations of how the tricks were actually done.

The four finally headed back to Piccadilly Circus, sleepy but happy after their peaceful, sun-soaked magical afternoon, looking up at the screens for the day's latest news, hopeful, expectant and a touch trepidatious.

And there it was . . . right next to an advert for an unnecessarily shiny watch and a bright energy drink.

Zack let out a yelping cry of joy, startling a pack of tourists, who ran for cover in Fortnum & Mason. In large letters, the huge headline shone down in dazzling red, white and blue at the throng of excited people gathered below, showering the crowd in dazzling light.

BREAKING NEWS:
NATION'S GOLD SAVED!

And then, with a jolt like you might get on a fairground ride if there was a sudden power cut, Zack realized that he'd been well and truly *had*.

The others saw this too as they watched, increasingly sullen-faced, while the headlines scrolled across the bottom of the screen:

DI CAULFIELD – THE GENIUS WHO SOLVED THE GREATEST
MAGIC TRICK EVER SEEN

And then, as if to rub it in further, the entire set of ginormous monitors was filled with the cheesy, immaculate face of the man himself, smiling down at them, waving, flaring out his lips saucily, making sure he was at just the right angle –

'NO!' exclaimed Zack. 'He's stolen my idea!'

They watched in dismay as the crowd around them nodded their heads, impressed. *How dare he not credit us!* Zack thought.

To add insult to injury, digitized animated drawings of Zack's very own handiwork, depicting how the thieves had set up the replica vault, were now on display. DI Caulfield's voice played loudly through the speakers:

'*Well, it's really rather straightforward when you think about it. I simply told myself to think laterally, and then it just came to me.*' He flashed a grin at the female reporter before carrying on. '*Obviously, everyone's hugely relieved we got to the real Bank of England vault just in time, but our main concern is that these tricky thieves are still at large. Who knows what they might be planning next.*'

The detective put on a sad face, before giving the reporter the tiniest fleck of a wink and handing her a business card, which blatantly had a personal message written on the back in deep, voluptuous red.

Sophie watched his lips as he mouthed something to her. Oh *please* – what a creep!

'I'm sorry, Zack, mate,' said Jonny eventually, putting an arm round his shoulder.

'It's just so unfair!' said Zack, his voice cracking. 'Why should *he* get all the glory?'

It was tough. Finally Zack had something that might have put him in the spotlight – and in a good way for once! Something that might have turned things around for him with the Magic Circle. But no, the 'proper authorities' had to go and take it away from him.

'*We* still know it was you who solved it,' said Alex.

That was true, thought Zack. He really *did* have a very special bunch of friends here.

'So the thieves are still out there,' mused Jonny. 'And if they've got *The Thieves' Almanac*, you can bet they'll already be planning something else.'

'I wonder how they felt about being rumbled out of the blue,' said Sophie as they wandered towards Charing Cross Station.

'Well, it serves them right,' reasoned Zack who, despite all his annoyance at DI Caulfield for stealing his thunder, was ultimately delighted that his powers of deduction had foiled the thieves' plot just in time.

'Not that the crooks themselves have been caught yet,' added Jonny darkly.

Alex looked over his shoulder. It was almost a reflex, a throwback to his playground days when he'd have to be on the lookout for anyone from Ben Beeston's gang that might be tracking him. Constantly on edge, sometimes cricking his neck painfully in the process, checking whether there was someone standing behind him ready to hurl abuse his way or not. Strangely, despite the pleasant day they'd had, Alex couldn't shake the feeling that they were being watched. He turned round again as they descended the steps into the Underground.

'Hey, fancy popping into Davenport's to cheer you up?' asked Jonny, smiling at Zack.

'Oh wow! Davenport's Magic Studio?' asked Sophie, her eyes lighting up. 'Is that down here?'*

'Sure is!' Jonny beamed.

Just off to the left, Alex could make out the greasy green entranceway to what looked like a store only adults were allowed into.

'Maybe another time,' said Zack, still feeling despondent. 'I never thought I'd say this, but I think I've had enough of magic for one day.'

Wow, thought Jonny. *Things must be really bad.*

All of a sudden they heard running footsteps, ragged breath and shouts behind them, the noise bouncing off the walls.

Alex turned as Henry – HENRY! – came hurtling round the corner past Davenport's, his cheek bruised, one eye puffy. 'What the –?'

'Henry?' Zack was freaked. 'What is it? What's wrong?'

'*Help!*' screamed Henry as he reached them and stood there panting. 'They thought I was one of you – one of your little *gang*!' the strange boy spat fearfully. He thrust a bloodied brown envelope into Zack's hand. 'I'm begging you . . . Just do as they say!'

He turned and stumbled away up the stairs, leaving the Young Magicians in a daze.

'What on earth was all that about?' Zack looked nervously around the now-deserted underpass.

* See Appendix 4 for more detail on this magical business.

'And what's in *there*?' asked Jonny, pointing at the crumpled and stained envelope in Zack's hand.

All of a sudden Alex started croaking, the sound slowly coming together to form words. 'There . . . there's a . . .'

'What is it, Alex?' asked Sophie, taking his arm.

'There's . . . There's a man looking out of the window at us,' he whispered, pale with fright. He was staring at Davenport's.

Sophie, Jonny and Zack slowly turned as metal shutters began to descend, obscuring the grey face of a hobbity-looking man now staring at them from behind the grimy glass. He lowered his face, continuing to watch them as the shutters dropped to the floor, barring him inside.

'Oh, that's . . . just Alton who runs the shop,' said Zack, trying to sound unconcerned – though in truth somewhat unsettled by the man's prolonged haunted stare.

'Probably disturbed by all the noise,' added Jonny casually. 'Henry sure likes drama, doesn't he!'

They all headed back up the stairs, glad to hear sounds of life above ground.

'So . . .' said Sophie, looking from Zack to the envelope and back again. 'Are you going to open it, or . . . ?'

He slowly peeled back the flap of the envelope, being careful not to rip the thin grainy paper. He delicately inserted his hand, pulling out a sheet of thick, yellowing parchment with his fingertips, peering into the envelope to check he hadn't missed anything, like it was his birthday and he was expecting a voucher. Along one side of the parchment was a roughly torn edge, followed by a thin margin and then – in jet-black ink – tiny spidery writing, scrawled all about the page, interspersed with hastily drawn pernickety sketches of bank vaults, ropes and pulleys. Beautiful in many respects, an antique perhaps, but somehow somewhat sinister. What on earth was it? And why had Henry delivered it to them?

Zack recognized the writing – the drawings too – but where had he seen them before? And then – in a flooding wave of excitement – he realized what it was they were looking at.

'These are the same as my drawings,' he said in a hoarse, incredulous voice.

'But this has been taken from a book,' said Sophie, spotting the page number (13) at the bottom of the page and running her finger along the torn edge. 'Why would a book contain the same –?'

But before she could finish, Zack interrupted, grabbing her hand excitedly. 'This is a page from *The Thieves' Almanac*!'

16

The four studied the densely packed sheet of paper, captivated, their breathing coming in short sharp gasps, amazed by the similarities between the method they could see outlined on the aged, textured page and the one Zack had described only earlier that morning.

'I told you, you could have written this book,' whispered Sophie.

'I promise I've never laid eyes on this book before.'

'That's not what I meant, Zack. I just meant you clearly have the same way of *thinking* as – well – whoever wrote this!'

'But why choose Henry to get it to us?' said Jonny, studying the writing more closely.

'Wh-what's that on the other side?' asked Alex.

Jonny cautiously turned the page, careful to keep it at arm's length, which – to be honest – was *more* than a sufficient distance to protect the reader from anything that might literally jump off the page.

The four drew in their breath as a globule of wet red ink dropped off the bottom of the page and landed on the subway steps like the first smatterings of a nosebleed. Across the top, on the reverse side of the sheet, were the words . . .

To: The Young Magicians
Re: Spoiling our fun!
Date: RIGHT NOW!

The four coursed through the page, baffled, terrified . . . transfixed.

Why, you interfering bunch of cunning minxes! HOW DARE YOU foil our plot? We had grand plans for that gold, you prime chunks of gunk. You weaselly crates of rotting fish! You FIENDISH FOUR! Don't force us to pay you ALL a visit like we did with Henry – you've seen what we can do to young magicians like you! (Tee-hee – that was quite fun actually. I wonder if he'll ever see out of that eye again!) He'll certainly be staying out of your way now.

Anyways, it's not all doom and gloom! Well, not for US at least. What's that? We're stealing the Crown Jewels tomorrow at exactly six p.m.? Er . . . YES! Yes we are. And no one can stop us this time! You can keep your pokey Bank of England gold, we're into jewellery now. Big, gaudy, depressingly expensive, unwearable jewellery. Feel free to run squealing to your prissy little detective inspector again – he won't be able to help you this time. No one will. Not even The Thieves' Almanac contains a chapter on how to steal the Crown Jewels! Oh, but we know how . . .

Hugs and cuddles,

The THIEVES X X X X (One kiss each & a big SLAP!)

P. S. Don't even think about trying to stop us this time – we're ON TO you. And don't you have an important audition to prepare as well? Priorities, priorities! ;-)

17

'OK, so let me get this right,' said Sophie as they wandered away from the station. 'These so-called thieves are planning on stealing the Crown Jewels but have told us *exactly* when they're doing it?'

'It seems that way, yeah,' said Zack, looking over his shoulder for Henry.

'But why would they do that?' asked Jonny.

It certainly seemed strange for the thieves to divulge the time, date and location of their next heist. Especially since their previous attempt had been so spectacularly foiled.

'It . . . It might be another double bluff,' said Alex, finding his voice again.

'True,' said Sophie, drumming her fingers together. 'In which case, they've told us exactly what we need to know.'

'Well then, why don't we go straight to the Tower of London and warn their security personnel right now?' said Jonny, overly pleased at getting to say the word 'personnel' for the first time in several weeks. 'I've got a membership card that can get us in for free!' He winked at Sophie like this was one of his favourite chat-up lines.

'But surely they'd never believe us,' said Zack, chewing his lip, a pained expression still on his face as they crossed the road towards the bustle of Trafalgar Square.

'Should . . . should we maybe go to President Pickle?' said Alex – although he wasn't sure what help the man might be.

'I don't know about that,' said Zack. 'I think someone at the Magic Circle *must* be involved somehow . . . The thieves seem to know so much about us. And they obviously got to Henry . . .'

'True,' said Sophie, frowning up at the fountains in Trafalgar Square. 'They even knew about our auditions tomorrow. But surely President Pickle wouldn't go to such lengths, would he?'

'I could try and ask Granddad – see if he knows anything,' said Jonny, checking his watch. 'Although he always seems to be out at the moment.'

'You know, I hate to say this, but perhaps we should pay DI Caulfield another visit,' said Zack with a sigh. 'It's too, well, *risky* telling anyone else.'

'No way, Zack!' said Sophie loudly. 'He's not claiming *this* victory for himself as well!'

'What victory?' asked Zack. 'We don't even know how the thieves are going to break in.'

It was true, the four of them hadn't the foggiest how one might enter the Jewel House inside the Tower of

London – an infamously impenetrable building since 1078, protected by at least a thousand members of Her Majesty's armoured army, with each orb, anklet, mood ring and whatnot shielded behind two-inch-thick shatterproof glass. And that's if you didn't set off one of the 25,000,000,000,000,001* bright green lasers crisscrossing the place like the web of some phosphorescent spider who only ate radioactive flies. Not to mention all the other unadvertised technology in place to protect these rare royal trinkets. Yep, these thieves sure did enjoy a challenge!

'I just feel like this is getting out of hand,' said Zack, hoisting himself up on to the wall, enjoying the wet spray of the spluttering fountains on his forehead. It was all very well sneaking about the Magic Circle library, getting into trouble with Cynthia and annoying a detective, but this was big. And these thieves clearly meant business. Zack shuddered at the memory of Henry and his oozing eye – what murderous miscreant does that to a minor?

'Why do you think they went after Henry? Why not come straight to us?' said Sophie, apparently reading Zack's thoughts (though actually just noticing the involuntarily movement of his arm towards his eye socket).

'I don't know, but I don't think Henry will want us asking him questions about it for a good while . . .' Zack gulped.

---

* A blatant mistake: they clearly only planned to install 25,000,000, 000,000,000, but someone must have miscounted!

There was something strange about the way the thieves were almost goading them into solving this next impossible crime. It was like they were being played and the last thing Zack wanted was to lead them all into peril again.

'Come on, let's at least stop by the Tower of London before it shuts,' said Jonny, wafting his membership card around.

'I . . . I agree,' said Alex, sounding only about thirty-four per cent convinced, but looking determined. 'It's . . . It's worth a look . . .'

'Well, only if we're all in it together,' Zack said, smiling at his three friends.

'Of course we are!' replied Sophie, giving him a bear hug and almost toppling him into the fountain. 'We're the Young Magicians, remember?'

Oh HEY! Long time! How are we all? Sorry to interrupt – but just to summarize the dilemma the four now face because – somewhat worryingly – I just need to get this all straight in *my* head too!

So then . . . Somehow the thieves have managed to get wise to the fact that our formidable four were the real brains behind solving the Bank of England plot and for some unknown reason have now decided to tell them exactly where and when their next bout of burglary will take place.

Why exactly they have done this is unclear. It *could* be a bluff, forcing the four to concentrate their efforts in one place while the crooks operate somewhere completely different. Or even a *double* bluff, forcing the four to think it's a straightforward bluff when in fact the thieves plan on doing *exactly* as outlined in their nefarious note. And then there's the whole issue of security surrounding the Crown Jewels . . .

The Tower of London is notoriously inaccessible. Not even the wickedest, most devious minds in history have managed to scale the mighty walls or penetrate the solid bedrock on which the fortress is built – let alone get anywhere *near* the Jewel House (located at the very centre of the complex within a series of inner walls, protected by myriad staff, dogs, ravens, and technology so advanced that it makes the Starship *Enterprise* look like the Nokia 3310). So by all accounts there's very little chance of tunnelling into the building or creating a nearby replica as in the Bank of England ploy.

And should one even manage to get inside, this isn't like a bank vault, where all the gold is laid out in piles. No, Her Majesty's Crown Jewels are each encased in a cube of Perspex so strong it can withstand the blast of a thousand nuclear bombs – though quite how this could ever be verified without destroying the entire galaxy is unclear. Nor is it clear why the Crown Jewels even *need* to withstand such a blast. Still, it's fun to imagine a cockroach holding up a pristine orb and sceptre, reigning over what's left of a barren, scorched Milky Way!

And what of *The Thieves' Almanac*? Well, at least the Young Magicians now know that the thieves have it and have been exploiting its devilish contents, just as Zack suspected. But how did they get their hands on it? Could President Pickle or another Magic Circle member be in cahoots with them, giving the thieves access to the book and its monstrous methods for some sort of financial reward, ensuring future funds for the

society? And why beat up Henry? Surely the thieves could just
as easily have approached the four friends instead. Or is this
all some kind of test?

 SO many questions!

 Yeah, tell me about it – and I'm the *author*! Better get back
to it . . .

18

They reached the great Tower of London just as the sun was starting to go down. Sophie marvelled at the four turrets and ornate stonework; it looked more like a cross between a cardboard cut-out and a boutique hotel than the medieval prison it had been described as in history lessons. Although, saying that, her history teacher seemed to drone on so monotonously and continuously that even if he were talking about skydiving he probably would have given the impression he was talking about some oppressive, medieval prison!

'Right,' said Jonny like an official tour guide, waving his membership card in the air so that the others wouldn't lose him in the half-term crowd. 'The portcullis comes down at four thirty sharp – and I mean *sharp*! – so we'd better get a move on.'

Sophie, Zack and Alex tried to keep up with Jonny as he darted through the main entrance, garbling something deliberately quick and inaudible at the Yeomen Warders along the lines of 'We'll be right back!' as they sped on through.

Zack grinned as they coursed against the general tide of tourists heading home, weighed down with expensive, nondescript and wholly unnecessary souvenirs (such as an axe that was also a lute, which was also a tea towel, a bookmark and a sweet). The four paced past the Bloody Tower like they were being persecuted by Henry VIII himself, and across the courtyard towards the entrance to the Crown Jewels.

'You'd better be quick!' shouted a greying member of staff, already regretting spending her retirement as a volunteer. 'The Jewel House closes in five minutes!'

'We'll be out in two!' hollered Jonny.

The four of them dashed into a labyrinth of glass cabinets, empty apart from a couple of American tourists, desperately trying to get a selfie with the Imperial State Crown without using the flash.

'OK, then.' Zack lowered his voice and tried to look inconspicuous. 'If we were here to steal these things, how would we do it?'

It was a good question. The jewels were encased in their thick, alarmed, bulletproof boxes, cameras and lasers trained on them as if they were being watched by a million marksmen.

Crowns encrusted with dazzling diamonds; plump cushions bearing gold necklaces covered in gems that wouldn't have looked out of place in Accessorize; egg cups and spoons covered in pearls – making them impossible to use – lined up in a row like they were waiting for a bus. Even the display cases were held together with ornate diamond screws.

'Bit showy, aren't they?' Sophie pulled a face at the royal treasures.

'Probably the most northern you've sounded all week!' said Jonny, giving her a big grin. Sophie shook her head at him, rolling her eyes as she coursed through the jewels, unimpressed.

'I think that's the point,' said the tired volunteer, sighing. 'But I'm afraid that's your lot for today. We open again at nine tomorrow morning.' She pressed a button, and a set of grilles descended from above, trapping the cabinets behind an additional thick mesh, accompanied by a continuous bleeping noise, like a reversing truck.

'Well, I guess that's us, then,' said Zack as they filed out, still completely flummoxed. Hmm!

'Any immediate ideas?' asked Sophie as they walked in the fading light back through the courtyard.

Zack chewed on his bottom lip thoughtfully. 'There's *something* at the back of my mind . . . Something the lady said, I think, but I can't work out how it's relevant yet – sorry.'

'*Very* helpful, mate!'

'OK, well, listen,' said Sophie, rolling up her sleeves like she was preparing to get her hands dirty. 'If we've only got twenty-four hours to solve this, then we'll need to be efficient with our thinking.'

They turned right towards Tower Hill Station as she outlined their homework for the evening:

'Zack, you try and work out how the thieves might get their hands on the Crown Jewels. Given what we've just seen, is there a weak spot, do you think? Or is it something we *haven't* seen?'

'Ooh, perhaps I could make some booby traps,' said Jonny all of a sudden, his eyes lighting up at the prospect of cracking open his new chemistry set, which was less an educational toy and more a collection of small but effective *bombs*.

'Brilliant idea, but not a priority right now!' Sophie turned to Alex and clicked her fingers. 'Alex, you need to look at what kind of locks the Tower of London might have. They'll be some of the oldest functioning locks in the country, so you'll need to read up on them!'

He nodded enthusiastically.

'And, pray tell, what are *you* going to be doing while we're all labouring away this evening, m'lady?' asked Jonny with a silly, unfurling bow.

'I, Master Haigh,' said Sophie, 'will be solving the ever-so-slight problem of being in two places at once – so that, if we need to be here catching the thieves at six p.m. tomorrow, we can also be on stage at the Magic Circle – remember what the note said? I don't think the timing is a coincidence – someone clearly wants to keep an eye on us.'

'Do you *really* think someone like President Pickle is involved?' asked Zack.

'I don't want to believe it,' said Sophie honestly, 'but the motive is there. The society is already in debt. President Pickle said so himself. We know he had access to *The Thieves' Almanac* while it was in the Magic Circle library.'

'Not that the thieves have managed to steal *anything* yet,' Jonny pointed out.

'Then let's hope we can stop them again!' Zack grinned, his enthusiasm for adventure back with a vengeance.

'Tree house at seven, then?' said Jonny, yawning so widely that a tiny bat from the tower careered towards him thinking his mouth was the entrance to a small cave.

'Yes. Tree house at seven to report back on our findings,' said Sophie.

'Yes, Your Majesty!'

'And remember – don't have nightmares!'

Alex looked over his shoulder as a flock of disturbed ravens took to the evening air with a loud caw.

19

Once again Alex had gone straight to his room (successfully bypassing his parents' bi-weekly wine-and-cheese evening) and spent his time swotting up on all sorts of medieval picks, practising on his wardrobe door and the rusty padlock he'd found in the garage. The thing with old locks, Alex was quickly finding out, was that, like a good cheese, they got better with age, what with the build-up of all the rust and grime. He sighed as, taking his penknife and a large stick, he tried to fashion some kind of pick. The pop of his parents opening another bottle of thick red wine sounded downstairs. Oh well, the night is young!

Jonny had once again travelled home via his granddad's, but just as before had been greeted with the faded red curtains drawn tightly across the windows, the only signs of life that of the evening birdsong drifting between the hedges of the front garden. He turned away, resolving to give Ernest a call later.

'Jonathan?' a voice whispered behind him.

Jonny turned back; his granddad was peering out from behind the half-closed front door.

'Can I . . . help with anything?'

Jonny looked into the old man's tired eyes. There was something in the way his granddad was standing that didn't seem quite right, something that was twisting his body, shielding one side from view, making him look suddenly very frail and vulnerable. 'I'm afraid I was just about to turn in for the night.'

For a fleeting second Jonny wanted to tell his granddad everything that had happened since the day before: their run-in with Henry, the thieves' horrible note, their suspicions about President Pickle – everything. He knew that the other three wouldn't mind. After all, if it weren't for Ernest, they would have been banned from the Magic Circle two days ago. And they could sure benefit from the man's ingenious magical mind with the Tower of London break-in. But no, figured Jonny, it was all too dangerous for even his granddad. They would have to tackle it alone. And in secret.

'I just wanted to check that you were OK,' said Jonny eventually. 'We missed seeing you today.'

Ernest gave him a smile, looking more like his old self. 'Well, I'm never far away, Jonathan – just remember that.'

And he quietly closed the door.

*

Having grabbed a plateful of breaded whatever-they-were-meant-to-be things from the hotel buffet, Sophie headed for her freshly cleaned bedroom. She plugged herself into a set of headphones and sat at the old-fashioned desk, which had been decked out to look like something belonging to Sherlock Holmes.

She sat back on the cushioned seat as the sounds of the rainforest filled her ears, helping her to focus, helping her to escape from the real world. She closed her eyes as an exotic bird called for a mate – or maybe told it to go away.

How can we be in two places at once? she wondered as the rain pattered and the thunder rumbled comfortingly in the background. Twins maybe? Body-doubles? No, too obvious! Her mother was a twin – not that that helped much: she'd barely seen much of her auntie, and her mum was all the way up in Halifax, convinced that Sophie was on a school trip! Her dad . . . Well, she didn't know much about her dad sadly, except that the last time she'd laid eyes on him was before she could really remember anything.

No, you're getting distracted, Sophie. Concentrate!

She scoured the books she'd packed for the journey for inspiration – *Mind, Myth & Magic, NLP, The Berglas Effects* – before finally picking up a biography of Houdini she'd borrowed from her local library.

Yes, Houdini, thought Sophie. He sure knew a thing or two about getting out of a tight spot! As the thunder got louder and the bird took shelter, she flicked through the pages, marvelling at the photos of a scantily clad

Houdini attempting his daredevil escapes. Sophie turned to a photo of Houdini standing alongside some suited and booted bankers with huge moustaches. She read the caption at the bottom – *Houdini Escapes from Magic Circle's Impenetrable Bank Safe!* Sophie turned the volume down as the bird began to squawk like it was being chased. She quickly skimmed the article on the opposite page.

Houdini amazes the world once more with latest daring escape . . . Audience wait with bated breath for Houdini to emerge from Magic Circle's airtight bank safe . . . It took the highly regarded escapologist just over two and half hours to step free from the iron vault, proving just how difficult such a feat must be . . . Audience give Houdini a standing ovation for his huge, painstaking efforts . . .

Sophie slammed the book shut just as the rain stopped and the bird emerged jubilant from her surroundings and with several newly acquired competing mates (Sophie presumed, given all the noise). She smiled to herself, removed her headphones and put the book back in her suitcase, satisfied that she knew how to get the four of them to be in two places at once the following evening.

Damn it, Sophie, you're good!

Zack was so swept up in a swirl of thoughts that he missed his Tube stop, meaning he'd had to take the 137 bus home. His head throbbed with questions as he plodded upstairs, armed with a huge chicken tikka sandwich. Why had the thieves been so uncharacteristically frank with them about the time and location of their next theft? Or was this presumed honesty a blatant act of *dis*honesty, a really basic way of leading the four astray. But then if the thieves wanted to ensnare Zack and his friends, why not simply get to them the way they'd got to Henry? he wondered. There was no need for it to be so elaborate. They were clearly very resourceful. And how did Henry really fit into all this, anyway? His ears had certainly pricked up the first time *The Thieves' Almanac* was mentioned – that was a given. But then surely all Henry wanted was eternal praise and respect from the upper echelons of the Magic Circle. Was the boy perhaps trying to foil the thieves' latest plot as well?

Now this made more sense, thought Zack, moving over to his bedroom window. What better way to ingratiate oneself further and deeper into pride of place on the Magic Circle shelf than coming up with a solution to an impossible task while simultaneously saving the Crown Jewels. Yes, perhaps that's exactly what Henry was up to, decided Zack somewhat competitively now. But he'd got in too deep with the thieves perhaps? It still didn't explain why the thieves had then come to the four, outlining their plan so explicitly, but still. Hmm . . .

Zack concentrated on the next question – which was . . . ? Ah yes: just the small issue of how to steal the Crown Jewels . . . Zack tapped his head against the window. *How, how, how?*

He leaned backwards off the edge of the bed so that he was hanging upside down, his hair grazing the floor. 'I just need to come at the problem from a different angle,' he murmured to himself. What was it the guide had said in response to Sophie saying the Crown Jewels were a bit showy: *I guess that's the whole point.* But what did that mean? It had triggered something in Zack's mind, but he couldn't put his finger on it.

He started to retrace his way through the Bank of England problem, hoping it might help him to think laterally. OK, so ... How do you break into the vault of the Bank of England?

Answer: you don't.

Hmm.

Zack started to chant the two words out loud: 'You don't, you don't, you don't!'

OK, so how do you break into the Tower of London?

'You don't, you don't, you don't!'

Right.

OK.

Is that it ...?

The upside-down Zack shook his head and tutted to himself. He gave a sigh and tried a different approach.

OK, what about *why* ...

Why break into the Bank of England?

To steal the nation's gold.

Why break into the Tower of London?

To steal the Crown Jewels.

Why steal the Crown Jewels?

Because they're worth billions of Great British pounds, if not priceless . . .

Zack's brain started to work at a crazy speed, spurred on by the blood rushing to his head, making him feel dizzy.

Why keep the Crown Jewels in the Tower of London?

Because it's one of the most secure buildings in the country.

What would protect the Crown Jewels even better?

If this wasn't where they were being kept at all.

20

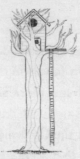

The Young Magicians stared at each other as a pot of porridge bubbled away in the corner of the tree house, filling the cosy space with the smell of oats and milk or – if you didn't like porridge – the precise smell of SICK!

'OK, so who wants to report on their findings first?' said Sophie. She looked around the room and then at Zack's leg, which bounced up and down like he was attached to a washing machine on the highest spin cycle. 'Zack, perhaps you have something you'd like to share with us,' she added sarcastically.

'OK,' he said, leg still twitching. 'So, hear me out on this one . . .'

'Naturally!' said Sophie.

'What if the Crown Jewels aren't actually kept in the Tower of London?'

'Uh-oh, here we go again.' Jonny raised his eyebrows while spooning out the thick, steaming porridge.

'I'm being serious! You said it yourself, Sophie – they're a bit *showy*. But what if that's the whole point? What if it's all for show?' said Zack. 'What better way to protect the Crown Jewels than pretend they're in a place where they're not?'

'OK, hang on . . .' said Sophie thoughtfully as Jonny refilled her bowl, spilling a splodge of porridge on to the tree-house floor, which slowly leaked through the cracks of the boards before descending miles down to the ground below, smothering some dawdler in a particularly intense and boiling bird poo. 'So you're saying we're looking . . . in the wrong place again?' Sophie felt both excited and confused.

'That's exactly what I'm saying!' Zack grinned at her.

Sophie chewed on her hot dollop of porridge pensively, her mouth glued shut by the sweet honey she'd squeezed generously over the white pulp, her eyes half closed as she considered this.

'But everyone knows the Crown Jewels are kept in the Tower of London,' protested Alex, quietly nibbling at the porridge – which was not his favourite. 'We saw them for ourselves!'

'Exactly!' Zack looked at them all in turn. 'What a great piece of misdirection! It's been going on for hundreds of years.'

'So you're saying the Crown Jewels have *never* been kept in the Tower of London?' asked Jonny, eyes wide. 'Whoa!'

'That's *precisely* what I'm saying!'

'What better way of keeping them safe!' Sophie exclaimed as it all clicked into place. 'So the ones you go and see – the ones we saw yesterday, protected by a million lasers and Perspex, are –'

'Fakes!' interrupted Zack.

'Oh, Jeez – of course, it makes perfect sense!' hooted Jonny, slapping Zack on the back with the porridge ladle and covering his friend's pullover in smatterings of slimy grey paste. 'Whoops – sorry, mate!'

'So . . . So does that mean the thieves are heading for the wrong place too?' asked Alex tentatively.

'It sure does,' answered Zack. 'I've no idea how they plan on getting into the Jewel House, but whether they do or they don't, it doesn't really matter – because the jewels on display there are fakes!'

'So where do you think the *real* Crown Jewels are kept?' Sophie put down her bowl and shook her head, infinitely impressed by Zack's powers of deduction once more.

'Ooh, I think *I* know where,' said Jonny suddenly, opening up the skylight so that they had a perfect view of Buckingham Palace, dressed finely in a pale coating of light fog. 'If *I* was Queen – or *King*, for that matter – I wouldn't let the Crown Jewels out of my sight!'

The others gazed out across Green Park. 'It's one almighty bluff . . .' whispered Sophie.

'I bet they're not even locked away,' said Zack. 'What better way to not draw attention to them than by making a big show of precisely where they're *not*!'

'OK, but we still need to tell someone about this,' said Zack, pulling the ceiling closed a fraction, the morning air a bit too crisp at this altitude for his liking. 'After all, the Crown Jewels may be safe, but the thieves still need to be caught.'

'We're not going to DI Caulfield with this again, surely,' said Sophie, wincing.

'What about your granddad, Jonny? Would he be up for helping us out again?'

'I just worry that he's getting a bit . . . well, too old for all this.'

'And there's his reputation to think of too,' said Zack. Ernest had already defended them once this week. 'What if we're way off the mark?'

'One thing we could do –' Jonny gave a mischievous grin – 'is go straight to the top. Why not go and see Her Majesty herself?' He gestured casually towards the building across the park.

'You're kidding!' Sophie wafted her hand in front of his eyes to check she hadn't accidentally put him into a trance.

'Nope!' he said, pretending to bite her hand off.

'Well, she's not in now.' Zack squinted at the bare flagpole.

'Yes, but maybe she will be tonight,' said Jonny excitedly. 'Why not tell her ourselves, and trap the thieves together? Let's face it, we can't trust anyone at the Magic Circle, our parents will just think we're making the whole thing up, and the last time we took this to the police, they took all the credit! But if we tell *her* that we know where the Crown Jewels are really kept, then perhaps she'll listen to us . . .'

'Only if my thinking is correct,' said Zack.

'Your thinking is *always* correct, mate!' said Jonny, walloping Zack with the porridge ladle and smothering his jumper once more.

'Oh man!'

'OK, OK!' Sophie stood up. 'I think we're getting ahead of ourselves. Let's just park that thought for now . . . But this brings us nicely to *my* findings.' The three boys looked up at her attentively as Sophie continued to speak. 'So whether we're heading straight for the Tower or to Buckingham Palace, we have to find a way of being in two places at once. We don't want President Pickle or anyone else inside the Magic Circle knowing what we're up to. Nor do we want to jeopardize our auditions.'

A common garden thrush rustled nearby, confused by the smell of porridge coming from inside her tree. She flew off, causing a few leaves to dislodge ahead of schedule.

'Go on, then,' said Zack. 'So how are we meant to be in two places at once?'

'Yeah, put us out of our misery!' exclaimed Jonny.

'OK . . . So, yes, we *do* need to be in two places at once, but only for a certain length of *time*.'

'Right,' said Zack slowly. 'And this helps how?'

'Houdini,' stated Sophie, like this single word held the answer to catching the thieves and whoever was colluding with them.

'Oh, come on, Sophie, stop teasing us now. Out with it!'

'OK. Are any of you aware of Houdini's bank-safe escape?' she asked, looking from one to the other. 'It took place in 1924 at the Duchess Theatre in London,' she added. 'It's the same safe that now resides in the council chamber beneath the Grand Theatre.'

Zack and Jonny looked blank, but Alex was nodding vigorously; he was familiar with Houdini's work, having made a fair few daring escapes himself.

Sophie continued. 'Like many of his escapes, it was all about the hype before and after the event and his ability to present himself as almost superhuman. He even got representatives from the Magic Circle to examine the safe to prove that it hadn't been specially rigged.'

'And so ... was Houdini ever in two places at once?' asked Jonny, still unsure where Sophie was heading with this.

'No, not as far as I'm aware. But he could have been if he'd wanted to,' Sophie answered cryptically.

Zack looked at Jonny and Alex, baffled.

'Let me take you through it step by step.' Sophie was clearly enjoying herself. 'What made Houdini one of the most famous people in the world?'

'He was good at escapology?' offered Alex.

'Partly. But also because of the publicity he generated. His escapes got more and more daring, more difficult; some – like the bank safe – were so tricky that it took him over *two and half hours* to get out!'

'My dear, sweet Sophie,' said Jonny. 'As impressive as your vast knowledge of this area is, I still don't see how this helps us.'

'But don't you see? That was the biggest illusion of all. The idea that Houdini found these escapes *difficult*. Who wants to see someone achieve something that's *easy*? Where's the fun in that? There's no intrigue, no tension, no point! We want to see the greatest showman of all time truly taxed; maybe even meet his end.'

'So you're saying that Houdini never really performed any of those escapes?' asked Zack.

'No, quite the opposite,' said Sophie. 'I'm saying that he did all the things we know and love him for, but that they weren't nearly as difficult as he made out.'

She sat down facing the others. 'Houdini was really, really good at picking locks. He could do it in his sleep. But he knew that if he made it look *too* easy, audiences would start to lose interest.'

'Oh, wow, I think I know where you're going with this,' said Zack suddenly, his leg starting to twitch again.

'So when Houdini finally escapes from his bank safe, exhausted, half dead, then ...'

'It's ... It's all an illusion!' Alex's eyes lit up.

'Exactly!' Sophie beamed. 'Houdini was out of that safe in five minutes flat; the real trick was in making the audience wait!'

'And so, if Houdini wanted to be in two places at once, he could simply nip off for a couple of hours or so while everyone thought he was still in the box!' Zack had it.

'Yup! Which is what he must have done on any number of occasions, I'm sure!'

Jonny looked at Sophie, smiling broadly. 'Wowsers! And so you're suggesting that we ...?'

'That we re-enact the bank-safe illusion in front of Council tonight. The safe is in the council chamber; I'm sure there'll be some kind of screen we can use in the Grand Theatre to shield us from view – after all it's what Houdini used to do. And, Alex, you can pick locks from the inside too, right?'

Alex held up the odd-looking implement he'd fashioned the previous night.

'There, see! And then, once we're out, we visit the Queen or whoever, catch the criminals, then return to the safe before bringing our act to a close and securing our place as future members of the Magic Circle . . . Or something like that!' Sophie added, knowing all too well that – like a space-shuttle launch – there were still a million things that needed to happen perfectly for this to be a success. And that even if 99.9% of their plan worked out there were still exactly a thousand things that would go wrong. That was stats for you. Always the bearer of bad news!

But this was not bad going, Sophie. Not bad at all! It was a starting point at least . . .

21

The four spent the rest of the time in the tree house hatching their plans in more detail as the light grew stronger and the branches of the horse chestnut swayed majestically, dropping conkers here, there and everywhere, like a schoolboy losing his marbles.

After a lot of deliberation Alex held up the scrap of paper he'd been writing on as Sophie dictated. It was the strangest to-do list ever!

1. Find out whether allowed to perform in front of Council as a group. If not, Sophie to 'persuade' President Pickle that it's OK.
2. Ask whether can borrow safe from council chamber. (Ask politely. Or persuade. Again.)
3. Find quickest escape route out of Grand Theatre. And quickest route to Buckingham Palace.

4. Alex to practise lock-picking from inside a pitch-black safe with the thing he's made.
5. Zack to think of how best to charm Queen of England with the news that the Young Magicians* know where her Crown Jewels are really stashed (without getting beheaded) so that she believes them about the thieves' latest plan.
6. Capture the thieves? Then do what with them?
7. Return to Magic Circle and appear to come out of safe after a significant period of time – impressing Council.
8. Zack to receive public apology from Council, having saved the country's millions on two occasions.
9. Cash reward/date of next Queen's Honour List ceremony?
10. Make sure DI Caulfield pays for taking the glory the first time round!
11. Ask Magic Circle Council to offer full membership to young magicians – access to library, etc.

'On point one . . .' said Sophie. 'I checked the constitution online, and there's nothing that says magicians can't perform as a group, providing they each give an individual performance as well.'

Alex looked a little deflated. *Oh well*, he thought, encouraged, he was a lot better prepared than at the start of the week.

* Alex had taken a special pride in writing these words!

'Right, now – regarding point three, getting to Buckingham Palace,' said Jonny. 'I might be able to help there. It'll be quick, but it might . . . it might be quite *dangerous*.'

Alex looked up. Given that Jonny was quite comfortable with leaping on to a rickety banister and pushing himself off without a care in the world, this was worrying.

'How dangerous?' asked Zack, smirking, his dark eyes shining over at his best friend.

'Well, I've been thinking about doing this for a while now,' said Jonny slowly. 'You know how we're pretty near the river?'

'Go on.' Sophie hadn't got a clue where Jonny was headed.

'Well, OK . . . It's a bit science-y, but just *bear with me on this*.'

'Fast becoming our motto!' said Sophie, laughing.

Jonny turned over the piece of paper Alex had been writing on and grabbed a thick crayon from the pot on his shelf. 'Let's imagine the Magic Circle is located *here*, say –' he drew a big cross at the top – 'and that Buckingham Palace is *here* –' another cross, but this time at the bottom of the page – 'and the river is *here* –' a thick wavy line at the very, very bottom of the page beneath Buckingham Palace – 'what does that tell you about these two locations?'

'That one lies north of the other?' offered Zack slowly.

'Yes . . . ?' said Jonny, suggesting that Zack was technically correct but that this wasn't the answer he was looking for. 'Think where the river is.'

'South of Buckingham Palace,' Sophie replied.

Jonny let the statement hang in the air.

'Which means . . . ?' she went on.

'Which means that since the river is the lowest point of the city, then travelling towards the Magic Circle is like going uphill.'

'How . . . How does that help us?' Alex was puzzled.

'Well,' said Jonny, 'it means that going from the Magic Circle to Buckingham Palace is *downhill*.'

The other three watched as he picked up a piece of extra-fine fisherman's wire to make it look like the porridge ladle was floating. 'Ever heard of a zip-line?'

Oh, you've got to be kidding, Jonny!

'Hang on, mate – are you suggesting we get a *zip-line* from the Magic Circle all the way to Buckingham Palace?' Zack couldn't stop laughing.

'There's no reason why not!' countered Jonny. 'Providing I use enough fixed locations to distribute the weight evenly, it's all downhill. We'll be there in no time! We can always come via this place if we want to alter our angle of final approach.' He banged on the side of the tree house with his fist, causing one of the small fixed panels to snap off and fall rapidly to the ground below, startling the dawdler again. Whoops! If Jonny was ever trying to impress them with his building skills, now wasn't the best time to show that bits dropped off his constructions every now and again.

'You won't have much time to rig it up,' said Sophie nervously.

'In that case, you guys go ahead to the Magic Circle and tie up things there,' said Jonny. 'I'll get going tying things up here!'

'Well, just be back in time for the auditions – otherwise we'll be well and truly –'

A fat pigeon landed on one of the nearby branches, causing it to sway and shower a load of conkers on to a baffled walker below. *Plop, plop, plop!*

'OK then!' said Zack, not quite believing their stint in the tree house this morning had culminated in a plan to pay the Queen of England a visit via a zip-line. 'Good luck!'

22

Sophie, Zack and Alex got off the tube at Euston and took the now-familiar route to the Magic Circle headquarters. It seemed odd to be walking without Jonny's tall frame casting shadows around them. They were strangely quiet as they thought about all the work they had to do. An *awful* lot of work!

Alex looked at his watch as he bounced along with a spring in his step. Of course, he was still petrified. Petrified of the amount of work they still had left to do, petrified of his impending performance in front of Council, petrified of having to perfect picking a safe in the pitch dark without sufficient time to practise on the moss-green safe down in the Council's chamber. Petrified of this zip-line Jonny was constructing . . .

A *zip-line*? *We must be out of our minds*. Sophie's brain was still buzzing with the million things they still had to do. She pictured herself climbing into her hotel bed for the last time that evening, before heading back up north, perhaps plugging herself back into the rainforest to find out how the exotic bird was getting on. Would they really have accomplished everything they wanted by the end of the day?

It seemed an almost impossible set of tasks, a whole mirage of blurry intertwined events that would only become clear at the final moment. Would she even get the place at the Magic Circle she'd so desperately fantasized about all her life ... ? Or was that strangely not as big a priority to her right now? Whatever the case, they were fast running out of time!

Zack couldn't help but smile. Not even he, with his sideways-thinking brain, could have imagined what lay ahead. He couldn't have wished for three better friends in Jonny, Alex and Sophie. Of course, he'd known Jonny since his first day at school when the boy (taller than his teacher, even then) had come over and shown Zack his dinosaur egg – which wasn't actually an egg but a stone wrapped in tinfoil – but it had been the start of a friendship for life. And now, with Alex and Sophie too, Zack felt that they were unstoppable! The Young Magicians ...

They headed for the blue door, looking at each other, taking deep, important breaths.

'OK,' said Sophie. 'Just remember to act normal. It's just an ordinary day here at the Magic Circle. Imagine you're palming a playing card, if that helps, Alex.'*

---

* Oh, HEY again! Just a bit of clarity on this ... Palming is the act of hiding a playing card in one's palm, ideally without anyone noticing. It's

The heavy door opened just as they arrived, revealing Cynthia, evidently a little stressed but pleased to see them again all the same.

'Jonny not with you, my dears?' she said breezily, holding the door open as they walked casually inside.

'Oh, no, he's just ... tying up a few loose ends,' said Zack innocently, smiling at the others.

'But he'll be back in time for the auditions this evening,' added Sophie, as if trying to reassure herself.

'Oh, good, good. Well, follow me then. You must all be very excited. How are you feeling, Alex?' Cynthia led them down the dim corridor, avoiding the now formidable number of rodent traps, which took up more space than the actual floor itself, it seemed.

'Erm ... I'm OK,' said Alex. 'The others have been ... helping me.'

'Wonderful! That's what it's all about,' said Cynthia. 'Right, let me just find my keys. New rules from Council apparently: the Junior Room is to be kept locked at all times, even when occupied.' She jangled around in her pockets and handbag as Sophie looked at Zack and Alex. So President Pickle and his cohorts were trying to exclude young magicians even further? *Interesting*, thought Zack darkly.

---

not so much the actual process of palming that's difficult; it's acting normal while you're doing it and thus not attracting attention. The last thing you want to do is suddenly start tensing up, which pretty much screams, LOOK AT ME AND MY HAND! OK, back to the main body of text, if you please!

Cynthia finally fished out her keys, which had somehow fallen through a hole in her pocket and looped themselves on to the inside part of her long skirt; Zack and Alex had to look away while Sophie helped her untangle everything without revealing too much bare skin. 'There we go. Brilliant – thanks, Sophie,' said Cynthia somewhat breathlessly.

'Actually, we were wondering whether it might be possible to rehearse on stage rather than in the Junior Room,' Sophie said politely as Cynthia started on the top lock.

'And *also* . . . whether it might be possible to perform as a group,' added Zack.

Cynthia studied them, mildly suspicious. She really was becoming rather fond of them, especially Sophie. But she was tired. Tired of having to defend their antics to her husband and others on Council. 'They're just being curious, Edmund,' she had constantly found herself saying over the past few days. 'You were a child once, remember?' (All over a steaming plate of roast dinner of course, with all the trimmings!) But her husband would never see reason. And President Pickle could humour his wife all he liked, but there wasn't a chance in hell that these four would ever be considered as future members of the Magic Circle. Not on his watch, at least.

Cynthia smiled at Alex. 'You know you'll still have to perform on your own, even if you do something as a group,' she said, believing this was behind Zack's request.

Oh, if only you knew the real reason, Cynthia, thought Zack.

Alex nodded politely.

'Well, we're going to have to run this by President Pickle, I'm afraid,' she told them. 'Follow me.'

Sophie grimaced as Cynthia hastily relocked the door, ignoring the sound of Deanna's yelps that had started to eke their way through the garish door (what *was* she doing in there?).

The four of them hurried down the corridor, increasingly conscious of time.

Strange, thought Zack as Cynthia led them through the Grand Theatre and down the spiral staircase – they'd never actually *walked* down it before. He tapped his fingers along the banister rail, catching Sophie's eye and grinning.

Nor had the Young Magicians seen the formal entrance to the Council's chamber, which was way less impressive than the title might imply, simply consisting of a plain wooden door smothered with a giant NO ENTRY sign. Still, better getting in this way than the spidery way. Alex shuddered at the memory of the double-sided cupboard.

Cynthia knocked lightly on the door, looking down at them. 'Let me do the talking, please.'

They nodded.

'Enter!' bellowed President Pickle.

Cynthia popped her head round the door, temporarily shielding the others from view. 'Do you mind if we have a quick word?' she asked.

'Of course, honeypot!' said President Pickle indulgently, smiling at her like he did when his dinner was nearly ready.

Cynthia opened the door to reveal Zack, Sophie and Alex.

'Oh!' He sighed, puffing out his cheeks. 'I might have guessed. What have they been up to this time?'

'Oh, nothing – nothing at all.' Cynthia beckoned them into the chamber. 'They just wanted to know whether it was possible to perform as a group as well, as part of the audition. It was their idea to come and ask you privately.'

Bless Cynthia, thought Sophie. Always trying to make them look good.

'Silence in the Council's chamber!' shouted President Pickle all of a sudden. 'Bill is counting.'

The three friends looked over towards the other end of the long table where Treasurer Bill Dungworth sat slowly counting odd bits of shrapnel, some of which had evidently long gone out of circulation. Beside him was the giant green safe, the door hanging open, revealing it to be completely empty. Zack swallowed involuntarily at the sight of the draughty safe confines – it sure looked pretty impenetrable!

Bill stared at them vacantly before writing something tiny on a scrap of stained paper and continuing, almost certain he'd lost count but writing down some random figure all the same for consistency.

'May I ask why you wish to perform as a group?' said President Pickle haughtily. 'You, little girl – you may now speak.' He waggled his fingers at Sophie.

She swallowed her anger. 'Well, we just want to do as much as we can to make a good impression on Council. Especially given all the *upset* we've caused lately.'

President Pickle sniffed pompously.

'We were actually hoping to perform a group escape from that safe there,' said Zack, gesturing towards it. 'If that's OK by you, that is?' he added with a quick, fetching smile.

President Pickle looked over at the safe and then at Bill, who had dozed off again, his drooling face knocking over a pile of rusting half-crowns. 'Bill!' he shouted, causing a sound wave to shoot along the length of the table and straight to the back of Bill's rotting teeth. The man woke with a start, jotting down another number before counting the coins again – starting with another number that he had blatantly just plucked out of the air.

'You know that safe has been around since the society was founded some hundred plus years ago?' the president said, getting up and patting it solemnly, like it was an ageing farm animal that had served them well, but was now at the end of its life. 'Its walls are constructed of eight-inch solid steel; only Bill knows the code that opens the locking mechanism, and he forgot it way back in the mid-seventies. It's completely airtight. It even took *Houdini* two and a half hours to escape!'

Cynthia looked down at the Young Magicians, concerned. They hadn't mentioned that their group efforts might be *dangerous*. 'You know what? Maybe this isn't such a great idea, after all,' she said, biting her bottom lip and trying to hurry the three back out of the room.

'Oh, no, no!' said President Pickle, rather joyful all of a sudden. 'I think it's a brilliant suggestion!'

Whether he was attracted by the idea of a group escape or by the prospect of keeping the four under lock and key – especially tonight of all nights – they couldn't tell. But they had his permission to go ahead, and that's all that mattered right now.

Well, that's items one and two ticked off, thought Sophie – and she hadn't even had to hypnotize anyone yet!

'Don't you want to double-check the constitution, darling?' Now that she realized what Zack, Sophie and Alex were suggesting, Cynthia was trying to put her husband off.

'No, that'll be all. I look forward to seeing the performance later. Of course, you'll need to get the safe up the stairs and into the theatre yourselves.' President Pickle couldn't help a giggle. 'But I'm sure you'll find a way,' he added, with a trace of his usual mean streak back. 'Good luck!'

Cynthia mothered them quickly out of the room, pulling the door shut. 'Now, listen here, you three!' she said, turning on them suddenly, her caring voice a little higher than usual. 'If this is another one of your little *errands*, then I don't want anything to do with it. I'm washing my hands of you! I will *not* help you get that safe up the stairs, do you hear me?' Cynthia looked like she was about to cry before tearing off round the corner and stomping up the spiral staircase. 'Dangerous magic!' Her voice echoed in the distance. 'As if my job isn't difficult enough without you four!'

Sophie, Alex and Zack looked at each other sadly. But right now there were bigger things at stake than Cynthia's feelings. She'd come round once she knew what they were trying to achieve.

23

'We need to get a good look at that safe,' said Sophie, glancing at Alex, who was super keen to see the mechanism he had to deal with.

'Yes,' agreed Zack, looking at his watch. 'And the quicker we can cart it up these stairs, the better!' He rapped lightly on the council-chamber door.

'Enter!' came President Pickle's booming voice once again.

Zack popped his head round. 'Do you mind if we grab the safe now and take it upstairs?' he asked, smiling his infectious grin. 'We'd like to get in as much practice as possible.'

President Pickle suddenly burst out laughing. A deep, large-man's laugh that shook his vital organs and made his chin jiggle about. The kind of laugh that he reserved for special occasions, when something really tickled him. Or like the first time Cynthia had turned the eggshell of her freshly eaten boiled egg upside-down, placed it back in the eggcup and served it to him on their finest, chintzy crockery as a joke. Oh how he'd roared! Truly one of the funniest things he'd ever seen. And now these little mites – one of whom was a *girl* – were asking whether they could take one of the heaviest things ever up a huge flight of stairs! Eventually he calmed down, mopping his brow theatrically, his cheeks and jowls all flushed. 'Be my guest,' he said, trying to suppress another wheezy laugh. 'Try not to wake Bill, though. He doesn't take kindly to anyone touching his safe.'

Could this man *really* be in league with the thieves? Sophie mused as they traipsed cautiously over to the safe. He was a complete clown, but the facts seemed to fit. He needed cash to save his floundering society . . . Could all this buffoonery merely be an act? A fantastic display of foolishness as he colluded and constructed some beastly plan with the nation's most-wanted to ensure his survival at the top?

Why, oh why did he dislike children so much? wondered Zack. It wasn't just a casual dislike; this was something bigger than that, something more deep-seated bubbling away under the surface. Perhaps they'd get to the bottom of it one day.

The three looked over at Bill, now lolling back, mouth gaping wide, his lungs working overtime to pump the stale air in and out of his decaying body.

The three friends swiftly sized up the safe as they approached. It sure was a chunky old thing, with easily enough space for the four of them to fit inside. Jonny would have to do something clever with his spine, thought Zack, but that's what Jonny always had to do whenever he got inside anything smaller than a blue whale.

Alex felt the cold, stinging metal walls – the kind of sucking, all-pervading cold that you could almost sense from a distance. He placed his hands on the door itself, which swung clunkily on its fat hinges, heaving and sighing. In the very centre on the outer side of the safe door was a series of circular dials, one on top of the other, with numbers and letters set round the grooved edges. Alex ran his fingers along them, glad to feel that the ancient mechanism had been well oiled.

'How do you want to lift it?' asked Sophie, looking at the bronze handles on the sides of the safe.

'I guess we just take one side each,' answered Zack, slightly overwhelmed by the dense weight of the object now they were this close. 'Alex, do you want to stop the door from swinging open?'

Alex pushed the door to, being careful not to shut it. Bill snuffled and adjusted his position but didn't wake.

'Careful!' sang President Pickle from the other side of the table, eyeing the three like they were a bunch of performers brought in for his amusement. 'He might look like a kitten when he's asleep, but he turns into a *wild cat* when startled.' He chuckled loudly, clearly trying to wake Bill.

Sophie and Zack took up their positions on either side of the safe and heaved on the handles, straining their shoulders as Alex supported the door. It was a mighty

effort. The sort only reserved for something like moving house; the kind you didn't want to do too regularly; the kind advised against by all qualified doctors.

'You couldn't ... perhaps ... give us a hand ... could you?' asked Zack between breaths as they inched forward under the monstrous weight.

President Pickle stuck out his bottom lip mockingly. 'As much as I would love to be of assistance,' soothed the man idiotically, clearly enjoying himself, 'I'm afraid I can't be seen to offer any preferential treatment ahead of your auditions in front of Council.' He smiled sympathetically before checking to see if Bill had woken up yet, frowning wildly like a pantomime villain. 'Uh-oh, he's stirring!'

'It's . . . all right . . .' managed Sophie. 'We've got this . . . Thank goodness society finances are so low . . . Otherwise this might be a *lot* heavier!'

President Pickle shot her a warning glance as they slowly manoeuvred the safe towards the doorway.

'Oh, now look – you've only gone and woken *Bill*!' shouted President Pickle all of a sudden. 'BILL! These children are trying to make off with your safe! What are you going to do about it?'

Bill rustled awake, his eyes blinking slowly as bits of dust and sleep fell out of his ageing eye-sockets and clattered noiselessly to the stone floor, catching the light – a faint dusting of DNA should someone wish to replicate Bill as a future science project. For a second they thought he was about to pounce. But no, not today. Today's frail Bill didn't really have it in him any more. He couldn't even see what President Pickle was getting so worked up about to be honest – everything was such a blur in this dimly lit cave. The only thing he knew was that he was meant to be counting . . . something.

Bill's shoulders sagged and he drifted back into a deep, deep sleep.

The three placed the safe down at the foot of the spiral staircase, glad to be out of the stuffy chamber. They looked up at the tiny speck of landing, way, way, way above their heads. If this was payback for their earlier treatment of the banister, then they'd been got back fair and square. How on earth were they going to get up with this cumbersome thing? They certainly hadn't figured this in their eleven-point plan!

Alex popped his head out, clearly embarrassed not to be bearing much, if any, of the load. He looked up at Sophie. 'I . . . I don't mind swapping places.'

Sophie couldn't help grinning. 'Well, that's very gentle-manly of you, Alex,' she said, stretching her arms for relief. 'But there's no *way* you're stronger than me!'

Alex nodded quickly and retreated.

Zack smiled at them. 'OK, well, let's just take it one step at a time, then, shall we?'

They heaved the safe up on to the first step with a solid *thud*. And then on to the next step. *Thud*. And then again. *Thud*. Three steps in a row this time. *Scrape, scrape, thud!* The whole staircase seemed to bend and moan at the colossal weight moving at tortoise speed, the banister creaking like a floundering ship, in serious danger of just giving up and falling apart.

It was a strange spectacle: Zack with his nose squashed against one side of the safe, his back to the curved stone wall; Sophie opposite, holding up the other side, her back jammed into the rail, which shone from the earlier polishing effects of the Young Magicians' slidey bums.*

Alex was doing his best at the downhill end of things, leaning forward to stop the safe door swinging open while

* Title of next book?!

231

offering words of encouragement. Still, it gave him the opportunity to study the locking mechanism in a bit more detail. 'The . . . The dial looks . . . difficult, but pickable,' he called out optimistically.

'Hang on . . . can we just . . . put it down a sec?' said Zack, wincing as he lowered his side of the safe.

'Not tired, are you, Zack, mate?' asked Sophie, a blatant edge of competitiveness in her voice.

'No, I just . . . I just heard something,' said Zack, lowering his voice and concentrating.

They stood motionless, about a quarter of the way up the spiral staircase, straining their ears.

Zack looked up as a cool breeze swept over him. Was it his imagination or was there a voice travelling down with it, spirit-like, freezing the three of them to the spot.

'Children . . . Children . . .' the whisper echoed, filtering through the air, cooing and beckoning them softly. Zack looked over at Sophie, his brow furrowed. 'What mischief are you up to now?'

Sophie gripped the banister, feeling it vibrate. 'I think there might be someone sliding down,' she said anxiously, looking over at the two boys.

Alex's face started to turn the colour of Greek natural yogurt (with no bits).

The voice sounded again, closer this time. 'Clever girl, Sophie! You'd be surprised how easily sound travels in this building!'

Zack opened his mouth to speak, but no sound came out. He looked around, wondering how to squeeze out from between the wall and the safe, and realized that he and Sophie were well and truly trapped. Should either of them move, the safe would topple back down the stairs, possibly taking the entire stairwell with it.

'Not like you to have nothing to say, Zack!' The banister started to groan under the weight of someone approaching, like some mournful chorus, dragged in begrudgingly to mark the arrival of this strange character. 'I've been watching you all for quite some time now,' continued the voice, which was arguably the most creepy thing he'd said so far. And then, as if to take the edge off:

'Not that I have much else to do, you have to understand!'

Although quite exactly how this made things any clearer or less unnerving was entirely up for grabs.

Alex looked up into the gloom, letting out a small cry as a dark figure whizzed round and round above them, facing forward on the banister (brave!), as if travelling by broom and caught inside a tornado. He was now only three or four turns above them, hugging the rail close, his whole body low and creeping, shooting forward.

'Now, now, don't fret, young Alex,' the voice said soothingly. 'Nothing to be afraid of, I promise.'

But as Alex knew all too well, people – his parents, for example – broke their promises all the time.

Sophie took a deep breath as the figure came to a halt, gripping the rail with his gloved hands, his nose stopping inches away from her shocked face. She looked disbelievingly into the kind eyes, for this was a face she'd never expected to see in a hundred years. For a hundred years was roughly the time when this man was last seen alive. There was even a painting of him up in the corridor above saying exactly when he died.

'Hi! I'm Alf. I'm here to help!'

ALF?!

24

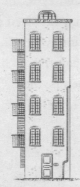

Sophie stared into Alf's face. Was this really the man who had died all those years ago at the opening of the Grand Theatre? Sophie didn't believe in ghosts, but if this *was* a ghost then it was incredibly realistic: the warm, minty breath, the smiling face – much older than hers but not grey or transparent. He looked so *real*.

Zack and Alex craned round the bulky safe for a better view.

'I do beg your pardon, Mr –' Zack began.

Alf already had a finger to his lips and was shaking his head. 'Like I said, you'd be surprised how well sound travels in this building . . . Let's get this monstrosity upstairs and out of the way first.'

The man-ghost jumped swiftly off the banister and on to the staircase above, grinning at their baffled expressions.

If this was a guy of 130, then he sure was nimble!

The three of them watched as Alf clambered over the top of the safe and down the other side, landing next to Alex – who moved away instinctively, causing the heavy safe door to swing open.

'Careful, young lad!' warned Alf, grabbing the door just in time so that it didn't whack Alex in the guts and risk hurtling him over the edge of the banister, or between the bars which – even though they were set fairly closely together – could still fit a thin, frightened Alex through if he were given a good, hard shove!

'Right, you two!' the man went on, peeping over the top of the safe at Zack and Sophie. 'Ready?'

Zack and Sophie looked at each other, at a loss for words.

'Come on!'

Alf heaved on his side of the safe, getting right underneath it, forcing Zack and Sophie to move up a few steps in rapid succession. And then they were off, moving steadily up the spiral staircase, the sort-of spectre taking the majority of the weight.

As Alex plodded along behind, he studied the man. This couldn't be a ghost! Ghosts didn't have muscles; ghosts didn't huff and puff with every step. Or maybe they did! Alex had never come into contact with a real-life, living ghost before. Maybe this was the kind of thing they got up to all the time!

After a short while, the four of them reached the landing. Alf let out a large sigh, reminiscent of the wailing sound they'd heard in the theatre only a few days earlier, as he lowered his side of the safe to the floor.

Sophie and Zack smiled at each other knowingly, instantly recognizing the sound as they stretched out their arms and legs, glad of the extra room finally.

'I take it you want this up on stage?' Alf asked, reaching down once more. As Zack and Sophie resumed their positions, Alex ran ahead to open the small green door.

With a bit of tricksy effort, twisting and – ultimately – by using Pythagoras, they managed to angle the safe through the doorway and up on to the stage. Zack and Sophie collapsed on top of it, breathing deeply, the muscles in their arms visibly pulsating.

'So,' said Alf, shining with sweat. 'Do you want to tell me what you're up to?'

In the dim house lights, the three young magicians looked up at him. He was tall – not as tall as Jonny or Ernest, but remarkably strapping. With his dishevelled hair, woolly jumper and brown corduroy trousers, he looked like someone more used to working backstage than in front of the curtain.

A fiddler and a worker, not a showy theatrical type, favouring bulky over graceful – someone who made the work of the pretentious prestidigitator possible. A wing man. Quite literally! A stage manager. The unofficial Patron Saint of Stagehands! That's how Zack had referred to him, wasn't it? *Always there for a magician in need*. Well, he'd certainly kept true to his word!

'If you don't mind . . .' Sophie didn't take her eyes off the man. 'Could you explain what *you're* up to first? I mean, who even *are* you?'

Alf smiled as he patted down his hair. 'Tell you what – why don't we all take a seat up in the gods?' he said, gesturing up towards the stage-left wing. 'I know a shortcut . . . And there's someone waiting for you!'

The Young Magicians looked at each other apprehensively. 'Oh, don't worry, he's one of the good guys!' And with that Alf disappeared into the darkness of the wings.

'Do you think we can trust him?' whispered Sophie, turning to Zack and Alex.

'Of course you can trust me!' came a raspy stage whisper out of nowhere, making them jump.

They moved forward slowly, still not entirely convinced they should follow.

'Come on, don't hang about! Sounds like you have an *awful* lot to get through today!'

They peered behind the gauze at the back of the stage and saw an iron ladder that rose all the way up into the flies, stretching up to a dizzying height.

Zack squinted into the darkness as, without another word, Alf began to climb. On the one hand, he thought, following this man could be the worst idea since Deanna was first given a magic set; on the other hand, who was waiting for them? Perhaps they knew something that might help them out today . . .

Sophie drew in a breath before moving forward and placing her foot on the bottom rung of the ladder. She turned towards her friends. 'Come on – we've got this far. I've got a good feeling about this!' She started to climb as Zack and then Alex followed guardedly behind.

After another full upper-body workout they reached the top. Alex glanced back down, gulping at the immense drop as Alf led them along a thin walkway that skirted the very edge of the stage walls, through a door and out into the upper gallery of the Grand Theatre.

This must have been where she first spotted the man's face, thought Sophie as she marvelled at the size of the auditorium from this soaring height.

And there, waiting for them, leaning on his cane with that familiar kindly glint in his eye, was Ernest.

25

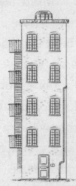

'Gosh, I love it up here, don't you, Ernest?' said Alf, sinking on to one of the aged cushioned seats. 'Nice place to keep an eye on everything!'

Zack, Sophie and Alex stared from Ernest to Alf and back again. What on earth was going on?

'OK, I guess we have a bit of explaining to do.' Ernest lowered himself carefully on to the seat next to Alf. 'I was hoping that Jonathan would be with you too – I do hope he's OK?'

They hastily took seats a few rows in front. Zack watched as Alf – for he really did look an awful lot like Alf, even this close – stretched his legs out to the sides, and placed his hands behind his head, completely at home, clearly quite enjoying the look of baffled confusion on the three youngsters' faces.

'You're not a . . . ghost, are you?' asked Alex, feeling it was best to get this question out of the way first.

The man answered with a wide grin.

'But . . . the picture in the corridor . . .' Zack hesitated. 'You look exactly like Alf Rattlebag.'

'And how do you know our names?' Sophie was both impressed and unnerved.

Ernest leaned forward in his seat as if he were about to watch Thurston vanish an elephant. 'Do you want to tell them or shall I?'

Alf removed his glasses and pinched his nose. 'OK, so there's a few things you need to know about me. Firstly, and most importantly, you don't need to be afraid – I'm not a ghost,' he said in a friendly tone, meeting Alex's gaze. 'Secondly, my name's not Alf, but it's fine for you to call me that. It's what Ernest has called me ever since I . . . first arrived.' He looked away for a brief second as his voice trailed off, his otherwise soft eyes suddenly downcast.

'And thirdly?' Sophie wondered if she could *influence* the man into giving away his real name.

'Now, now, dear,' said Ernest with a twinkle, reminding her instantly of Jonny. 'We're coming to that.'

'And *thirdly*, I've been living in this theatre for the past five years. Using it as a temporary . . . shelter, I guess.'

'You're homeless?' said Zack .

'Well, not any more!' Alf looked around the theatre. '*This* place is my home now. I have everything I could ever want: a roof over my head, the run of the building, a library of books I'll never read! And Ernest has been sneaking

biscuits out of the council chamber for me for years now!'
he added, patting his stomach.

'And so you've known about Alf all along?' said Sophie,
looking at Ernest.

'Oh yes, Alf's been my eyes and ears for a good while
now. Mine aren't what they used to be – and as you've seen
for yourself, there are things happening in the Magic Circle
that need to be kept an eye on.'

'And your resemblance to the *real* Alf?' Zack asked Alf,
wondering if perhaps sheer coincidence had played its
part here.

'Deliberate,' he replied, pulling at the collar of his shirt –
identical to the one in the painting. 'After Ernest found me,
he reckoned that capitalizing on the legend of Alf might
help keep me safe, in case I was ever spotted. And naturally,'
he continued, 'once mysterious "sightings" were reported
back to the Council, President Pickle was only too keen to
endorse the idea that the theatre was haunted – hoping to
scare off any trespassers, no doubt!' He waggled his fingers
in imitation of the president. 'Not that it ever stopped *you*
wandering about the place of course, young lad!' He
flashed Zack a grin.

'And so all that wailing when we first stepped in here . . .
Was that *you*?' asked Sophie.

Alf nodded enthusiastically. 'But only so you knew that
Cynthia and President Pickle were heading towards the
theatre. Otherwise you might have been caught snooping
even sooner, do you see?'

'And what – if you don't mind me asking – have *you* lot been up to?' asked Ernest. 'Alf tells me that you've been up to *something*!'

Zack looked at his friends. Was it time for them to come clean and share their plan? Jonny hadn't wanted to bother Ernest, but here he was! And this wasn't like telling any old granddad. This was someone with a shared sense of adventure, someone who knew that magic could be mischievous as well as miraculous. Ernest was pretty much one of them already . . . Hadn't his defence of them already proved that? He was the oldest and wisest Young Magician of the lot! Yes, it was time for them to share their theory.

Sophie and Alex nodded back at Zack, giving him the go-ahead. He took a deep breath . . .

It was a long tale, full of mishaps, run-ins, adventures, theories and false assumptions that would have sounded like a piece of fiction were it not all completely and utterly true. But Ernest sat listening intently, hardly even blinking, lapping it up like a child tucked up in bed listening to their favourite night-time story.

It was strange hearing it all. Sophie could hardly believe that so much had happened since the four had first met only three days ago.

Zack covered everything: *The Thieves' Almanac*; their theories on how someone inside the Magic Circle – possibly President Pickle himself – must be working with the thieves in order to secure funds for the society; Zack's solution to the Bank of England plot; DI Caulfield and his betrayal of their trust – everything.

He paused before going on to tell Ernest about their run-in with Henry, about the thieves' sinister note detailing how they planned to steal the Crown Jewels, and how the four of them planned to escape from the Magic Circle and inform the Queen themselves this very evening.

At last, after what seemed like a whole book-load of storytelling, Zack finished.

Ernest nodded solemnly. He'd been listening intently, nodding on occasion, taking everything in, making mental notes, pausing every so often, holding up his hand while he processed a particular thought before gesturing for Zack to continue. Alf too had sat there, transfixed, glad of the extra company, for this was the most group conversation he'd had in years!

'And Jonathan?' asked Ernest quietly. 'He plans on finishing this contraption in time for this evening?'

Zack nodded.

'And you're *sure* the thieves are heading for the wrong place?'

'Yes,' answered Sophie. 'All being well!' She looked at Ernest and Alf. 'Does this ring any bells? You must see and hear so much of what goes on here.'

Alf frowned. 'It's true that something strange is going on within the society.'

'Oh, but don't for a second think that you're alone!' said Ernest suddenly. 'Cynthia, for one, is on your side.'

'Well, maybe she *was*, but not any more.' Zack remembered her parting words: she was washing her hands of them.

'Ah yes, but not everything is as it first appears in this place,' said Ernest wisely. 'Either way, it's imperative that the society is allowed to nurture young and brilliant magical minds like yours . . . If only President Pickle weren't so damn *stubborn*!' He banged his cane on the tattered carpet.

'Listen,' said Alf, suddenly standing. 'Who knows exactly what's going on here, but it seems the society is in real trouble, and I for one don't want to lose a roof over my head! You just keep on doing what you're doing – you're clearly on to something. Just tell me how I can help.'

The three Young Magicians looked at each other. Perhaps adults weren't all that bad after all! Well, certainly not adults like Alf and Ernest.

'Well, in that case,' said Zack slowly, 'two things: one, we need someone to keep an eye on President Pickle this evening – he of all people can't know what we're really up to.'

'Consider it done,' said Ernest.

'And two,' continued Zack, 'you don't happen to know a quick way up to the roof, do you?'

Alf beamed. 'I'd be a lacklustre theatre ghost if I didn't know something like that, wouldn't I? Secret, sneaky passages and tricksy hiding places are my bread and butter!'

And with that he got up and headed back towards the little doorway. 'Follow me!'

Sophie, Alex and Zack leaped up, trying to keep up with the man, who moved like an ambidextrous mountain goat as they headed back towards the gangway high above the stage.

In the doorway Zack turned back to look at Ernest, who was still sitting peacefully in his seat, like he was enjoying some quaint sea view, content with life. 'Thank you, Ernest,' he said. 'Your help means an awful lot.'

The elderly gentleman nodded conclusively. 'You're welcome, Zack. You're most welcome.'

Alf dashed along the walkway to the other side of the theatre, the youngsters following cautiously, holding on to the rail.

Ahead of them, he came to a stop and reached up above his head, pulling on a short thick rope knotted gracelessly at the end, like a really basic toilet brush. 'Mind out!'

They watched as a small ladder unfolded on to the walkway, reminding Alex of the time when his parents had taken him to the Conways' family home and he'd found his way to their loft via a similar ladder (while the adults got intoxicated in the tacky lounge on cheap peach schnapps).

'This way will take you straight to the roof,' whispered Alf. 'From there you can use the fire escape at the side of the building – or whatever mad contraption Ernest's grandson has put together!'

The three of them smiled nervously, dreading to think precisely what their gangly friend might have fashioned during his time away.

Well, as you asked . . . !

26

Jonny was making good progress. Sure, it wasn't his finest work – that prize would have to go to the log flume* he'd constructed one hot† summer's day in the Lake District two years ago, but still, this would do. He hoped!

He figured it was best to work backwards, tying off the zip-line at Buckingham Palace – or as close to Buckingham Palace as he could get – before working his way north ('uphill') towards the Magic Circle. There was only a ten-metre difference in elevation between the two sites, so the incline of the zip-line wouldn't be too steep. However, once they built up sufficient speed, it might be tricky to slow

---

* Calling it a log flume is not quite right, by the way, but that's how Jonny referred to the small raft he'd hammered together and connected to a series of pulleys, before launching it, along with himself, into Rydal Falls. Please don't try this at home! (Though quite how or why Rydal Falls would be churning its way through your house I have no idea!)
† Implying that the Lake District is ever hot during the summer is also, arguably, not quite right.

down as they hurtled towards the finishing post. Oh well! Their plan was to get there as quickly as possible.

Although he missed his three friends and couldn't wait to find out how they were getting on (Oh, just you wait, Jonny!), he enjoyed working on his own in this way, at his own pace, without interruption.

Jonny had begun his course a stone's throw from the walls of Buckingham Palace. As he couldn't get into the gardens, he'd figured that if he made a nearby tree his endpoint, then – all being well – their momentum would carry them over the wall. And to stop them from breaking their necks once they'd left the zip-line? Ah yes, everyone's favourite piece of safety equipment: the humble umbrella. Four large black umbrellas, in this case, which he'd found at home, along with everything else he needed.

Jonny had scaled the tree next to the wall of Buckingham Palace with great ease, taking care to stay out of sight of the security cameras posted at intervals along the garden's perimeter.

Jonny tied off the end of the wire by looping it around several low hanging branches before leaping to the ground, landing on all fours like a particularly giant cat. He picked himself up, grabbed the rucksack containing a huge coil of fine wire,* and started to spool it gradually out along the ground as he moved across Green Park.

---

* The kind used to make David Copperfield fly: it's almost invisible to the naked eye but can hold the weight of an elephant. DISCLAIMER: David Copperfield does not weigh the same as an elephant. YET.

And from there Jonny continued, making his way towards the Magic Circle, literally moving as the crow flies but at a snail's pace, trying to remain inconspicuous – constantly pretending he was doing up his shoelaces – picking out the most direct route, occasionally stopping to check that the wire was tucked securely away along the sides of buildings, making sure he left just enough slack, but not so much that the wire was noticeable by people, pigeons, police or the press.

It was a lengthy task – perhaps even longer than this description does justice – and Jonny would only know it had worked once he reached the roof of the Magic Circle and yanked firmly on the end, hoisting the wire up into the air in one swift movement – hopefully without decapitating any startled starlings or belligerent businessmen along the way.

As he bent to retie his shoelaces outside the BT Tower, Jonny ran the numbers through his head once more. The physics of the situation certainly looked good on paper, and that was all Jonny usually needed to put his mind at ease – but so much was resting on this. There was a lot more at stake here than getting something wrong in a science exam! What if this contraption got them into serious trouble? Or, worse, if it put an end to the Young Magicians? And a very painful end at that! *Still, the idea of a man walking on the moon must have sounded bonkers at the time, right*, thought Jonny, trying to reassure himself.

He kept on going . . .

27

Back at the Magic Circle, Zack, Sophie and Alex were hard at work on the airtight safe.

'OK, let's just run through the plan one more time,' said Zack as Alex continued to fiddle with the lock, now sat inside the safe with the door swung open, his legs dangling off over the edge. Alex had now successfully managed to pick the lock on several occasions, but Zack had refused to let the lad completely lock himself inside – just in case!

'We're going to have to rehearse it fully at some point, though,' said Sophie, checking her watch again.

'OK, fine, well, let's just talk this through first . . .' Zack paced across the stage like a student director. 'As soon as we're all locked inside, Alex will then move into position to pick the lock.'

'And so . . . so maybe I should get in last.' Alex's voice sounded even more frail as it deflected off the inside walls of the safe, thinning it slightly.

'And I'll be keeping an eye on President Pickle!' whispered Alf from directly above. The three of them smiled up towards the flies, just about making out Alf's ghoulish silhouette, leaning over the walkway like a prying poltergeist.

Sophie craned her neck to see if Ernest was still up there too.

'He's gone to the toilet,' whispered Alf loudly, correctly interpreting Sophie's neck straining and causing the sentence to echo about the theatre.

Sophie smiled, wondering if Alf had ever considered a career in mind-reading, as Zack continued . . .

'Now, as in Houdini's original escape, once we're all inside and the clock has started, a screen will be placed in front of the safe, shielding us from view. Hopefully, shortly after that, Alex will have picked the lock.'

'Which is when we make our escape to the roof,' said Sophie excitedly, moving upstage towards the gauze curtain.

'Precisely!' said Zack. 'And from there on, we're in Jonny's hands, I guess!'

'How long do you think before anyone suspects that something is up?' asked Sophie eventually, wondering how long President Pickle might leave it before having the safe door surgically opened.

'Well, knowing President Pickle's love of us lickle children, I suspect he might leave it a good while. Long enough for us to get a decent head start at least!' said Zack.

'What about while everyone thinks we're inside?'

'I don't know . . . Maybe Deanna could perform one of her dance routines –'

Clunk.

It was a frightening, conclusive sound. The metal door had slammed shut, securing its contents safely inside which – in this case – happened to be a small boy with blond hair named Alex Finley.

'No!' cried Zack as he and Sophie tried to prise the door open – to no avail.

Alf leaped off his watching post in an instant and hurtled his way down the ladder at the back of the stage, slipping down the last few rungs like wet paint, deliberately missing his footing to speed up his descent – a manoeuvre he'd had to do on many occasions when he was in danger of being caught out and needed a quick getaway.

'Alex! Alex, are you OK? Talk to me!' shouted Zack, desperately fiddling with the dials.

'Tell us what to do, Alex!' screamed Sophie as Alf joined her. The three of them strained to hear Alex's muffled voice.

'What's he saying?' Zack looked around for something to force the door with.

'How much oxygen in that safe?' Alf looked at his watch.

'I don't know, I don't know – we haven't worked that out yet!' shrilled Sophie; perhaps, in all their excitement, they'd overlooked just how dangerous trying to escape from an airtight safe might be. It was all very well Alex saying he could pick the lock, but could he do it in the dark, as the air slowly ... ran out?

All of a sudden the safe door clicked and pinged open like a microwave.

'I ... I said,' said Alex, pushing the door further open with his little foot, his voice cool as a refrigerated cucumber, 'please don't turn the dials or bang on the door while I'm trying to pick the lock from the inside!'

The three let out a huge gush of laughter as Zack and Sophie dragged Alex out of the safe and gave him a tight, squishy hug.

'How ... How did I do? Was I quick?'

'Faster even than Houdini, by all accounts,' said Alf, impressed. 'Which certainly bodes well for tonight.'

Suddenly they heard footsteps on the landing.

'Quick – President Pickle!' rasped Alf, recognizing the sound of the man's trot instantly, the steady footsteps carrying the unmistakable weight of his pride and no doubt several large slices of recently digested chocolate torte.

He vanished in an instant, like a real-life ghost, just as President Pickle appeared through the green door by the stalls and stared up at the three children beside the safe.

'Oh, you managed to get it up the stairs, I see,' he said, stopping in his tracks, clearly rather baffled. He sucked on his lower lip like he'd just popped in a particularly sour cherry drop. 'You children are full of surprises, aren't you?' he said, almost impressed, before realizing and reverting to his usual haughty self. 'But you can't be in here unsupervised any longer, I'm afraid, and council members will be starting to arrive soon. Follow me!'

'But, sir, we need to rehearse,' pleaded Sophie.

'*I know!*' said President Pickle, pretending to understand and pouting sympathetically while batting his eyelids. He beckoned them off the stage and away from the safe before frogmarching them up through the stalls and out of the theatre. He led them back towards the Junior Room, grumbling about the traps, annoyed at having to watch his step all the damn t– OUCH!

Sophie looked at Zack and Alex apprehensively. OK, so they hadn't quite rehearsed the escape as a group, but at least Alex had managed a dry run with the door closed. He could do it again, right?

Alex smiled reassuringly as they hopscotched down the corridor. On his *life*, he would get them out of that safe.

Careful with your choice of words, Alex!

Zack glanced at his watch. 'Jonny should be here by now,' he whispered to the others as they reached the Junior Room, the heady warm air already spilling through the gap under the door.

'What was that?' asked President Pickle, turning on the spot, annoyed at having missed something potentially incriminating. He opened the door wide to reveal Jonny toying with a set of multiplying billiard balls, chatting animatedly to an enraptured Max.

'Oh!' said Zack, beaming at his best friend before turning to President Pickle. 'Nothing to worry about!'

28

Jonny had worked with increasing speed as he approached the Magic Circle, placing his wire through Mayfair, Soho and Fitzrovia, desperate to know whether this was going to end in success or outright, accident-causing disaster! Finally he clambered up the fire escape of the Magic Circle headquarters, dangling his coil of wire over the edge so that it didn't get tangled in the criss-crossing iron banisters.

Eventually he reached the roof, looping the wire around a solid metal pipe, temporarily tying it off, before putting on a pair of thick flowery oven gloves that his mother had given his father for their second wedding anniversary. He looked out over the roofs of London, surveying the various landmarks like a superhero catching his breath. (*Planet Earth, may I present ... OVEN-GLOVE MAN!*) Now came the tricky part ... Jonny knew that lifting the mile-and-a-half length of wire lying between here and the tree next to the wall of Buckingham Palace meant one almighty tug. He

braced himself, then, slowly, carefully, untied the wire, making sure it was still looped round the metal pipe, and began to wrap the end around one of his gloved hands.

Cautiously he began to pull as, bit by bit, the wire started to give, curling around the metal pipe like a thin snake.

Jonny leaned over the edge, wrapping the wire around his hand frantically, and watched the slack being taken up. Finally he stepped on to the ledge, heart racing. If there was ever a time to trust in science, then it was right now!

He leaped off the tall building with all his might, but thankfully, rather than freefalling, he found himself gliding smoothly as the wire – through Fitzrovia, Soho, Mayfair and Green Park – lifted up and into the air with a faint *swish*, gliding seamlessly high above the buildings of London, pulling taut just as Jonny's feet gracefully touched the ground outside the Magic Circle. I mean, if this wasn't a superhero moment, he didn't know what was!

At the other end of the wire, one and a half miles away, the tree next to the wall of Buckingham Palace shook slightly, as if to say, *Yes, all fine this end too!*

Jonny tied off the wire at the bottom of the fire escape, hiding the slack as best he could with a quick Farrimond friction hitch, which he'd discovered in a fascinating book about knots. And from there, Oven-Glove Man jogged round the corner of the building and entered the Magic Circle through the blue door as if nothing had happened.

29

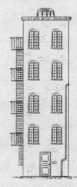

Zack, Sophie and Alex had practically thrown themselves into the room towards Jonny, immediately hijacking his conversation with Max (who had dutifully wandered off to practise his appearing egg routine, happy as a hippo), desperate to hear about the zip-line and to fill him in on everything – from Alf to Alex's miraculous escape.

Jonny couldn't believe his long ears at everything that had gone on since they'd parted company. 'Oh, wow! So Alf's *real*?' he whispered excitedly. 'I knew Granddad would have a trick up his sleeve!'

The others nodded, glad to be a four again.

'Well, he's not the actual Alf who died all those years back, but he's a sort of Alf!' answered Sophie, sitting next to him.

Jonny lowered his voice. 'And we can definitely trust him?'

'Yes, he's one of the good guys, like your granddad,' said Zack. 'I can feel it.'

For the rest of the afternoon the four talked through their plan, drilling the sequence of events again and again so that they wouldn't even have to think when the time came.

Sophie looked around at her friends. Had it really only been three days since they'd first met? That was when you knew you had friends for life, she thought; when a new friendship felt like it had already lasted a lifetime. Like there wasn't even a time before the Young Magicians and *The Thieves' Almanac*!

'Of course, once we're inside Buckingham Palace, then it's a case of . . . improvising!' said Zack, trying to sound confident but hardly daring to think that far ahead. Were they really planning on going to the *Queen* with all this? He looked around at the other young magicians getting ready, some equally nervous but for different reasons Deanna was already beginning her warm-up routine, which was less of a warm-up routine and more of a full cardiovascular workout. *No Henry*, Zack noted, feeling a touch of guilt. Had his run-in with the thieves actually driven him away for good?

'And . . . the zip-line can definitely hold all our weight?' asked Alex nervously.

Jonny nodded, and was about to launch into a detailed run-down of the superlative strength of the Farrimond friction hitch – but was thankfully interrupted by Cynthia calling for their attention.*

'Right,' she said, taking to the small raised area once again. She levered herself up with a bit of effort, smiling down at them all. 'Now, if I can give any final word of advice, it would be to just do your best. Council aren't expecting miracles, they just want to see that you have a firm grasp of the basics. After all, this is all about making a *good first impression*.' Her eyes lingered on the four at the back. 'Now, I know we've got a group performing tonight, along with everyone's solo efforts . . .'

The four looked across the room as the posh lads, all dressed in their finest top hat and tails, clad in pristine white tie, clapped each other on the back.

'All I'll say to those particular people –' Cynthia's eyes flashed at the four – 'is do please try and keep to the schedule, and *be careful*. After all, you are the future of magic.' She smiled a tired smile. A smile that summed up a lifetime of effort at the Magic Circle.

'OK,' she chirped, clicking her fingers, a bout of her usual energy back, 'on the subject of the schedule, I've got some rules that apply to your solo performances so that we don't overrun.' She lifted a grotty page of yellowed paper, the kind you might find in the loft, buried under a

---

* I promise to write another book *specifically* about this hitch and nothing else, so please don't worry!

pile of old records that should have been binned in the late sixties. The kind of paper that hadn't seen much daylight. She held it tightly between her left thumb and finger as her other hand flailed around for the glasses bouncing around her belly, having a whale of a time. 'These rules come straight from the top, so please pay attention . . .

'No *apprentice must perform his set for longer than eight minutes. Should he run over, he will be immediately disqualified.*'

Sophie tried not to shout out at the language – like female magicians didn't even exist! Like this set of rules had been written before the very *idea* of a woman!

Cynthia continued reading. '*To assist with timings, the Right Honourable Treasurer, Bill Dungworth, will ring a bell at six minutes, ring three bells at seven minutes, and then sound a continuous foghorn from eight minutes onwards. Should any apprentice attempt to continue his performance past eight minutes and one second, President Pickle has permission to launch a . . .*' She trailed off. 'Well, I don't think any of us plan on performing for longer than eight minutes, do we?' She hastily crumpled up the piece of paper.

'Right, well . . .' Cynthia looked at her watch nervously. 'Perhaps we should all go through to the theatre – it's almost time.'

The four Young Magicians exchanged glances. Yes, it was almost time!

Cynthia led the parade of juniors down the corridor and through the poster of the entranceway, the four forgetting for a moment that the peculiar experience of walking through a picture into the Grand Theatre of the Magic Circle was unfamiliar to most of their peers, who ooh'd and aah'd at the optical illusion and the size of the auditorium, just like Sophie, Alex and Jonny had done before.

'Oh wowwwwwww!' exclaimed Jonny, pretending this was the first time he'd seen it too, but overacting dreadfully.

Zack gave his sleeve a tug. Now wasn't the time to attract attention!

It was strange seeing other people in the theatre, thought Sophie as Deanna, Max and the group of boys, who looked like a royal quidditch team, traipsed down the aisle. This had been *their* place – whether they were meant to be in here or not!

Alex craned his head up to the gods where they had been sitting earlier that afternoon. It was hard to make out much in the dim lighting, but he could just see the faint outline of Alf, his white teeth twinkling at them like faint stars through the gloom of space.

Jonny followed Alex's gaze, giving the distant figure a surreptitious wave. 'Nice to meet you, Alf!' he mouthed.

Zack watched as a few greying council members began to take their seats, filling the stalls haphazardly, like the remains of an unfinished chess match, pieces dotted about willy-nilly, delighted to see Jonny's granddad taking a seat near the front. Ernest bowed his head at them reassuringly.

'Right, this way, please!' Cynthia gathered everyone together and led them into a glass partitioned room at the back of the stalls, away from the inquisitive eyes of council members – most of whom looked at the young magicians as if this was the first time they'd ever seen one. *Were we ever like them? Surely not!*

The four friends entered the temporary 'green room' (green with mould), which was about the size of a downstairs bathroom, the walls covered in cracked wallpaper, the odd decomposed good luck cards from times gone by still visible through the dust.

'This is where I'd like you to wait until you're announced on to the stage,' said Cynthia, flicking a light switch and causing one of the few remaining bulbs to immediately pop and shatter. 'Oops, watch out for all that, of course!'

Zack, Sophie, Alex and Jonny moved into a corner of the room, away from the others.

'Are we all set?' whispered Zack.

The others nodded.

'Just remember to breathe.' Sophie used her hypnotizing voice. 'We can do this!'

'There's a running order on the door . . .' said Cynthia, busily trying to tack a sheet of paper on to the crumbling door, the peeling paint coming away under her fingers like it was never meant to be there in the first place, like it was shedding its skin, preventing the tack from adhering.

'Oh dear, I'll just read it out, shall I?' she said eventually, catching the list as it fell to the floor for the tenth time. 'So first up, to get the ball rolling, as she was already inducted last time, we have Deanna.' Deanna's mother was now massaging her daughter's shoulders like she was about to enter the boxing ring. 'Henry is sadly not feeling well and can't be with us, so let's just take his name off the list to avoid any confusion, shall we?' She took one of her glittery pens to the sheet, obliterating Henry's name in a fantastic mess as Zack and the others shared a knowing look.

'Next,' continued Cynthia, 'it's Max!' The boy waved a fat wand in the air.

'Then it'll be Hugo, then Jackson, Charlie, Salisbury and then Mayhew,' she said, moving her finger down the list of names.

The kid with the floppy, bouffant hairdo coughed irritatingly and sneered across at his competitors.

'Then we have Jonny, Zack, Sophie, Alex, and finally – you four – we'll end with your . . . escape thing. Everyone OK with that?'

Cynthia gave them a tight smile, clearly unsure as to why her latest protégés felt the need to perform such a reckless effect. She bustled out into the theatre and down towards the stage.

The four looked around as the rest of room checked and rechecked their pockets and props, preparing for their performances and practising their patter.

It was strange, thought Zack as he surveyed the other magicians: usually he would be pretty nervous by this point. In fact, it had been at this point last time that he'd been escorted off the premises for 'stealing' President Pickle's gavel, so he'd never even got the chance to perform in front of Council. But all that paled into insignificance compared to the journey he and his three friends were about to embark upon.

They synchronized their watches and Alex's mind began to race at the prospect of giving his first ever solo performance. He wiped his damp hands down the front of his shirt. *No, come on – you can do this, Alex! Pinkie break, reverse cull, palm off selected card, double lift, pressure fan . . .*

'Oh, and by the way,' said Cynthia, poking her head round the door like an inquisitive emu. 'Tomorrow we'll be having a little party to celebrate, so do feel free to bring along any family and friends . . . regardless of what happens tonight,' she added a touch too pointedly.

All of a sudden a dusty brown speaker hanging from the ceiling began to pop and squeal – decades-old dirt shooting out of the object like it was clearing out its lungs. Steve's friendly but distorted voice echoed into the room, barging its way about as if the overzealous man was at the back of the stalls himself. 'Is this on?' *Tap, tap, tap, pop, squeak!* 'Ah yes, there we are.' He cleared his throat loudly, causing the audience to wince in pain. 'That's better. Great. Right, please pray silence for Mr President Pickle!'

They heard a smattering of applause as President Pickle took to the stage, grabbing the mic off Steve (*pop, squeak, rustle, tap tap tap!*) before letting out a loud sigh.

Everyone fell quiet. The Young Magicians huddled in the doorway, looking out at the stage as the society's foolish figurehead – the society they so desperately wanted to reform – began to speak.

30

'Well, I must say, I didn't expect to see so many of you!' he began.

Zack, Jonny, Sophie and Alex looked at one another as they surveyed the packed auditorium.

'Oh wow!' said Sophie in a low voice. 'Perhaps Steve was right. Perhaps there *are* members who'd like to see young magicians let in.'

'I don't know why my wife insists on getting this young lot in,' President Pickle continued. 'Most of them can't even tie their booties!' The audience chuckled on cue, as if this was a routine they'd seen before.

Zack shook his head at the clear disgust in the man's voice.

'They'll probably have gone off magic by the time they come of age.' More laughter (and a couple of wheezy coughs from the older members). 'You know what kids are like nowadays – always going through phases. Not like in our day.' Groans of approval from the wheezers. 'No, in our day we took magic seriously: we read, we studied, we understood, we were *patient*. We didn't have it nearly so easy. But see what we became!' Cheers from the aged crowd.

Sophie studied Cynthia, who was standing beside her husband. How she managed to stop herself from clopping her husband around the head every time he spoke, Sophie didn't know.

Jonny was frowning. 'He knows we can all hear him from back here, right?'

Sophie shrugged. This was hardly the encouraging pre-performance pep talk they had expected.

'Still,' said President Pickle, sounding more solemn now, 'it would be wrong to deny these youngsters the opportunity of performing in front of Council, even if only to separate the wheat from the chaff.' More groaning nods and nodding groans. 'And my wife will have my guts for giblets if she doesn't get her own way on this!' The audience roared with laughter, always pleased to hear any rousing speech end with a slightly inappropriate remark.

Zack looked at his watch, anxious for the president to get on. Didn't he know they were on a tight schedule? Or was that the whole point of this tiresome, protracted address.

'Anyway,' bonged President Pickle eventually. 'Before any of that, on to far more important matters: let us all please be upstanding and remember the many members who have passed away, which, this year –' the four listened as President Pickle pulled out a piece of paper to double-check the figure – 'is more than the number of people who've died in train crashes. Ever.'

Cynthia looked towards her youngsters at the back of the stalls, gesturing for them all to lower their heads as the members in the auditorium got to their feet, their chairs squeaking and crackling, some seats retracting back if their aged hinges were still strong enough.

Zack, Jonny, Alex and Sophie listened as crackly music filled the auditorium: luxurious, elegant and moving, while a slideshow of black-and-white photos projected on to the back wall of the theatre. Melvyn Shalks, Arthur Russell, Cliff Lount, Ron Spencer, Ray Shirley, Ali Bongo, Paul Daniels, Tony Clarkson . . .

The list of names seemed endless as the music ebbed and flowed, many members moved to tears judging by the soft sound of sobbing Alex could just about make out, punctured occasionally by the odd little cheer or cackle as a particular photo reminded them of a forgotten good time. A time when the people projected on to the back wall of the theatre – their friends – were still alive and playing the fool, making goldfish appear inside duck eggs, acting up – seemingly invincible, until age finally caught up, their bodies slowly decaying like old apparatus that once functioned so perfectly but now couldn't quite do what it was intended to do, the moving parts beginning to rust, the varnish starting to chip and fade.

Zack noticed a tear swelling in Cynthia's eye. And in that moment he was adamant. Adamant that they would do everything they could do to keep this magical society alive. Whatever it took. And despite what those who thought they knew better said. There was just so much life ingrained in these walls, so much to celebrate and continue, it was simply too cowardly to give in. Surely it couldn't be what all those 'Broken Wands' projected on to the wall would have wanted. No, they needed to be remembered, in the way that one day hopefully Zack, Sophie, Jonny and Alex would be remembered by progressively younger generations who would stand where they now stood looking on (albeit in hopefully more accepting and accommodating circumstances!). Yes, that's what it was all about. And if it meant overthrowing the presiding president – then so be it!

Eventually the music began to fade, slowly replaced with respectful, mournful silence as President Pickle and Cynthia took their seats at the front.

Tap, rumble, thump, squeak ... The sound of Steve being reunited with the microphone at the side of the stage. 'Ladies and ... sorry ... *gentlemen*, please welcome your warm-up for this evening ... *Deanna*!'

31

Talk about a change in mood!

I mean, in many respects, you couldn't fault Deanna who – given the somewhat questionable build-up – had pinged on to the stage twirling her sticks and ribbons like she was headlining her own show in Vegas and this was a Saturday night! It wasn't clear exactly what kind of magical skill was on display here, but the stunned audience lapped it up all the same. As a finale (not that she'd done anything yet but *move*), Deanna grabbed a pile of coloured handkerchiefs, blatantly hiding something beneath them, and took position centre stage. With a flourish, she whipped away the glittery fabric to reveal a small bottle of champagne, holding it aloft like it was the Olympic torch. She faced her audience, angry that no one had applauded yet, waiting for the music to finish. Which it did after a while, triggering a massive pyrotechnic so forceful it blasted her chin, causing her to drop the champagne, which smashed splendidly on the floor. Deanna's mother ran on to the stage to rescue her daughter, who was already up on her feet looking for the individual who had mistimed the pyrotechnic, pacing back and forth like she herself was about to explode.

'Why doesn't she just go into cheerleading or something?' asked Jonny, baffled as to why she'd chosen magic.

'Maybe she wanted to be in an environment where she was the only girl,' said Sophie, wincing.

'Wow!' chimed Steve over the microphone as the shocked applause slowly dribbled away. 'What wonderful stuff!'

Max was up next, waddling on to the stage like he was a prize turkey, making eggs appear, one at a time, inside an otherwise empty bag. Not much by way of technical skill, noted Zack, who could see where the eggs were coming from, but he sure did admire the boy's appetite as Max devoured each appearing egg with increasing speed, finishing with a massive Scotch egg. Finally he produced a series of different-coloured soft drinks out of a kettle, which he also – unnecessarily – chose to consume. Jonny applauded enthusiastically, the others joining in for good measure as Max was escorted off in a daze.

Hugo, Jackson, Charlie, Salisbury and Mayhew were up next, one after the other, Steve rattling off their names like a racing commentator. Each performed a veritable smorgasbord of overly expensive, over-hyped tricks, Mayhew's huge forehead reflecting the footlights like a polished trophy as he burned and restored a £5 note, then a £10 note, then a £50 note and finally his parents' stocks and shares portfolio. Last came Hugo, his teeth shining out over the audience like the keyboard on a tiny but expensive grand piano, who said that he, 'speaking on behalf of *all* the juniors', was grateful for the chance to perform in front of Council and delighted to see so many members present.

Ugh, thought Jonny, trying not to make the sound out loud.

President Pickle gave a polite nod of approval (more an acknowledgement of the posh boys' impeccable manners than some hint that they would secure future membership – no way, not on his watch!) as they tottered down the stairs to take their places in the front row of the stalls to suss out the competition.

Jonny was up next, Steve introducing him as 'Ernest's grand*dad*' by mistake, causing several gloomy council members to suddenly perk up in a fit of hysterics before growing tired and slumping back in their seats again.

'Good luck, mate!' said Zack, shaking his friend by the hand.

'Give them hell!' Sophie punched him in the arm, while Alex gave a tiny thumbs up.

Jonny walked confidently on to the stage before launching into his patter, his effortless charm making his grandfather grin from ear to ear with pride.

'He is *such* a natural,' whispered Zack to Sophie as Jonny breezed easily through his first two routines, including hydrostatic glass and a needle through a balloon.*

'Yeah, it's making me feel a bit sick actually!' joked Sophie in her thick northern accent.

Jonny ended with a delightful effect whereby he got Steve's old broken watch working again.

'Well I never!' boomed Steve, tapping the glass front with his stubby forefinger as the second hand ticked back to life.

'Magnets!' heckled President Pickle loudly from his seat in the stalls. 'But nice try!'

Jonny looked down at him. If this guy really *was* working with the thieves, now hours away from their second daring raid of the week, then he certainly wasn't giving anything away. Jonny leaped off the stage and sat down next to a freshly recovered though positively egg-filled Max, giving him a quick and somewhat painful high five as he sat down next to him. He turned towards the back of the auditorium to give his three friends an encouraging wave.

'Well, you're never going to believe this,' said Steve, clearly enjoying himself as resident MC, 'but we've only gone and got *another lady*!' People gasped as Sophie walked

---

* This works by sticking a couple of pieces of Sellotape to the parts of the balloon that are to be pierced. Except that every time I try it I always end up . . . *BANG!* Just like that!

276

on to the stage, beckoning several audience members – including Jane – to join her.

Within seconds she had read their minds, made them forget playing cards they'd just remembered and feel taps on their shoulders that weren't there; Jane had a strange hallucination in which she believed Steve had turned into a unicorn.

The Council watched on in near silence, frowning, many clearly deeply unimpressed by the female of the species in general – especially the one on display here, who was toying with 'dark arts' that 'verged on Satanism'.

President Pickle cleared his throat loudly, prompting Bill to sound his foghorn, warning Sophie that she was nearly at the end of her allotted time, even though she wasn't. (Although it's fair to say that dear endangered Bill had actually consistently forgotten to start the clock on every single occasion so far.)

Sophie finished with a dramatic snowstorm of white confetti, which, presumably because it looked quite pretty, earned her a smattering of applause. She sighed as she took a seat next to Jonny. *Jeez, what is it with these people?*

'You were great!' mouthed Jonny.

'Like my mother-in-law says about the Brussels sprouts every Christmas dinner – we're getting through 'em!' said Steve. Silence. 'Please welcome to the stage . . . some of you may remember him from the last one of these, except he, erm – Well, anyway, please welcome *Zack Harrison*!'

Zack gave Alex a final look of encouragement, sad to leave the boy alone at the back as he made his way down the slope towards the stage.

A dark figure stuck out his leg, catching Zack in the shins as he passed and causing the boy to stumble forward awkwardly, which made some of the audience titter. He looked back, frowning, but whoever it was had disappeared into the darkness . . .

Zack kept walking forward and up on to the stage, the only sound that of Sophie and Jonny applauding amid a sea of stony faces and crossed arms.

The young magician turned to face the crowd, surveying the array of aged, glum faces.

He took a deep breath as he readied himself. *Well, here goes. Here's my chance to show Council and the members of the Magic Circle what I can do. To prove that I'm not just some pickpocket but a proper magician like the rest of them!* He noticed Bill, snoozing merrily in the front row. *Yes, well, here goes!*

He brought out a length of thick rope, locating the middle and cutting it in half with a large pair of scissors. With a flick of his wrist the rope was suddenly whole again and the scissors had vanished.

Jonny, Sophie and an elated Max applauded encouragingly as the council members looked away, feigning boredom, some trying to see President Pickle's reaction, keen to take his lead.

Zack tried to make eye contact with the president, but the man only stared back, seemingly genuinely bewildered. This was unquestionably accomplished magic, but how could that be when the practitioner was ... a *child*?

Meanwhile, at the back, Alex was trying to applaud without causing too much of a distraction. He checked his pockets once more, his hands starting to twitch as he prepared for his own performance. *No, Alex, you can do this*, he told himself. *Think how far you've come. Just imagine the others are here beside you. It's all going to be just fine!*

The dark figure approached from behind, leering and looming over the boy with his arms outstretched, as Alex, completely oblivious, continued to watch his friend on stage ...

Zack ended by performing his own miraculous version of Any Card at Any Number,* bamboozling his entire audience – including Jonny and Sophie, who couldn't fathom how their friend had managed to get a randomly named card to appear at a randomly named location in a shuffled, borrowed deck.

Zack stood on stage, almost breathless, not quite knowing how to interpret the staggered silence.

---

* Please feel free to check out Appendix 5 for a more thorough analysis of this baffling effect.

It was Cynthia who began the applause, much to her husband's annoyance and Zack's delight, as several others – and not just those younger than ninety – began to join in, undoubtedly impressed by what they'd just witnessed despite the protestations of their presiding president. They hadn't seen stuff like this in *years*! This was the stuff of legend, surely. No one did that kind of stuff any more – did they? What was this lad's name again . . . ?

Zack stood soaking up the applause, hands hanging awkwardly by his sides. For a moment it was like nothing really mattered any more. *To hell with trying to catch some thieves – this feels great!* He eventually skittered off the stage, grinning and proud – proud to have finally given this performance, even if it was six months later than planned. This was where he belonged, and finally, this might now mean his slate could be wiped clean.

President Pickle raised an obnoxious arm, calling for silence as Steve took the microphone again.

'You absolutely nailed it, mate!' said Jonny, reaching over and giving his friend a firm thump on the thigh.

Zack plonked himself down next to Sophie, turning round to give Alex a final nod of encouragement.

It wasn't just the shock and speed of the dark figure's appearance that had frightened Alex, but the roughness with which he'd been dragged behind the glass partition and over to some desolate, hidden stairwell, the man's slimy hand smothering Alex's mouth firmly, preventing the boy from screaming his guts out, the sound of Zack's finale fading into oblivion. With all the aggression of a striking snake the man turned Alex round to face him, switching on with a swipe of his hand a single light bulb that flickered and swung on its fraying wire above, causing the space to vibrate terrifyingly. Alex kept his face to the ground, heart pounding, not daring to look up and into the glowering eyes of ... No, it couldn't be ... But he looked so ... *different*?

Henry?!

The swinging light bulb illuminated his attacker's face again, casting strange shadows over the sneering features.

'H-Henry?' managed Alex eventually, hoping this might just be some joke.

The nightmarish figure grabbed his hand, crushing it and causing him to buckle at the knees in pain.

'Who's H-H-Henry?' said the man mockingly.

Alex stared into the boy's – no, the *man's* – crazed eyes. What on earth was happening?

'Oh, sorry – do you mean *this* guy?' The man smoothed back his hair, pulling his skin taut, making himself instantly more youthful. 'Henry can't be with us right now,' he said, affecting Henry's high-pitched voice and pacing back and forth.

And at that moment – amid all the pain and the panic – it dawned on Alex. The strange behaviour, the severe look, the snooping and the sucking up:

Henry was not a child.

Henry was not one of them.

Henry was not a young magician.

Henry was . . . an *adult*!

Suddenly another sensation, as something sharp pierced Alex's palm. Excruciating, nerve-wrenching pain shot up his arm as blood oozed out from between his fingers.

'Oh, I'm sorry, does that hurt?' sneered Henry, squeezing his hand hard. 'Did you really think I was going to let you and your little gang escape from here, tonight of all nights? Did you really think you could outwit *me*? Oh, you think you know so much, but you don't know a *thing*! You fiendish four!'

This was even worse than Alex had feared . . . Henry was one of the *thieves*!

And then, with a squelching pop, the man let go, sending the boy tumbling to the floor like a broken puppet. Alex rotated his wrist, struggling to unfurl his fingers as the remains of a red rose, its thick gothic thorns deeply embedded in his flesh, twanged at his nerves like guitar strings. Damp petals fell around him gracelessly like some sour afterthought. Alex looked up, speechless and terrified, as the man slunk away, like a spider resuming position in his web, his work done – for now.

'I'm sure the others will manage *just fine* in that safe without you,' he whispered, pulling the door shut and plunging Alex into deep, desolate, devastating darkness.

32

'And *now*!' roared Steve dramatically. 'Please, please welcome your penultimate act of the evening ... Alex Finley!' He started tapping on the top of the microphone to simulate applause, filling the auditorium with a deep rhythmic thudding, like the monitoring of a foetal heartbeat.

Jonny, Zack and Sophie clapped enthusiastically, craning their necks towards the back of the theatre. They all knew how much this performance meant to Alex; how much it would help his confidence if he could just get through these next few minutes. He was ready.

But Alex didn't appear.

Steve tapped the microphone again as the applause dwindled to nothing, several council members beginning to fidget in their seats, already yearning for their beds. 'This is still *on*, isn't it?' Steve said, fiddling with the microphone cable, making it squeal some more, his voice echoing around the auditorium and answering his own question. He tried again: 'Alex Finley, everybody!'

Steve, Cynthia, Zack, Jonny and Sophie began a second round of applause, but still he didn't appear.

Alex's three friends stared at each other, confused and worried.

Meanwhile Cynthia was already out of her seat, heading up towards the back room, hoping that the boy's nerves hadn't got the better of him.

President Pickle suddenly stood and turned to face his councillors. 'Well, I'm afraid it's automatic exclusion if you fail to appear in front of Council when summoned. That's what the constitution says.' Several of the sleepy members began to snore their assent as Bill accidentally let off the foghorn again, oblivious to what was going on and what was required of him. 'Bill!' joked President Pickle, ribbing him like a child. 'Stop rubbing it in! Poor lad must have got a bout of stage fright!' As he spoke, a bit of spittle flew out of his rubbery lips, landing flat on Max's head. The unfortunate boy ruffled through his hair like he'd just been pooped on by a sparrow in the upper circle.

Zack, Jonny and Sophie watched in dismay as Cynthia returned to the stalls, shaking her head. *No, not after everything they'd taught him – surely not!*

'Oh well, never mind!' boomed President Pickle. 'Let's move on to the final group piece ... I've been looking forward to this!'

'Excellent idea, Mr President!' sang Steve, taking the reins again. 'OK, so if we could welcome Zack, Jonny and Sophie back onstage, please?'

The three of them looked at each other as the realization hit them like a cold shower – they couldn't break out of the safe without Alex!

'Come on!' shouted President Pickle at the top of his voice. 'We haven't got all day!' He looked over his shoulder, grinning around at everyone, searching for laughs.

Zack turned round to face the greying audience, desperately trying to think on his feet, glancing at the others for some sense of guidance. He cleared his throat. 'Erm ... We've decided *not* to go ahead with the group piece after all,' he said, his thoughts tumbling out of control ... *This ruined everything!* If they couldn't get out of the safe, then they couldn't achieve anything tonight! He sat down and motioned for Sophie and Jonny to do the same.

'Nonsense!' President Pickle was already making his way to the end of his row. 'Come along, you three, back on your feet. You're scheduled to perform now.'

'We absolutely can't get inside that safe without Alex,' whispered Sophie urgently as they stood up again. 'We'll suffocate!'

'I know,' said Zack quietly, his mind racing, searching for a solution. 'But what about the plan? Where *is* he?'

Sophie looked up to the gods for an answer, but what could Alf do at this distance without giving himself away? No – they were on their own again. *Where was Alex?* Perhaps one of them could go and find him . . .

'Hurry up, will you?' called President Pickle, a note of irritation beginning to show in his voice.

Jonny looked at his granddad. Could it be that he was nodding at him, encouraging them to press on? Glancing back at Zack and Sophie, Jonny cocked his head towards Ernest, who gave them all another reassuring nod and a smile.

Well, if Ernest has our backs, thought Sophie, *then surely everything will be OK. Maybe!*

'Let's give them some encouragement, shall we?' said President Pickle, grabbing the microphone from Steve – *thunk, pop, thud*.

He started a slow hand clap, the kind reserved for ironic entrances or for marking the tempo change in the slow movements of long symphonies. Its effect was hypnotic though as all the council members began to join in; even Bill rang his bell and sounded his foghorn in time (well, not quite!), creating a strange, hypnotic sound that filled the confines of the drab theatre.

Zack, Sophie and Jonny slowly climbed up on to the stage – almost as if they were out of control of their own bodies – as President Pickle went over to the safe.

Was it her imagination, Sophie wondered, or had the safe been moved slightly?

Jonny stared at it. It was the first time he'd laid eyes on it properly . . .

It certainly looked a lot less enticing than during their rehearsals this afternoon, thought Zack as they gradually approached, already fearful of what might be coming up.

The repetitive thudding stopped as President Pickle spoke. 'Lights!'

A magnificent spotlight suddenly shot down from above, coating the safe in an intense white light, like it was about to be beamed up on to some imaginary spaceship.

'So, as you can see,' began President Pickle, like he was a kid again performing in a parochial hall, 'here we have a solid safe.' He bashed the sides and there was a low *bongggg!* 'It's completely airtight and – as most of you will be aware – has resided in the council chamber ever since Houdini was here almost ninety years ago; I myself can vouch for its authenticity.'

Bill sounded his foghorn loudly, making the three friends jump.

'As can our longstanding treasurer, who was in fact alive at the time. Thank you, Bill!' The president twizzled on the spot to face the Young Magicians. 'And so if you want to get inside and we'll start the clock – nothing like a hearty bit of escapology before dinnertime!' Several council members tittered in agreement, goading them on.

Jonny frowned at his friends. Where, oh where was Alex? There's no way he'd leave them in the lurch like this. Something must have happened. But what? And how? Or was it just stage fright, as President Pickle had suggested?

They looked up to the gods again, hoping for reassurance from Alf, but were blinded by the spotlight.

'The thing is,' Zack began in a quieter voice, looking up at President Pickle, 'we *physically* can't do this without Alex.'

President Pickle stared down, at him, grinning. 'After you!' he said, holding open the safe door like a refined gentleman might at a particularly swanky hotel and causing one particular audience member to laugh so hard their hernia exploded.

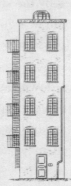

33

Zack, Jonny and Sophie silently weighed up their options. On the one hand they could attempt the escape without Alex, putting their lives at risk . . .

Or . . . they could refuse and not go ahead. President Pickle couldn't force them into the safe in front of all these people. But then how would they warn the Queen about the thieves? There were much bigger things at stake here.

All of a sudden, like a fairy godmother, Ernest appeared onstage too. 'I must say,' he said coolly, 'I do find myself in agreement with President Pickle for once.'

Sophie, Jonny and Zack looked at each other, confused, while President Pickle and Ernest eyeballed each other over the safe.

Really, Granddad? thought Jonny, hoping Ernest hadn't finally lost it. *You* really *think this is a good idea?*

'Well, you certainly took your time,' said President Pickle respectfully, 'but I'm glad to see you've come round to my way of thinking.'

Zack and Sophie looked up at Jonny's granddad, not quite knowing what to do. It was clear that Ernest was on their side, but what he was suggesting this time was – frankly – too dangerous! But then, wasn't this Ernest all over, always keen to inject a bit of theatre into proceedings, never giving away the full story all at once – a master of deception.

'OK, let's do it,' said Zack, half to his two friends (*where, where, where was Alex?!*) and half to the audience, prompting Ernest to give him an infinitesimally brief nod.

'Excellent news!' shouted President Pickle, bringing his hands together and grinning out at the crowd. 'In you pop, then!'

Ernest turned and shook his grandson's hand firmly. 'Good luck! Stay safe!'

Jonny felt something hard being pressed into his palm as his granddad gave him a long, meaningful look before ushering them all into the safe with the words: 'Jonny, perhaps you should squeeze in first so you're *at the back*.'

Obediently Jonny hunched over so that he could squeeze inside, scrunching up against the smooth metal walls.

'The screen . . .' said Sophie suddenly, turning to Zack with one foot on the lip of the safe.

'The *what*? What was that?' hollered President Pickle over the mic, determined not to miss anything important this time.

'Erm . . . We need a screen to shield us from view, so the audience can't see how we do it,' said Zack innocently.

'Poppycock!' baulked President Pickle. 'Where's the fun in that? We're all magicians here, young lad!'

'It's what *Houdini* used to do,' offered Sophie tentatively.

But the president was getting impatient. 'No. Sorry – all of you *in* please. And I think you'll find these weren't around in Houdini's day either,' he added, plucking the torch from Zack's back pocket and dangling it from his fingers as if he'd just caught a rat by the tail.

Ernest gave them a final confidence-boosting smile before clambering back down into the stalls.

Leaning out of the safe to watch him go, Jonny suddenly realized that the old man had managed this brief spell on stage without the help of his walking stick. There was life in him yet!

Zack and Sophie squeezed into the safe. Even if they did manage to escape, what was the point if they were in plain sight? thought Zack with renewed frustration. This was almost the exact opposite of what they had planned! And where on *earth* was Alex?

'Right then!' announced President Pickle. 'We'll see you in a few hours, I expect!'

And with that he shut the door with a loud, deafening *thunk* that rang in their ears like they were inside a massive bell. The last thing they saw was President Pickle grinning like the Cheshire Cat as they were plunged into deep, stifling darkness.

34

If any of them thought they knew what it would feel like being trapped inside an airtight safe, they were wrong. The pitch dark was so intense that it reminded Jonny of a picture he'd once seen of the universe before the Big Bang in the Science Museum, before even the concept of light. Stark, thick, suffocating, noise-cancelling darkness that seemed to press in on them, as if the iron walls were slowly oozing together.

'Ow!'

'Is that your foot?'

'No, that's *your* foot!'

'What?'

They crawled over each other as Jonny tried to squeeze his way towards the front, like a giraffe trying to fathom his way out of a box of cereal. 'Granddad gave me a pick!' he told the others enthusiastically.

'Oh, I *knew* he was up to something!' said Sophie, invisibly punching the air. 'You brilliant man, Ernest!'

'But what happened to Alex?' wondered Zack anxiously, his breathing becoming increasingly rapid.

'Just remember to breathe,' said Sophie, trying to stay calm. 'As cruel as it sounds, at least we've got a bit more oxygen without Alex – we can worry about him later.'

'OK, I'm in place ... I think!' said Jonny, who had successfully wriggled forward and was now searching about blindly for the central dial mechanism. 'Does anyone know what I'm feeling for?' He inserted the pick into what he hoped was a keyhole.

'I think you just jiggle it about,' said Zack, trying not to laugh despite their desperate situation. 'That's what Alex seems to do, anyway!'

'Why was your granddad so insistent that you go in first, Jonny?' asked Sophie, having a sudden thought.

'I guess because he knows I'm not that great at palming,' said Jonny, twisting the instrument this way and that.

'Yes,' said Sophie. 'Or maybe ...' She moved herself to the back of the safe.

'Ow – again!'

'Mind!'

'Careful!'

'Or maybe,' Sophie continued, ignoring the boys' dramatics, 'there's a back way out!' She started to search for a lever, a catch, an orifice – anything to yank and twist. If there was ever going to be a safe with a secret opening, then it had to be the one Houdini had once used!

She ran her fingers along the wall, her fingers exploring the corners, searching, hoping . . .

Nothing.

'How long have we been in here?' said Zack quietly, trying not to panic. It was a good question. Surely it couldn't have been that long, but then again – they felt so cut off from the rest of the world right now – they could have been floundering in here anything between ten seconds and ten minutes.

Keep going, keep going.

'Any luck, Jonny?' said Sophie, still trying to find a hint of a secret opening.

He shook his head, forgetting that not even an owl could see him in this light.

'Jonny?' prompted Sophie again, her voice sounding oddly flat, muffled by the thick shock-absorbent walls and lack of air.

'Oh! Sorry!' answered Jonny. 'No. Nothing. Not yet – you?'

Sophie continued to scour the back wall. Surely this was what Ernest had been getting at, she hoped. Another way out, something that would put them back on track, free once again, free to scupper the thieves without giving themselves away in front of President Pickle and the entire Magic Circle Council. But – what was that? She couldn't tell whether it was just a patch of rust, but it was worth a try.

'Hang on, hang on!' she said suddenly. 'Jonny, pass me the pick.'

'Say please!'

'Come off it!'

'Here.'

'Where?'

'*Here!*'

'Ow!'

'Is that the pick?'

'Yes.'

'It's *warm*!'

'I've got warm hands!'

Sophie felt for the slight indentation again – yes, no ... there was definitely *something* there! She toyed with the pick between her fingers, feeling for the sharp end.

She took a deep breath, unknowingly reducing their oxygen supply by about a quarter in one fell swoop.

'What is it? What have you found?' asked Zack frantically.

But Sophie was concentrating, pushing the pick carefully into the small recess, not wanting to force it.

She put her ear against the back of the safe, rotating the pick clockwise, then anti-clockwise, still not quite sure what it was she was listening for.

'Come on, Sophie – you can do this!' whispered Jonny, even though he didn't know what she was doing either.

Sophie remembered what Alex had told her about picking locks. How had he phrased it? *You just* know *when it feels right ... And then, just when you think there's too much resistance –*

Click.

With a faint rush of incoming air, the back door opened on hidden hinges, flooding the safe with its first thin shaft of light in twelve minutes. They all remained completely still.

Sophie put a finger to her lips as they tuned in to the low-level bickering between Cynthia and her husband – live onstage.

'If they're not out in another three minutes, we're opening that door!' shrilled Cynthia.

'Oh, come on, darling,' crooned President Pickle. 'We should give them a *bit* longer than that – it's meant to be entertaining! Could Deanna do another stint while we wait?'

'It's *dangerous*!'

'Well, I did warn you what would happen if we let children into the society!'

'Oh, just give it a rest, will you, Edmund?'

Sophie, Zack and Jonny tried to silently work out what to do. With Cynthia and President Pickle still onstage, their exit might be seen. But what choice did they have? It was either this or just waiting around. They were just going to have to be quick and hope that Cynthia and President Pickle's argument was sufficiently distracting.

'Slowly,' mouthed Jonny at Sophie, his lips forming wild, over-exaggerated shapes.*

* Not that Jonny had the time to explain in detail (hence its inclusion down here) but the human eye is much more adept at spotting fast movement than slow movement – presumably a hangover from when

Moving at a snail's pace, Sophie leaned on the door, easing it open smoothly. The three of them blinked as the safe filled with more light and Sophie swung her feet silently, cautiously over the lip of the opening and lowered herself out on to the stage floor. Zack and Jonny followed.

The thought entered Zack's head before he felt the sensation: *This would be a really,* really *bad time to sneeze! Oh, Zack – why did you have to think that thought now?* For – as he'd correctly anticipated – all he now wanted to do was sneeze his face off. The kind of sneeze that dads would make: the loudest sound in the universe (after a giant supernova explosion). The kind of sneeze that marked the start of hay-fever season. The kind of sneeze that needed a thousand tissues to clear up. *Oh, Zack, why did you have to think of this now!* The tickle rose up his throat, fluttering about way, way back in his nostrils, making his eyes sting. There were no two ways about it . . . it had to be done.

Zack sneezed so loudly that Jonny and Sophie felt the blast on the back of their heads, as a billion bits of mucus

---

the caveman and cavewoman had to watch out for hungry velociraptors and other such speedy beasties looking to catch them for their din-dins! In fact, this principle is something magicians exploit all the time: that a bigger, quicker movement will always be noticed much more readily by a spectator over a smaller, slower movement, which itself becomes relatively hidden, even when in plain sight, allowing the magician to do the real dirty work at his or her own pace. And so the saying 'The hand is quicker than the eye' is in fact a blatant misnomer – a piece of misdirection planted by magicians to filter into the psyche of the general public to make their jobs a notch easier!

flew through the air, landing in their hair in a messy clump. He instantly placed his hand over his mouth, his eyes pleading with the others. *I'm so, so, so, so, so sorry!*

Sophie peered round to see – alarmingly – that President Pickle was now staring right at them. She opened her mouth to explain, but was immediately interrupted. 'What the devil was that?' said the pompous gent, striding towards her.

Sophie, Jonny and Zack turned to face President Pickle, looking forlorn.

Well, that was that then; there goes making a good impression on Council or rumbling a bunch of thieves. Zack pinched himself in exasperation. How could he have been so stupid!

35

President Pickle looked at them strangely.

'What is it?' Cynthia asked anxiously, appearing at his side.

Zack was just about to answer when Jonny placed a hand on his and Sophie's shoulders, silencing them both. There was something in the way that President Pickle was staring that just didn't add up; his eyes were roaming around, out of focus.

Oh, Granddad, you haven't, have you? thought Jonny, feeling like he might be in a dream.

'Must have come from inside,' grumbled President Pickle, walking away from the safe, shaking his head.

Jonny looked at Sophie and Zack wide-eyed, a wild grin across his face. They were inside a one-way mirror tunnel!*

---

* A WHAT?!

OK, well, as you asked . . . So, a mirror tunnel is used in many theatrical illusions – the point being, you can't actually see it at all! It's a way of

'Ernest must have set this up when we were in the Junior Room,' whispered Zack.

creating space that doesn't actually exist. Well, that's not strictly true: the space *does* exist, but it's a reflection of some other space from elsewhere – the mirror just places that space somewhere it *isn't*! Using these clever mirrors, it's possible to make it look like there is an empty space when in fact there's a hidden pathway extending all the way from the safe – in this instance – to the back wall of the stage. This particular construction was a *one-way* mirror tunnel, meaning that the three could see President Pickle, Cynthia and the rest of the theatre as if they were looking through a pane of glass, while remaining completely invisible. No wonder Zack's sneeze had unsettled those on the other side!

OK, as you were . . .

'I *knew* the safe had been moved,' whispered Sophie, marvelling at the illusion. Jonny tried his luck by pulling a silly face at President Pickle, who went on arguing with Cynthia, oblivious to the Young Magicians on the stage behind him!

Zack smiled, thinking how Alex would have loved seeing an illusion like this in action.

The three reached the gauze curtain at the back of the stage, squeezing underneath, careful not to disturb it and give themselves away.

'Which way to the roof?' asked Jonny quietly.

'This way!' said Sophie, twinkling and grabbing the rungs at the bottom of the tall, sturdy ladder that stretched above them.

Up they went, high into the flies, climbing stealthily.

They reached the top, turning a sharp left without breaking stride, and paced along the lofty walkway towards the second ladder, pleased to see that it had already been unfurled – *Thank you, Alf. Not far to go now!*

Sophie pushed on the wooden boards, firmly opening a kind of trapdoor, and swung through out on to the roof.

Wow, they were high!

The three of them stood on the rooftop, surveying the dusky London skyline. Had they really come this far already? Way, way ahead in the distance, Jonny could just about make out the magnificent outline of Buckingham Palace, the tiny flag flapping in the wind. At least the Queen was in. Imagine if they'd got all this way, only to find out she'd stayed at Balmoral tonight. *Sorry, come back another day. Off with their heads!*

'What about Alex?' said Zack thickly, glad to finally speak at full volume.

Jonny and Sophie stared at him, frowning. No, they couldn't possibly go ahead without him. They'd hatched the plan as a foursome; without Alex they simply weren't the Young Magicians!

'I'll find him,' came a voice – an adult voice – behind them.

They turned with a start as Alf walked casually towards them, his eyes shining in the dwindling light.

Phew!

'Will you?' said Zack passionately, letting out a sigh of relief. 'Thank you! Something must have happened to him – he wouldn't just leave us in the lurch like this.'

'Don't worry. I promise to keep him safe. But he'd want you to keep going – you know he would.'

Zack chewed on his bottom lip; the man was right – Alex would want them to complete what they'd set out to do. More than that, he would hate to think they'd altered their plans because of him.

'Oh, erm . . . Hi, I'm Jonny by the way – nice to finally meet you!' said Jonny, extending his hand. 'I hear you've been a real help today!'

'And it looks like *you've* been busy too, young lad!' Alf said with a nod towards the zip-line. 'But if you're going, then you must go now,' he added pressingly, looking over his shoulder. 'There's no way Cynthia will let them keep that safe door shut much longer. And once President Pickle sees that you're not where you're supposed to be, who knows what he might do?'

Sophie sensed that Zack was struggling with this. But Alf was right: they had to go on! She stared at Zack.

Finally he nodded.

Jonny took a deep breath. 'OK,' he said, sounding rather officious all of a sudden. 'It's a one-and-a-half-mile trip to BP from here, and there's an overall descent of about ten metres.'

Zack and Sophie nodded dutifully, as if they were being given a safety briefing before a flight.

'It might not seem like we're going very fast at first,' continued Jonny. 'But by the end we'll have picked up quite a pace!'

He handed them each what appeared to be an over-thickened coat hanger (partly because that's exactly what they were). 'OK, so this end goes over the wire like this . . .' He hooked them over the fine wire and squeezed the tops round into a continuous loop so that they couldn't come off. 'And then the only rule is . . . hang on tight!'

'Great. Now go!' Alf encouraged. 'And look after yourselves.'

Sophie frowned as he headed back towards the attic, her heart and head suddenly a strange mix of emotions. 'Wait!' She ran over, whispering something before backing away, biting her lip. Alf gave her a quick smile before vanishing down into the attic.

'What was all that about?' asked Zack.

'Never mind.' Sophie was keen to change the subject and get going. 'Now, Jonny, are you *sure* this thing is safe?'

Jonny twanged the fine wire, glad to find that it was still super taut. He looked back at her like this proved it. 'Oh yes, it's completely safe!'

Sophie gulped.

'Ooh, almost forgot!' said Jonny, grabbing some large black umbrellas he'd stowed under an air vent. 'These should help break our fall when the time comes to leap off.'

Sophie stared up at him, eyes wide. 'We *leap off*?' she repeated. Surely this was madness!

'You'll soon see – don't worry about it!' said Jonny, taking up his position on the ledge again and alternating the coat hangers with the umbrellas, hooking them on to the wire like clothes on a washing line. 'Hmm, that's odd . . .'

'Oh no, what now?' said Zack, fearful of what Jonny might have forgotten to do, or forgotten to tie up or . . .

'No, it's just . . . I thought I'd packed *four* umbrellas, but . . . Never mind – I must have miscounted!'

Zack rolled his eyes, his heart pounding. Now wasn't the time to be questioning any of these calculations, Jonny!

'OK – please make sure that your umbrella stays in front of you at all times!' said Jonny, mimicking a flight attendant. 'And please ensure it remains closed and in an upright position until the very end!'

Zack and Sophie looked at each other disbelievingly. It wasn't that they didn't trust their friend; they were just nervous about putting Isaac Newton directly in charge. Slowly, cautiously, they stepped up on to the ledge beside Jonny high above Stephenson Way, gripping their coat hangers tightly.

Far below, the rush hour was well underway, commuters fighting past each other, scrabbling about to get the next tube or bus home. Didn't they know there were quicker, more direct modes of transport?

'Well . . . Here goes!' Jonny hopped off the edge. For a second he just remained there, hanging, the wire humming in the breeze, the darkening sky preventing him from being seen by those below. Well, the wire seemed to be holding at least . . .

One and a half miles away, the small tree next to the wall of Buckingham Palace gave another reassuring shake.

Slowly, inch by inch, Jonny started to glide away from the roof of the Magic Circle, sliding down the wire with increasing speed as physics started to do its thing.

'It works, it works!' he cried.

Zack and Sophie shook their heads disbelievingly . . . Jonny had only gone and done it! Sophie suddenly pushed herself and Zack off the ledge.

'Oh great – thanks, Sophie!' shouted Zack, petrified, as they bounced along the wire towards Jonny.

'Not a problem!' said the girl, trying not to look down and keen to get the journey over with.

'Why, welcome aboard, comrades!' said Jonny as Zack and Sophie caught up with him. 'Do hold on tight now!'

It was a beautiful, terrifying journey and without doubt the best of Jonny's science constructions to date. The zip-line was already head and shoulders above the Rydal Falls project (in that this actually *worked*, and didn't make him feel like he'd been attached to the underside of a bull for the whole day).

Zack and Sophie held on tight, trying to ignore the strain in their arms, transfixed now by the buildings below

as the lights flickered on and off through the windows, blinking and winking up at them, like they knew something was going on, but keeping shtum.

Surely this was the best way to see London, thought Zack, his confidence growing as he flew past the BT Tower, zipping along at quite a speed now, the wind rushing in his face and causing the tops of his ears to glow.

And so the Young Magicians Minus One continued . . .

Over the roof of the American church near Goodge Street where a wedding had just taken place, the remnants of some windswept confetti catching in their faces, over the glowing billboards of Piccadilly Circus where they'd first learned of DI Caulfield stealing Zack's idea, over the Ritz and its dazzling top-floor suites that cost thousands to reserve and even more to clean up afterwards by the look of the military operation currently in progress, and into Green Park – picking up speed all the time as they sank closer and closer towards the tall trees, their feet now beginning to skirt the tops of branches, flicking off leaves like they were verge trimmers.

Jonny looked down at his feet as the ground beneath continued to rush past. He didn't want to say it out loud just yet, but they were going way too fast. Way, *way* too fast! Maybe he hadn't factored in exactly how smooth their journey would be, or perhaps the wind was behind them – but whatever the reason, they were travelling too quickly. And Buckingham Palace was approaching rapidly.

There was no way round it – they'd have to use the umbrellas to slow them down on the wire. Which meant they'd have to travel the last hundred metres one-handed.

Jonny raised his voice. 'We'll have to open the umbrellas now to slow us down! But don't let go of the wire until we reach the end . . . Obviously.'

'What? What did he say?' cried out Zack, aware that Jonny was trying to tell them something but only really able to make out the vowels over the noise of the wind: '*Aaaa eee iii ooouu!*'

'He says,' shouted Sophie, trying to keep her voice steady, 'that we're to open our umbrellas now to help slow us down. But stay on the wire!'

'You mean we're supposed to hold on with *one hand*?'

Neither Sophie nor Jonny answered, which Zack took as a 'Sadly yes!' *Oh great!* He tried to ignore the pain already mounting in his arms.

Jonny freed his right hand and reached forward, carefully unhooking the umbrella trailing just in front of him, his left arm already starting to twinge as it took his full weight. With a flourish he shook open the umbrella, which caught the air in an instant, slowing him down but causing Sophie and Zack to crash into him so strongly that he jerked off to the side.

Instinctively, Jonny let go of the umbrella, needing both hands to resteady himself on the zip-line above. 'Damn it!' he said as he watched the umbrella plummet down into

Green Park, narrowly missing a jogger, who was convinced she'd just seen a UFO.

'Let me try!' said Sophie, opening her umbrella, decelerating immediately and causing Zack to come crashing up against her. But the rushing wind was too much for the brolly, causing it to invert like a cheap cocktail stick. Regretfully, Sophie let go, reaching back up towards the zip-line, spreading her weight evenly across the hanger with both hands – a welcome relief ... of sorts! The umbrella flapped to the ground gracelessly, like a blackbird with a broken wing.

'Let me try and pass you my umbrella!' screamed Zack as they picked up speed again. 'It's no good me trying to slow us down from the back!'

Jonny could see the small tree that marked their end point coming into focus as they rushed towards it at a terrifying speed.

'Here!' called Zack as he thrust the umbrella at Sophie.

She twisted round as best she could and in one swift movement took it from Zack and swung it in Jonny's direction.

He grabbed hold of it carefully. If this brolly failed as well, then there would be no doubt they'd have enough momentum to send them hurtling over the wall of Buckingham Palace – but not in the slow, graceful Mary Poppins-style way Jonny had envisaged. And then what? Crushed bones, twisted necks, sprained hips – hardly the etiquette when presenting oneself in front of Her Majesty! What had he been *thinking*?

As Green Park sped past beneath his feet, Jonny held the umbrella out in front of him, figuring that it was better to try and open the dreaded thing slowly, rather than catch the breeze in a blast like last time. Gradually it began to unfurl . . . they were closer to the ground now, like a plane speedily cruising over the start of its landing strip.

But it was impossible to keep the umbrella from catching in the turbulent air, and – like a perfect sail – it dragged Jonny's right arm behind him, causing the boy to rotate almost 180 degrees so that he was now face to face with Sophie, travelling backwards. Not ideal! But at least it was slowing them down. As before, Zack came crashing into Sophie, who was now sandwiched between the two boys, both of whom screamed a million apologies to her over the billowing wind.

Now that he was the only one who could see where they were going, Zack began the countdown. The tree was approaching at a terrifying speed. He gulped as he spotted the wall beyond it. 'Let go on *three, two . . . one*! *LET GO!*'

They careened through the air, skimming over the wall of Buckingham Palace wondering – fearfully – what might be on the other side. Concrete? Gravel? Spikes and fireworks? Hydrangeas?

A billion thoughts flashed through Zack's mind as, out of the corner of his eye, he watched their last brolly flap and crash headlong into the wall. Was this how they met their end? Impaled as a three in the grounds of Buckingham Palace, found dead the next morning by some drippy corgi out for his first poop of the day before duty called?

Jonny didn't know *what* to think. Was this all *his* fault? Should he have tested the contraption first? But they'd simply run out of time. It was amazing that they'd got this far.

Sophie actually stood the best chance of surviving the fall, being presently cushioned between the two boys, but it was hardly an ideal situation.

The three of them closed their eyes as they sensed the ground approaching, the smell of a well-kept garden fast filling their nostrils. Damp mulchy leaves, moss, pine cones and bark, freshly cut grass, twigs, compost ... *Soft, cushioning compost*.

They landed together like they'd just arrived at Sophie's hotel and were trying out the giant, feathery bed for the first time.

The three cautiously opened their eyes, not believing their luck.

Standing over them, like a tiny urchin chimney sweep, was Alex, his right hand wrapped in a filthy bandage, his left hand holding a garden hoe, panting, sweating, but *smiling*.

ALEX!

36

They didn't wait for explanations. They just pulled him roughly on to the compost heap – bandaged hand, hoe and all – squashing him into a tight hug.

All of a sudden Sophie leaped to her feet, dusting herself down with aching arms. 'Alex, what the *hell*?' she said breathlessly. She didn't care about being quiet. It didn't matter that they were trespassing in the Queen's actual back garden, she had to get some answers. They *all* had to get some answers!

Alex struggled back to his feet, using the hoe as a support, desperate to tell them why he'd left them. They needed to know that he was still a good friend. Still one of the Young Magicians.

'Henry . . . Henry is *one of the thieves.*'

'He's *what*?!?' piped the three others in unison, Zack and Jonny standing up at the same time like this was some poorly acted soap opera!

'*And* . . . he's an adult!'

Alex held up his hand, the bandage already blotched with fresh blood. 'I must . . . must have passed out for a few minutes, but by the time I came round you three were already locked inside the safe!' He was clearly trying to fight back tears. 'And I just thought . . . if you three couldn't stop the thieves, if you couldn't get out of there without me, then I'd have to finish things myself!'

'You travelled along the zip-line all by *yourself*?' asked Jonny, impressed.

'I took one of the umbrellas and tied myself on – I hope that was OK.' Alex looked down, embarrassed by all the attention.

'And you put together this crash mat of compost so that we would land safely?'

Alex nodded. 'Just in case you *did* manage to escape, I . . . I figured it might help. My umbrella only just held out!' He pointed to the battered brolly lying beside the compost heap.

The others laughed incredulously. Alex had saved their lives and they would always remember this. Whenever anyone had a go at Alex, or barged past him in the street, or took the mickey out of his flattened side-parting, they would be there, standing up for him, protecting him the way he'd protected them.

'But . . . but how did you manage to get out of the safe?' asked Alex, baffled.

Jonny explained how his granddad had sneaked him a pick so that they could escape through the secret back way out of the safe. Alex's eyes widened in wonder at the sound of the mirror tunnel just the way Zack had anticipated.

'You'd have loved it, Alex,' said Sophie, grinning. 'Anyway, we can catch up on all this later. What's important right now is that we find the Queen and warn her about Henry and the thieves.'

'Who, with any luck, are well on their way to the Tower of London!' said Zack.

The four of them looked around. They were actually being concealed by a number of tall rose bushes that grew parallel with the wall.

'OK, well, let's go and find the Queen of England,' said Zack, his body pumping with nervous energy as he looked at his watch . . . It was almost six o'clock!

'These . . . these bushes go all the way round to the inner courtyard,' Alex told them. 'If we stay close to the edge, we won't be seen.'

They set off cautiously, dreading to think what might happen if they were caught.

'Her bedroom window will face the inner courtyard, not the street,' Sophie reasoned as they crept through the undergrowth, Alex leading the way, trying not to snag their clothes on the thorny bushes.

All of a sudden she heard a sinister, threatening growl and stopped.

'Please tell me that was your stomach, Zack . . .' said Jonny quietly.

Another growl, louder and longer than the first.

Sophie peered through the bushes, eyes still adjusting to the dark. Beside her, Alex was panting.

Except that the panting wasn't coming from Alex at all, but from a pack of very angry corgis, now staring Sophie in the face, their hackles raised, their group growling rumbling like thunder.

37

The Young Magicians stood there, petrified, as five canine heads pierced through the rose bushes, their teeth glinting in the pale moonlight.

Jonny gulped. *Wow! They never look like this when they're being paraded about by the Queen!*

'Everybody just stay calm,' said Sophie quietly, not taking her eyes off the princely pack. 'I'm just going to *try* something ... There you go – good boy, *goooood* boy!'

The dog furthest to the left let out a snapping bark of warning.

'Easy, *eeeasy*.' Sophie didn't move a muscle.

'Does anyone have any food?' asked Zack hoarsely.

'I don't think now is the time for a picnic, mate!' said Jonny.

Zack shook his head incredulously – Jonny made jokes in even the most *delicate* of situations!

'Don't worry, you two,' said Sophie a bit more confidently, slowly raising her hand towards the dogs' eye level. 'I've got this.' And then, all of a sudden, Sophie barked.

Alex allowed his eyes to drift over to the back of Sophie's head, wondering if she'd suffered some kind of blow when she fell off the zip-line.

With a tiny movement of her arm, Sophie changed the tone of her bark, causing the dogs to blink in unison, now following her every move like she was wafting some delicious bone in front of their noses. With another wave of her other hand and a little grunt they sat down, somewhat droopily, their teeth now hidden behind thick, drooly gums, their tongues lolling. And then, with a final click of the fingers and a tiny celebratory howl, that was it – they were under her spell.

Zack, Jonny and Alex looked at her, gobsmacked. 'Oh, you've got to be kidding me!' said Jonny slowly as he looked at the dozy dogs.

Sophie gazed back at them and lowered her hands. 'Didn't think that would work, to be fair.'

'You really are quite extraordinary!' said Jonny. 'But you don't half bark like a girl!' he added.

'Yeah, save it for later, Haigh. We've got work to do. This way – quick!' Sophie took off again as the dogs began to wander dreamily across the lawn.

The four of them crossed a gravel path, trying to keep as light on their feet as possible, passing under a large archway that led to the inner courtyard.

Zack looked up at the windows on the first and second floors, searching for a clue as to where the Queen might be at this time of an evening. 'There!' he said excitedly, pointing up to a small lit window in the far corner of the courtyard.

Alex cocked his head, looking a little like one of the corgis. Was that *humming* he could hear? The others strained their ears as he held up a cautionary hand.

'Do-doo-doo *gracious Queen*, do-doo-doo *noble Queen*, do-doo-doo *Queen, DO DO DO DO!*'

The four stared at each other as the sound of a flushing loo drowned out the rest of the National Anthem. From the same lit room came a scraping sound as someone lowered the window before pressing down on what had to be a giant can of air freshener. *Pfffffffffffffffffffffffffffffffffffffff*. And then again. *Pfffffffffffffffffffffffffffffffffffffffffffff*. Followed by a second flush.

Jeez, thought Jonny, grinning at Zack.

All of a sudden the light went out and the next three windows lit up brightly. The Young Magicians could just make out the silhouette of a small lady with perfect hair bobbing up and down as she walked along the corridor, switching lights off as she went towards . . .

'That must be her bedroom right there!' Zack pointed to a dimly lit room a few windows along. 'Look – the curtains are different to all the others.' It was true: whereas the other curtains were royal blue and creamy white, these were distinctly more garish. And perhaps even patterned with dogs and horses.

'This way!' Zack took off again, desperate to reach Her Majesty before the clock struck six.

The four hugged the wall, Alex still with hoe in hand (which he could have easily put down but had actually grown rather fond of), as they traversed the edge of the inner courtyard, keeping to the shadows, their light steps making little impact on the perfectly laid gravel.

Zack slowed down as they approached the area directly beneath the window. Did Buckingham Palace really have this little protection? wondered Jonny, worried that their current progress seemed a bit too good to be true. He needn't have worried, for just at that very moment a long line of Buckingham Guards paraded through the archway where the four had just been standing, marching around in a large square looking a bit like some strange breed of Chinese dragon.

'Quick – over there!' rasped Jonny, spotting a small door in the wall ahead set behind a freshly planted patch of marigolds, which the slugs were already fiendishly devouring. (OFF WITH THEIR HEADS!)

Alex rushed up ahead as the guards approached, their heels scraping up the gravel in quick-time, like the trot was beating out a countdown to them being caught. *Crunch, crunch, crunch.* Alex reached the doorway, fishing the tool he'd fashioned the night before out of his pocket. He stared at the keyhole in front, assessing its shape carefully, biting the end of his pick like a famished rabbit and carefully altering its shape. He slowly inserted it into the keyhole of the polished, metal-studded door.

There was no doubt about it, if they were caught now, then this really *would* be the end, Alex thought. No amount of hypnosis was going to work here.

Jonny, Sophie and Zack caught up with him and huddled in the doorway, breathless. 'Not that you need to redeem yourself, Alex,' joked Jonny, 'but if there was *ever* a time for picking a lock in record quick time, it's now!'

Sophie punched Jonny on the arm, but couldn't help grinning.

Alex gave Jonny a confident nod as he twisted the piece of dowelling and pushed the pick deep into the lock. Almost instantly the door clicked open like the locking mechanism had simply melted away.

They rushed inside, closing it silently behind them just as the guards crunched past.

'Nice one, Alex!'

'Yeah,' said Jonny. 'I think we can call it quits now!'

'Right then,' whispered Sophie, taking charge. 'Upstairs, is it?' Ahead of them she saw a beautiful staircase leading to a long corridor.

'And keep an eye out for, erm . . . the lady!' said Zack, feeling apprehensive now they were actually inside the Queen's house, for this was *Trespassing* with a capital T! Perhaps even the definition of the word, thought Sophie alarmingly, imagining some old Royal coming up with the term in a fit of rage several thousand years ago when he saw some unwanteds crossing his luscious gravel pathways and beautiful plush carpets. TRESPASSERS, OFF WITH THEIR FEET!

The others grinned nervously. Could the lady they'd spied earlier really be *that* lady? The only lady that had her own piece on the chessboard. The only lady they so desperately needed to see right now.

'This way!' said Zack, hurrying them on excitedly.

The four tiptoed up the stairs, Jonny quickly taking off his shoes and leaving them neatly at the bottom, partly to stop him from clomping about, but also because he didn't want to get his muddy size-eleven footprints strewn all over the soft, thick carpet. Plus it only seemed polite when (breaking and) entering into the Queen's home!

They reached the top of the stairs and moved silently over the long landing, trying to stay low every time they passed a window. Alex couldn't believe they'd made it this far. It was one thing to have survived his solo flight across Jonny's zip-line, quite another to be standing on a landing, about to invade the Queen's bedroom.

Despite everything though, for all his previous worries, all Alex could now feel was excruciating excitement. Perhaps it was the adrenalin of having survived his ordeal with Henry and being reunited with his three best friends ... Whatever it was, he wanted to bottle the feeling!

The four of them stood facing the corridor ahead of them. Light spilled in through five windows, making the doors on the opposite side glow like choices in a game show. 'Will it be ... door number *one*? Or maybe door number *two*? How about door number *three* ... ?'

Zack turned to the others, whispering, 'I guess we just try them all.'

They crept slowly down the corridor towards door number one. With a careful hand Zack rotated the gilded, crested knob. *Nope, not this one. Locked.*

And – more tellingly – *cold*, observed Sophie, placing her palm against the fancy metal door-plate. No, this room hadn't been used in a while. Perhaps it was one of the grandchildren's.

They continued to door number two – *nope, locked again* – before pausing outside door number three. A small shaft of light filtered out from underneath the door. Sophie took hold of the doorknob, withdrawing her hand almost immediately and nodding her head. *Warm!* It had to be this one!

Zack pressed his ear against the – frankly *gorgeous* – bedroom door, listening intently. Was that more singing he could hear? He removed his ear, rubbing away the oily mark left on the polished surface with a grubby sleeve, sort of making it a bit worse. He nodded at the others. There was only one way to find out . . .

Cautiously he inched the door open and a warm, floral wave of air wafted out, reminding Alex of a particularly intense brand of putrid bubble bath his mother sometimes used to chill out.

Zack pushed the door open a smidgen further, just enough to allow the four of them to squeeze through one at a time and close the door behind them.

It was a truly glorious sight! The kind of room that you dreamed might be waiting for you on the other side of the door when you checked into a hotel. The kind of room that you could only really upgrade to if there were *exceptional* personal circumstances! The kind of room fit for a queen.

Zack, Jonny, Sophie and Alex gazed around, mouths open. It was a room of spectacular proportions, its four-poster, queen-size (naturally!) bed surrounded by antique chests, cushioned sofas, costly cabinets, ornate coffee tables boasting large bouquets of flowers. Zack smiled at how the duvet had been folded back to reveal a couple of neat, brilliant white towels – complete with a tiny bar of fine soap – on top. There were even some mint chocolates on the bedside table should Her Majesty desire a naughty little night-time treat. Even though he couldn't see it, Zack was sure that the end of the toilet paper would have been folded into a triangle – like you might find in a B&B to categorically *prove* that the owners were making an effort.

Sophie studied the coffee table more closely, spotting a copy of the *Radio Times* beneath the bowl of potpourri, the string of pearls and the textured stationery set. What on earth were they going to say to the lady when they finally came face to face?

From behind the bed, on the far side of the room, came a voice: 'What the bloody 'ell do you four want?'

The Young Magicians froze as a lady in a dressing gown and frilly pink slippers strolled out from behind the large bed, rubbing moisturizer into her small, aged hands.

There were no two ways about it. The lady they now faced, the lady whose bedroom they had invaded, was the lady they watched after lunch every Christmas Day: none other than Her Majesty Queen Elizabeth II.

'Well? Come on, then!' she shouted. 'I'm waitin' for a bleedin' answer!'

38

All four of them stood staring at the Queen, mouths hanging open, at a loss. *No, come on*, thought Zack. *This is what everything has been leading up to – don't choke now!*

Zack bowed deeply, the others following suit. HM the Queen gestured with the back of her hand, as if shooing away a fly. 'Ah, don't bother with any a' that! But I'm tellin' ya – ya got less than a second before I scream for my guards!'

Her *voice*! It was like someone had taken the Queen and inserted the entire cast of *EastEnders* into her mouth. What was it with the accent?

The Queen noticed their quizzical expressions. 'Not what you were expectin'? Nah, I guess not – no one ever does! But then, no one ever gets to see the real me, does they? Except when they storm into my bedroom like this! What if I didn't 'ave me nightie on?'

Zack slowly straightened up. 'Ma'am . . . Erm . . . This is going to sound a bit . . . Well, just bear with me on this! The thing is . . . we believe the thieves who tried to steal the nation's gold earlier this week are now after the Crown Jewels. Ma'am.'

The Queen looked at Zack, motionless for a few seconds, inscrutable as her waxwork at Madame Tussaud's, the noise of the clock ticking suddenly sounding more like cannon fire. None of them dared to move or speak. 'What, is that it?' she said suddenly, with an almost toothless grin. 'You came all this way to tell me that?'

'Oh . . . Erm . . . No, ma'am,' continued Zack. 'You see, the thing is, it was actually me – well, *us* – who solved the Bank of England case in the first place. We told DI Caulfield what we knew, but then he claimed all the glory for himself.'

'Yeah, that sounds 'bout right, knowin' 'im!' she said, a look of mischief on her face.

Zack continued, more confident now. 'So when the thieves told us exactly when they were going to steal the Crown Jewels, we thought it best to come and tell you in person.'

'You thought . . . it best . . . to come and tell me in person,' repeated the Queen, as if this was one of the most ridiculous things she'd ever heard (save for some of her husband's jokes!).

'Well, also,' Zack piped up again, 'because we don't believe the Crown Jewels are kept in the Tower of London at all . . . We think they're here with you, and that the Tower of London is just a bluff.'

The Queen was silent for a moment, before gesturing to a chaise longue. 'Sit,' she said, like she was talking to one of her dogs. 'All four of you – *naow*!'

They obeyed at once while the Queen dragged a chair across to face them. She sat, hitching up her dressing gown and kicking off her slippers, making herself comfy.

'And what makes you fink the Crown Jewels ain't at the Tower a London, where they've bin for a hundred years?' she asked casually.

'Well, from a magician's point of view, it's the perfect bluff,' said Zack, looking her squarely in the eye, trying to see if she might give anything away.

'You're *magicians*?' said the Queen, looking between the four of them inquisitively, an optimistic trace in her voice. 'Like 'Arry Potter?'

'Well, not quite, Your Majesty. We're the Young Magicians,' answered Sophie, trying to sound confident.

'Oh, I see – and what's that?' asked the Queen, smiling.

'Oh, well, it's just . . . nothing.' Sophie was lost for words for once.

'Nah, come on, girl,' jibed the Queen playfully, 'don't be shy, what is it?'

'Well, it's just what we call our group . . . gang . . . thing.'

'You four?'

'That's right.'

'And you are . . . ?'

'Sophie, ma'am.'

The Queen looked at Alex and Jonny and Zack.

'Oh, erm, I'm Jonny and this is . . .'

'Alex.'

'Zack.'

The three boys gave her a nod before lowering their heads politely.

'My Charlie used to be into magic,' said the Queen. 'Even got 'imself a place at that Magic Circle up the road.* That's goin' back decades, o' course.'

Zack carried on, like a true raconteur, explaining to the Queen everything that had happened – from their initial

* COMPLETELY true!

discovery of *The Thieves' Almanac* to their zip-line journey to Buckingham Palace.

The Queen listened, entranced, digging into a couple of mint chocolates as Zack spoke.

'All right, so 'ang on!' she said eventually. 'So you – Zack – you're the one who dreamed all this up. Jonny, you built the wire thing that leads to my 'ouse. Alex, you picked my locks, and – Sophie – you hypnotized my dogs? Is that about right?'

'In a nutshell, yes,' said Zack, daring a smile.

'And you're . . . the Young Magicians?'

They all nodded.

'I like it! But what the 'ell do you want me to do about it?'

'Well . . .' Zack hadn't anticipated this question. 'Maybe you could alert the security people at the Tower of London. We didn't think they'd take us seriously, and we didn't want to have to go to DI Caulfield again.'

'Nah, I don't doubt it!' The Queen smiled at them – a warm, genuine smile. 'It's nice havin' a bit of company up 'ere. The 'ouse is so quiet when the family are away.'

Zack, Jonny, Sophie and Alex stared at her, shocked. Sophie had never taken much interest in the royal family, but this wise woman was very special. Her voice for starters! Sophie smiled at the thought of her delivering her Christmas Day speech in this voice.

'One question, though,' said the Queen, drumming her fingers on her lap thoughtfully. 'If you lot have managed to work out the real location of me Crown Jewels – hypothetically speaking, o' course – then what's to stop these thieves from working it out too?'

'Well, precisely!' said a deep, snarling voice from the doorway.

39

The Queen looked up, suddenly alert, all sense of cosiness wiped away in an instant as they turned to see Henry – the mature, scarred Henry that Alex had described – now leering at them.

'You four thought you were so clever!' he snarled.

Jonny stood, furious with Henry for what he'd done to Alex, among other things.

'Uh-uh!' warned Henry, suddenly brandishing a screwdriver. 'Not so fast, beanpole! I've got someone here who'd like to say hello; someone I'm sure you'll all be *very* surprised to see!'

The others stood too as Henry reached into the darkness of the corridor and pulled someone into the room: a man in a suit with a bag over his head, his hands tied behind his back. Henry flung him on the floor, causing the man to cry out in pain.

'Now, you listen 'ere, mister!' barked the Queen.

'No, *you* listen here!' shouted back Henry, his lips flailing about sinisterly. 'Don't you want to know how I've done it? How I've managed to pull off one of the greatest thefts in all of history?!'

'Yes, Henry,' said Sophie, acting oddly calm. 'Why don't we all sit down while you tell us?' She returned to the chaise longue, encouraging the others – including the Queen – to sit down too.

'Hey, hey!' cried Henry, waving the screwdriver around. 'Don't any of you move a muscle! And don't try any of that relaxing mumbo jumbo on me, idiot girl! I've seen what you did to those dogs!'

'Fine, fine,' said Sophie, holding up her hands and standing back up, trying to ignore the Queen's slight glance of disapproval. 'We just want to know how you knew to come *here*.'

'What? You don't think I've been one step ahead of you all the time?' said Henry with a smug laugh. 'What better way to outwit a bunch of clever children than to let them outwit themselves! All I needed to do was tempt you in and now look where we are . . . Oh, what – was this not part of your plan?' He pouted insanely at Zack, looking like an unhinged baboon.

'But what . . . what about the rest of the thieves?' said Zack, feeling empty all of a sudden.

'What *thieves*? There were never any *thieves*. It was only me. And *this* man, of course!' Henry kicked the man on the floor, causing him to let out another muffled shriek.

'President . . . President Pickle?' wondered Jonny.

'Oh, you *wish*, beanpole! You couldn't see it, even though it was staring you in the face!'

Jonny stared at the figure on the floor, the aged suit, the smart tie . . .

'Ladies and gentlemen,' screamed Henry as if he was on stage at *The Royal Variety Performance*. 'Your Majesty, *children*! May I present to you the real mastermind behind the madness . . . ERNEST HAIGH!'

40

The Young Magicians watched in horror as Henry unveiled a broken and beaten Ernest, pulling back the sack from his head with an aggressive flourish, as if he was just some prop in a hack stage routine.

For a second all anyone could hear was Ernest gasping for air – until Jonny murmured, 'Granddad?'

'Jonathan . . .' he sighed. 'It's not what you think.'

Henry suddenly rounded on him, putting the screwdriver to his neck. 'Oh, but it is, old man! Why don't you tell them? Why don't you tell them *everything*?'

Still wheezing away, and hardly daring to look at the Queen, Ernest got to his knees. He studied the four of them sadly. 'It all . . . It all started a while ago . . .' he began. 'But I never meant it to lead to this, I promise you.'

'No, Granddad. *No!*' Jonny didn't want to believe what he was hearing. All eyes were now trained on Ernest as he started to explain.

'Henry was expelled from the society a number of years ago. You don't need to know why, nor do you need to know his real name, but it was a nasty affair.'

Henry smacked Ernest across the back of his head, causing Jonny to step forward involuntarily. Once again, Henry raised the screwdriver. 'Stay where you are!' he barked ferociously. 'Continue, old man!'

Ernest cleared his throat before carrying on. 'About a year ago I came up with a plan. A plan to save the Magic Circle from falling into financial ruin. You all heard what a state it's in. And all President Pickle and his council can do is brush things under the carpet! But I couldn't carry out my plan alone, I needed assistance. And then I remembered Henry and his talent for . . . *misbehaviour.*'

The Young Magicians looked on as the truth slowly sank in; the vast, luscious room suddenly felt overpowering and claustrophobic.

'Council stopped listening to me years ago,' Ernest went on. 'It was time to do something practical to ensure the future of the society so that it could allow young magicians like yourselves to flourish. Like I flourished. Back then.'

'And so you decided to *steal*?' said Jonny, his voice breaking.

'*Yes*, steal, Jonathan! But not to harm. Not for personal gain!'

'And Henry . . . what? He would simply share the prize – was that it?' Jonny's voice was hollow with anguish.

'Yes. At least, that was the plan. But you have to believe me when I tell you that I did it for the likes of *you and your friends*. To keep the society I once loved from crumbling away. But I never meant for you to be involved!'

'Explain to the other boy how he's been played,' said Henry, turning to Zack. 'I want him to see how *foolish* he's been!'

'You were trying to get me involved,' Zack realized all of a sudden, his face blank. 'Six months ago, when I first arrived, you were sizing me up to see if *I* could help you, weren't you?'

Ernest looked up at Zack, nodding sadly. 'I'm afraid to say we were, young lad, yes.'

'But . . . *why*?'

'Because of your *brain*, don't you see?' said Ernest. 'There hasn't been a magical brain like yours for generations! How else were we to commit these impossible crimes?'

'What about *The Thieves' Almanac*?' said Sophie, still trying to piece everything together. The Queen looked over at her, trying to keep up.

'It doesn't exist,' said Ernest flatly. 'Or if it does, I don't know where it is. No, we needed to look for the really bright magical minds, innocent . . . unguarded.'

'Hence Henry posing as a kid at the first ever induction week,' said Zack, shaking his head.

'But you were getting too nosy.' Henry fixed Zack with cold eyes and paced to and fro behind Ernest, clearly enjoying the effect his performance was having. 'And since you weren't willing to come on board, since you *rejected* my friendship . . .'

'We just needed you out of the way while we put our heads together,' continued Ernest.

'And so you had me framed!' Zack swallowed.

Ernest nodded again. *I can't believe this man is my granddad*, thought Jonny, feeling completely disorientated.

'And when did the rest of us become part of your plan?' asked Sophie bitterly. She had *trusted* him.

'Right from the moment you first stepped into the building,' answered Ernest. 'I knew I had another chance of getting to Zack on learning he was a close friend of Jonathan's, but we had to be less obvious this time round. Now that we had everything in place. He couldn't get a sense that he – or any of you – were being . . . *groomed* by Henry and me.'

'You got me into magic just to get to Zack again?' spat Jonny, running his hands through his hair.

'Yes, but . . . I . . . I . . .' Ernest trailed off. There was nothing else he could say.

'And the Bank of England plot – what went wrong there?' asked Sophie, grabbing Jonny's hand.

'Nothing. That was just . . . a test. To see if you would take the bait. We were always after the Crown Jewels . . . Not that we had the foggiest idea how to get to them,' answered Ernest as Henry grinned behind him.

'And so you see,' said Henry, almost salivating at his success, 'while you were confiding all your brilliant solutions to Ernest, you were simply showing us the way, doing our job for us! Of course, we had to put you on the right track every now and again, let you know that you were on the right lines without being too obvious, make Zack think it would all lead to him *clearing his name* so to speak . . .'

'The bookmark in the restricted section,' whispered Zack. 'The page from *The Thieves' Almanac* . . .'

'We could have suffocated inside that safe!' screamed Jonny, tears streaming down his face, trying to lash out at his granddad as Sophie held him back.

'But, Jonathan, that's why I gave you the pick. I didn't know that Henry was going to disable Alex like that, I swear. Henry was out of control. I wanted out, I promise you! I wanted to tell you when you came to visit me, but he was behind the door. I never meant it to come to this!'

Henry glared over at Alex, causing the boy to squirm and shake once more. 'To think how guilty you all felt believing the thieves had got to "Henry"!' He threw his head back, touching the eye that had once appeared horribly bruised, but had clearly just been more make-up and theatrics. 'And now you know everything,' he said smugly. 'Apart from how I never planned to accept a mere portion of the prize, even at the beginning – just the prize itself! The greatest theft in all of history! The theft of the *Crown Jewels*!'

'I should never have trusted him!' said Ernest pleadingly, his body now contorted towards the four youngsters, his back arched, like he was physically begging – bent double – for their forgiveness. The room fell quiet as Ernest hung his head in shame, sobbing.

'Pathetic old man.' Henry sneered down at him. 'You should have seen him on the zip-line – he almost wet himself!'

Zack bit his lip. The two men had certainly pulled off an elaborate scam, but then . . . Hmm. What if . . . ? No, surely they would never buy it. But then again, you never knew – just *maybe* . . . ?

'There's just one little thing to add,' he said, meeting Henry's gaze.

Sophie and Alex glanced at each other, puzzled. What was Zack up to now?

'And what's that, Brains?' spat Henry. 'Worried I might blame all this on you again? Don't worry, that's already covered. It's all very straightforward: "Young magician fails Magic Circle induction *again* and so turns to crime!"'

'Nope, not that,' said Zack casually. 'I'm just wondering why you didn't suspect the bluff?'

Henry's eyes suddenly narrowed, like he needed to be on guard. Had he been too complacent? 'What bluff?'

'Well, it goes without saying – why just settle for a bluff when there's the double bluff? What better way to protect the Crown Jewels than to pretend they're somewhere they're not . . . But for that to be pretend too!'

Jonny looked up. Was his friend being serious?

'You mean . . . ?' began Sophie.

'Yes. Sorry to drag you along for nothing,' Zack went on, 'but it was the only way to get the thieves – or whoever – as far away from the Crown Jewels as possible. Didn't you think I knew I was being played, Henry – or whatever your name is? I'm just so pleased you and Ernest took the bait!'

Jonny, Sophie and Alex stared at each other, agog. Was Zack telling the truth or was this more invention?

'No!' shouted Henry angrily. 'You're bluffing! They *must* be here!'

'Why?' said Zack, goading him. 'Because some *children* said they were? What if I'd said they were stored on the moon – would we be standing *there* now?'

Henry was boiling with rage, his screwdriver pointed at Zack. Instinctively, Alex, Jonny and Sophie moved in to protect their friend.

The Queen suddenly stepped forward.

'I'll be honest, right. I ain't really followed much o' this, which is why I ain't spoken much, but the kid's right – they're not 'ere. And even if they were, you wouldn't be able to find 'em, 'cos they don't even exist! They never 'ave done!'

WHAT?!

Now it was Zack's turn to gasp. Could this be true? The Young Magicians turned to face the Queen as the veins in Henry's neck began to pulse and bulge.

All of a sudden Ernest began to laugh. A deep, hearty laugh that ran up from his bowels and exploded out of his mouth. Henry glowered at him. Had the old man deliberately led him astray or was he as shocked by this revelation as the rest of them? It was impossible to tell who was bluffing any more, and the room – like Henry's head – was beginning to spin. Was everyone here taking him for a ride? Didn't they know what he was capable of? Didn't anyone know? Ah, but he still had the screwdriver.

As Ernest continued to guffaw, Henry slowly raised the screwdriver high above his head.

The others all looked at Ernest, then up at Henry ... and then just to the left of Henry as someone began to approach rapidly from behind with a frankly remarkable choice of weapon: the garden hoe.

41

DI Caulfield walloped Henry on the back of the head – hard enough for it to have an immediate effect, but not so hard that it made a mess of the Queen's nice carpet. The screwdriver dropped to the floor, and the inspector quickly scooped it up, before disabling its owner with a pair of Scotland Yard's finest handcuffs.

'DI whatever your name is!' exclaimed the Queen in her famous fruity voice. 'I've been hearing all sorts of fantastic stories about you this evening, but I'm most glad you showed up when you did. Pray, what brought you here?'

The inspector garbled a response as his brain tried to deal with the sight of Her Majesty in Her Nightie. 'Well, Your Majesty – it's DI *Caulfield* by the way – C-A-U-L-F-I-E-L-D. So, erm, yes, it's a long story, but a curious man named Alf tracked me down in a rather swish restaurant this evening with the news that these four youngsters were on their way to see you regarding the attempted theft of

343

the Crown Jewels. He thought I might be useful as backup. Love the nightie, by the way!' The detective flashed the Queen one of his press-pleasing grins, garnering zero response.

The Young Magicians stared at each other. So *Alf* had sent DI Caulfield – but how had he known where to find him? Zack wondered.

'And where is this Alf fellow? I'd like to see him,' said the Queen politely, like the drama of the last fifteen minutes hadn't just played out *in her bedroom*.

'Well, the thing is, I'm ever so sorry, Your Maj – but he just kind of . . . disappeared once we got into the grounds.'

Sophie and Alex smiled at each other, knowing all too well how Alf had the strange habit of vanishing into thin air.

'Why weren't you honest about who really solved the Bank of England plot?' asked Zack, standing firm and cocking his head at the preening inspector.

DI Caulfield opened his mouth to answer, but only the noise of him trying to come up with an excuse came out, making him sound a bit like a Geiger counter.

'I think you owe these children an apology,' said the Queen, folding her arms haughtily.

'Oh . . . *absolutely*!' The inspector squirmed. 'I was just about to do that. Whatever you think best, Your Maj!'

'And stop callin' me Maj, you 'ear me?' she hollered, forgetting to use her pretend voice.

'Oh, sure!'

Ernest had stopped laughing and was now looking exhausted, his eyes unfocused.

Jonny couldn't bear to look at him. They had *trusted* him, thought he was on their side. But only so they could unwittingly carry out his grand plans.

DI Caulfield dragged Ernest to his feet as Henry began to come round.

'Take them away, please – they're making a smell,' bossed the Queen, gesturing towards Henry and Ernest. 'I believe we five have some unfinished business.' She gave the four friends a mischievous smile. (The kind you might see if you folded a fiver in a particular way and held it at an angle!)

42

It was a rather strange journey back to the Magic Circle. Her Majesty had initially wanted to try this famous zip-line everyone kept on banging on about – until she learned that this would require them to slide uphill, making it quite impossible. And so instead, at the Queen's insistence, the five of them had travelled by private horse and carriage (INCONSPICUOUS!). As they bounced up The Mall and headed north towards Stephenson Way, she demanded Zack show her a trick she could teach her great-grandchildren.*

It had been a startling series of revelations. Everyone was stunned – and no one more so than Jonny, who stared out of the window, uncharacteristically quiet. What should

---

* There were many tricks Zack could have chosen, but he obliged by piercing the face of the Queen on a five-pound note with a pen, causing the real Queen to scream like it was a genuine act of Voodoo, before cawing with laughter as he removed the pen from the other side of the note to reveal her face, perfectly intact once again. Wonderful!

he tell his mother and father? Maybe this was what they'd
been hiding from him all along – the fact that his granddad
was a criminal.

Alex, his hand now freshly bandaged in fine royal linen,
looked at Zack. 'You ... You were bluffing, right, when
you said you'd brought us to Buckingham Palace
deliberately.'

Zack smiled at him. 'I wish I was that clever! But no, it
was a bluff. A triple bluff, I think that makes it. Or maybe
a double double bluff – I don't know!' Sophie and Alex
laughed as Zack turned to face the Queen.

'Your Majesty, do you mind me asking whether the Crown Jewels really exist?' he asked.

The Queen stared at him as the carriage rocked from side to side, weaving in and out of traffic. 'Well, the fakes certainly exist,' she said.

'Yes, but do the real ones?' probed Zack.

'Well, that'd be tellin' now, wouldn't it? But who's to say the fakes aren't as valuable at the real 'uns?'

Zack smiled at her, happy for it to remain a mystery.

'Yeah, it's not just you magicians who like to misdirect,' the Queen continued as they headed up Shaftesbury Avenue. 'Take that flag of mine always goin' up and down. She's in, she's not in, she's in, she's not in! None of it means a bleedin' fing – it's completely random! I come an' go as I please. Keeps everyone guessin', though, don't it?'

'Ma'am,' enquired Sophie. 'What is it with your voice?'

The Queen looked at her. 'I just don't like givin' too much away ... When you're on display all the time, it's nice to keep some fings ... secret! After all, what is it they say about royalty ... a queen is just a person playing the part of a queen!'

Sophie smiled back at her. That sounded familiar – what a great way to put it!

Eventually the horse and carriage pulled up in Stephenson Way. The Young Magicians hopped out, Alex courteously turning to offer the Queen a hand – which was batted away with a snort. They headed towards the blue door again.

'Nah, I thought we could go in the other way you talked about!' said the Queen, already heading for the side of the building and heaving herself up the fire escape.

Just one last climb and then we're almost done, thought Zack.

43

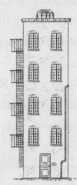

In the Grand Theatre of the Magic Circle a variety of weird and wonderful things had been going on, things that might have been described as a 'cabaret' if it weren't for the fact that it was ABSOLUTE PANDEMONIUM!

President Pickle had taken off his jacket and was now desperately scratching at the circular dials on the safe door. At his side, Cynthia whimpered in his ear, begging him to prise it open – the two of them still oblivious to the mirror tunnel extending behind it. Meanwhile Deanna's mother had taken it upon herself to inflict a) bowls of e-number-riddled snacks and b) another performance by Deanna on the ageing onlookers.

And as if this wasn't enough, Bill – perhaps finally having conked it – was now slumped over his foghorn, causing it to sound endlessly, filling the auditorium with a rich continuous wailing. The audience looked on, oddly hooked, their faces a mixture of alarm and disbelief, as if they were trapped inside some bizarre dream which seemed to go on and on and on and on and . . .

With the tiniest *pfft* – which cut through the cacophony of sound almost like magic itself – the safe door nudged open.

The room fell deathly quiet as Steve and Jane finally shifted Bill (who was *still* alive – phew!) off the foghorn, but which still rang in everyone's ears like an unpleasant, unwelcome reminder. Even Deanna couldn't help but turn and look; for once not annoyed that all the attention wasn't on her and her frantic mindless antics.

All eyes were now on the safe door. President Pickle took a step back, arms outstretched, his sweating face showing both relief and confusion. Had he actually managed to crack the code and open the safe? Despite the circumstances he couldn't help being impressed by his efforts. Oh yes, he thought, his mind already racing. This would look brilliant splashed across the society magazine: EDMUND SAVES THE DAY ONCE AGAIN! But what if the safe's contents had . . . perished? No, that wouldn't sound so good. Not good at all. He began to go pale . . .

Cynthia was biting her lip. How long had it been? she wondered. Well over an hour . . . Surely *one* person couldn't survive in those airless confines for an hour, let alone *three* . . . Oh, why had she allowed them to go ahead?

Slowly but surely, the safe door opened another fraction . . . And then some more . . . And then a hand . . . A HAND! Thirteen-year-old Zack Harrison's hand, to be precise. The boy emerged from the safe grinning from ear to ear as the audience gasped and began to applaud. President Pickle stepped back as if Zack was an apparition, come to haunt and taunt him for the rest of his days.

The ovation grew louder as Sophie appeared – for this was magic of the highest order! Next out was Jonny, who looked like a daddy longlegs emerging from a Smarties tube.

Zack and Sophie looked at each other knowingly as they turned back towards the safe. All eyes returned to the heavy door as a small hand felt round the edges of the safe. Cynthia's concern gave way to a broad smile as Alex – ALEX! – popped out boasting a small smile.

The crowd got to their feet as the tilted chandelier high above shook in time with the thunderous rapture echoing about the theatre. Sophie glanced up to the top gallery, just making out Alf guffawing and applauding from the gods.

She gave him an emphatic wink, smiling back at the others.

But there was still one more surprise!

The Young Magicians turned once more to face the safe as first a shoe, then a knee, then a midriff, and finally the entire bulk of Her Majesty the Queen of England stepped out to face the crowd, causing President Pickle to belch so loudly that a tiny bit of sticky toffee pudding-flavoured bile crept up his oesophagus, which he had to swallow back down with a noisy, incredulous GULP.

The whole room fell silent again, many of the aged members rubbing their eyes. Like they were out for a meal and had just been served an entire gazelle in place of coffee and mints. No, this was *not* what they were expecting at all!

President Pickle grabbed his jacket, trying to tidy himself up while bowing respectfully.

'Oh, there's no need for any of that!' said the Queen in her usual voice. Everyone gasped. *It was really her!*

'Your Majesty, we – erm . . . we weren't . . . expecting you.' President Pickle tried to sound like he was in charge.

'No, I'm sure you weren't!' answered the Queen jovially. 'And I wasn't expecting to be confronted by these four earlier this evening.'

For a second Pickle thought he had found an ally; that the Queen was here to reprimand these four delinquents. Perhaps he would even be up for a knighthood! But his thoughts were quickly dashed.

'Do you know that these four have saved the country's fortunes not once but twice this week?' she asked him.

Pickle began to stutter liked a struggling engine. 'We . . . I . . . didn't know that, no, ma'am.'

'It seems that there's a whole load of things you don't know, Mr Pickle.' The Queen gazed out into the theatre, shielding her eyes from the bright lights. 'Gosh, where are all the other youngsters? Most of these people are older than me!'

'Well . . . the thing is, ma'am, the Magic Circle constitution states that –'

'Pah! Constitutions are made to be broken!' said the Queen with a twinkle in her eye.

'N-no, yes, absolutely . . .' stammered President Pickle, ignoring the pointed look from his wife.

'And while you're at it, a few more women wouldn't go amiss either!'

'Hear, hear!' shouted a crusty gent in the stalls, missing the point entirely and causing the Queen to roll her eyes.

'Well, I can't hang about,' she said, nodding at them all politely.

Deanna's mother suddenly raised her arm. 'Sorry, Your Majesty . . . You wouldn't mind if my daughter Deanna sang you her version of the National Anthem, would you?'

The Queen looked at her kindly. And then looked at Deanna. She paused for a second, before offering her verdict. 'It's a bit late, I'm afraid.'

Sophie smirked at her friends – *Aww, what a shame!*

'Oh – one last thing, Mr Pickle!' sang the Queen as she headed back towards the safe. She heaved on the heavy door and reached inside.

The Young Magicians watched as she dragged out a single gold bar and set it down on the wooden floor with a gratifying *thud*. A GOLD BAR!

'A present from the Bank of England – courtesy of these four, I might add.' The Queen nodded at Zack, Jonny, Sophie and Alex, who looked at each other agog. When had she managed to fetch *that*?

354

She turned to the president. 'Now, be a good man and get your house in order, yes?'

Pickle rocked on his heels, not knowing what to say. 'Erm . . . no, yes, absolutely. Thank you, ma'am!'

'Don't thank *me*!' The Queen held out her hand to the four friends. 'Well, it was lovely to meet you all. What a strange and wonderful place this is!'

They shook her hand and bowed.

'Oh, and congratulations,' said the Queen loudly, 'on becoming *members of the Magic Circle*!'

Cynthia looked over at her husband, who was now furiously chewing on his lower lip like a goat munching on fresh hay.

'The thing is, ma'am,' said President Pickle awkwardly. 'Only when an apprentice *comes of age* can he be –'

'Nonsense, man! I think these four have already proved their worth, don't you? They are *the Young Magicians*, after all!'

Zack, Jonny, Sophie and Alex watched, awestruck, as the Queen clambered slowly back into the safe. She turned and beckoned to Jonny. He walked forward hesitantly.

'Naow, listen 'ere, you!' she said in a low voice, smothered once again in her thick Cockney accent. 'I know it's been a tough evenin' for ya, but it sounds like your gramps was just doin' what he thought were right. Don't make it right, o' course, but still.'

Jonny smiled at her. Though it pained him to think about it, he knew she was right.

'Oh, and also,' added the Queen conspiratorially, 'be sure to take down that zip thingy you made, will ya? Don't want any old Tom, Dick or 'Arry comin' to see me in me nightie!'

'I'll take it down right away, Your Majesty,' said Jonny, flashing her a grin, a notch of his typical cheekiness back.

'Only after I've tried it out, o' course!' The Queen winked at him.

And with that she barged him out of the way, grabbing the safe door and closing it behind her with a conclusive *thunk*.

The Young Magicians stared first at the safe, then at President Pickle, then at Cynthia and all the members of the Magic Circle gathered in the Grand Theatre as the applause and cheering began to thunder in from all sides.

44

The Young Magicians stood facing the blue door. Behind them, a flock of Friday morning pigeons scrabbled about the wheelie bins along Stephenson Way, searching for a discarded crust – or even an entire crayfish, as had once been the case.

'So,' said Jonny. 'One thing I've been wondering . . .'

'*One* thing?'

'. . . is how Alf knew where to find DI Caulfield.'

'Oh,' said Sophie, her fully packed rucksack ballooning out from behind – having checked out of the hotel and suitably undone any traces of hypnotic influence on the staff. 'That'll be because I told Alf where to find him.'

'Naturally! And might we know how *you* knew?' said Jonny with a smile.

Sophie mouthed something at him.

He paused. 'No, sorry – no idea what you're saying.'

'I was saying,' said Sophie casually, 'that I can *lip-read*.'

'Oh, right. Oh, *right*! *Coooooooool!*'

'Ah, so when DI Caulfield whispered to that journalist the other day . . . ?' began Zack.

'I knew exactly where he was taking the lady on a date, yes!'

'Ha, brilliant! I bet he loved that!' said Jonny.

'Tell you what the inspector's going to love even more –' Zack was bouncing from foot to foot – 'is when the Queen finds out he took a few bits and pieces from her bedroom!'

'Oh, Zack mate, you *didn't*!'

'Well, I had to get back at him somehow, didn't I? Don't you remember the final points on our plan? And it was just too easy sneaking it all into his pocket. He didn't notice a thing.'

'Do ... Do you think Henry and Ernest will go to ... prison?' Alex asked hesitantly, lowering his eyes when he saw Jonny instantly bristling at the mention of his granddad's name.

'I don't know, Alex,' answered Sophie. 'I'm sure Henry will.'

'We're safe from him now – that's the main thing,' said Zack.

'So,' said Jonny, changing the subject, 'shall we go and partay?' He gestured towards the door.

'Yeah – I mean, we *could* do that, Jonathan,' said Zack mischievously. 'But, you know – as we're now *members of the Magic Circle* and all that – I was hoping we could have a proper wander about the place ... I'd love to check out that second set of stairs past the library, for example.'

'Oh, now, that sounds like a *much* better idea!'

And with that the Young Magicians raced through the blue door, slamming it shut behind them and causing the flock of nearby pigeons to fly high into the air, and straight into the path of a rapidly accelerating monarch who had categorically refused for the zip-line to be taken down in the end as it was plain and simply too much fun getting to soar above one's country like this. Even in broad daylight!

SWOOSH!
SMACK!

feathers

45

Well, there you go! I do hope my interruptions haven't been TOO annoying! I won't keep you much longer; I for one am in *dire* need of a long candlelit bath. But I just wanted to tie up any loose ends that I failed to address in the main body of the book. This, I hasten to add, was totally deliberate on my part, so that I had an excuse to pop up again at the very end. Either that or a MASSIVE career-ending oversight. *You* decide!

So firstly, yes, Frank *is* still at large in Euston Station, so please watch out. He now doesn't work Wednesdays or Sundays, though, so maybe just travel on those days?

Secondly, the characters in this book are all real, apart from the ones I've completely made up. Such as . . . the ones I've completely made up. But none of that is deliberate.

Thirdly, no pigeons were harmed during the writing of this book, but several thousand were intentionally killed. A LONG OVERDUE JOKE!

Fourthly, and finally ... Many of you have been asking (clearly an outright lie!) whether *The Thieves' Almanac* exists or whether it is genuinely the stuff of myth. Well, it doesn't *completely* not exist. That's to say, if it does exist, it has been rather well *hidden*. Whether anyone has read it ...? Well, that's another story!

Of course, from what Zack told us, and from Sophie's dream, we know that *The Thieves' Almanac* must contain solutions to impossible crimes, anatomical drawings, diagrams of intricate mechanisms, locks, picks, dangerous contraptions, glossaries of strange terms, chemical formulas, appendices upon appendices, a book within a book ...

A book within a book.

Hmm!

One other thing we know about *The Thieves' Almanac* – *if* it exists, that is – is that page 13 was removed by the character who called himself 'Henry' and given to the Young Magicians outside Davenport's Magic Studio. So, if we *were* to inadvertently stumble across *The Thieves' Almanac*, we'd be looking for a book with no page 13. *flicks back and checks*

Hmm! (Again!) Who's with me?

And of course the final thing to say on this matter is that the clue – like the solution to many a magic trick – is often in the title ... Often something staring you in the face the whole time.

Take this book, for example ...

'What are you reading at the moment, young lady?'

'Oh, just *The Young Magicians and the Thieves' Almanac*.'

'Sorry, I didn't catch the name of that *second* book . . . ?'
'*The Thieves' Almanac.*'
The Thieves' Almanac!
A book within a book.
Oh, it exists all right . . . And you've just finished reading it.

GLOSSARY OF TERMS

Charlier cut – A one-handed cut. Using the foot. (KIDDING!)

Cut and restored rope – *Uncannily* similar to torn and restored newspaper (see below!)

Dealer's grip – The standard way of holding a deck of playing cards. Completely and utterly boring.

Double lift – A card move whereby the top card is displayed, but actually two cards are lifted and so the face of the card displayed is actually the second card down. If the playing cards in use are particularly sticky, you may find yourself lifting all 52 cards at once – though it can be rather tricky trying to pass this off as a single playing card. GOOD LUCK!

Expert Card Technique – The go-to book on card magic. The one every magician better than you tells you you *must* read. Since it is very big, it also makes a handy lap-tray when eating snacks in front of the television.

False deals – The act of dealing a playing card from somewhere other than the top of the deck. So fiendishly difficult that it is sometimes easier to just deal the card from the top of the deck and then not continue with the rest of the trick.

False shuffle – A shuffle that appears real, but in fact doesn't disturb the order of the playing cards in any way. A tidy person's shuffle. Or for someone with *extreme* OCD.

Hypnotic induction (handshake method) – A type of hypnotic induction that exploits the reflex action of shaking a hand. Works on most people when perfected, though probably best not practised when greeting your gran – or on anyone who has dirty hands. Not saying that your gran has dirty hands by the way! (Unless she does.)

Mentalist – A practitioner of mental magic. And/or a mad Derren Brown fan.

Muscle pass – Technique in which a coin is transferred from one hand to the other; the muscle at the base of the thumb is used to propel the coin into the air. Looks like real gravity-defying magic when performed properly – and so not when performed by me.

Pinkie break – Insertion of the little finger to maintain a 'break' in a deck of playing cards, allowing the magician to cut the deck at a specific point, usually to bring a selected playing card, assumed to be in the centre of the deck, to the top ('the pass'). Can be a bit obvious if your little finger is the size of your big toe.

Pressure fan – A perfect fan of cards, made possible through application of pressure and a slight bending of the cards. For the record, my version of a pressure fan looks more like a half-eaten taco.

Reverse cull – The act of secretly sliding ('culling') a playing card under a spread of cards to the bottom or top of the deck – i.e. a fun way to show off; i.e. I have no idea what this means.

Thumb tip – Essentially a fake hollowed-out thumb that can be used to hide handkerchiefs and other such small objects (though NOT wasps), allowing items to seemingly disappear and reappear from the closed fist at will. Stands out like a sore thumb if the thumb tip you use isn't the same colour as the rest of your hand/face/body.

Torn and restored newspaper – The act of destroying a newspaper through tearing, only to show – seconds later – that it has magically restored. Relies on hiding a duplicate newspaper. Either that or – like all of the above – it needs to be accomplished by purely magical means.

APPENDICES

1. THE MAGIC CIRCLE HIERARCHY

The President of the Magic Circle

Please be upstanding for Mr President Edmund Pickle!

President Pickle has never had to do a proper day's work in his life and consequently devotes the hours he's awake (and sometimes asleep – which can often be very similar!) to magical politics, both national and international. In the 1800s his ancestors were huge landowners, and there's a rumour going round that you can still walk from London to the West Indies on Pickle-owned land without getting your feet wet.

The Magic Circle Council

These are the wise old magicians who run the organization, and – given that magic is based on the premise of making

Members of the
Inner Magic Circle

Associates of the Inner Magic Circle

Members of the Magic Circle

Young Magicians

the impossible possible – you'd think it might be a rather smooth affair. Sadly, NOT A CHANCE! For one is forgetting that a lot of magicians are self-important buffoons who like making rules about how their society should be run and how their art should progress just as much as they like turning a dove into a mess. If not more so.

Council are the boffins behind rules like 4.10.1 (part of clause 108, 'recently' – in 1971 – revised under subheading C), which states that one must wear cufflinks when on society premises and that buttoned shirtsleeves are UNACCEPTABLE attire for the modern-day conjuror. CUFFLINKS please! Or the suggestion that – during a society convention – a lady named Beryl should provide the lady partners of magicians with Sussex cream teas, entertaining them with anecdotes about her watercolours and the invention of lipstick while the men go to a lecture on plate-spinning and elephant vanishes.

In short, Council is largely comprised of outdated stuffy stiffs and stiffy stuffs!

Magic Circle Membership

Once you're in the Magic Circle, there are three tiers of membership that separate magicians like Steve and Jane from the real working pros like Jingles the Jester.

There's your bog-standard Member of the Magic Circle – or MMC for short (which many magicians choose to cite after their name on fancy business cards, as if to say: *Hey, look at My Magnificent Credentials!*).

Then there's an Associate of the Inner Magic Circle or AIMC. This usually means that a magician has achieved a higher level of technical skill and would like other members to know about it. It's the 'I'm slightly better than you' trademark of the magic world, and – although the acronym is meaningless to anyone other than a bunch of petty conjurors (and the Association of Internal Management Consultants, of course, who I'm told are a *right* laugh!) – gives you access to certain books in the Magic Circle library. Which is handy, even if it means you just pretend to read them while sneering at all the lowly MMCs scrabbling around on the floor looking for old playing cards.

But, HANG ON – who sneers at the AIMCs, in that case? Well, apart from the Holy God of Internal Management Consultants, it's the Members of the Inner Magic Circle or MIMC. This little clique is reserved for members who boast skills indistinguishable from those of Dumbledore, but who exist in an otherwise normal non-Hogwartsy world.

How one actually becomes a MIMC is still shrouded in mystery. However, rumour has it that the lucky magician is sent a formal A5 letter, printed (using an inkjet printer) on plain white paper in Papyrus font, stating – in no uncertain terms – that they are invited to become a member of the Inner Magic Circle. MYSTERIOUS!

No, that's just a shrewd guess. It may well be written in Times New Roman or even – heaven forfend – Comic Sans. Anyway, it's a real privilege. Until you turn the letter over and see the COST of the privilege! (I'm not suggesting that COST is now an acronym, by the way, just that it should be said LOUDLY. Same true for LOUDLY and MYSTERIOUS, etc.!)

Cynics would say that the Magic Circle are desperate for money and that this is merely an easy way of persuading an existing member to part with yet more cash. Others (namely Council) would say that this is just the cost of physically changing MMC into MIMC for correspondence with the particular individual, but this – like most of Council's logic – is clearly, oh yeah, BONKERS!

By the way, there's currently no Inner Inner Magic Circle. But given the choice of shape, there's no reason why they couldn't just sneak one in and keep going with this idea. Had they chosen a pyramid, there'd be a very obvious end point. But as it currently stands, this Circle could very well spiral out of control and just become a filled-in dot!

Women and the Magic Circle

'*The first lady magician was let into the Magic Circle in 1991 – but only because she needed the toilet!*' once said President Edmund Pickle during a council meeting.

OK, so if you don't mind, let's just examine a brief history of the human race.

Let's start with the wonderful fact that half the planet is female – which is fantastic news. There's definitely a certain comfort in knowing that, at least metaphorically speaking, for every Santa Claus – say – there's a Belinda Carlisle.

Anyhow, let's now take a look at the rather disheartening figures currently boasted by the Magic Circle: in a population of around 1,500, less than 5% is female.

Less than 5%.

This means that if you're a different species – particularly if you're an *Oryctolagus cuniculus* (rabbit) or *Columbidae* (dove) – then you're more likely to find yourself in the building than some random XX human chromosome combo. What the deal is for female rabbits and doves I have no idea!

It's not so much that females are actively discouraged from joining the Magic Circle; more that they might feel as if they've gatecrashed the wrong party. And – as if a T. Rex added you as a friend on Facebook – there's just something not quite right about it.

Now, there are a small handful of ladies within the organization who, it has to be said, *adore* this male-heavy environment. Sophie evidently isn't one of them. Sophie wants to be in the Magic Circle because she is a magician. Not a *female* magician or – worse – a *magicienne* (YUCK!). She's here because she deserves to be. Which can't always be said about the 95% men who frequent these premises, making spells, smells and dreadful puns – marking their territory!

'Under Act 13 of the constitution, children may not join the Magic Circle, nor benefit fully from its facilities, until they come of age,' says President Edmund Pickle, all the time.

2. THE LEGEND OF DOUGLAS AND ALF RATTLEBAG

There were once two brothers, both born in 1893 (not twins, though). The first was named Douglas after his late great-grandfather (who was also, crucially, called Douglas). The second was named Alf – but only because the name Douglas was now taken.

The two boys couldn't have been more different – apart from their love of magic. Every day they'd perform for their family, each trying to outdo the other as they learned increasingly complicated tricks, perplexing their parents with pitch-perfect patter, confounding their cousins with cards and coins, annoying their aunts with anything.

As the boys grew, so did their interest in magic – until, on coming of age, they decided to forge a career in the craft.

Deciding that they might be more successful as a double act, the two young men began travelling from town to town as 'Douglas and Alf'.

However, it soon became clear that Douglas – the more suave and confident of the two – was coming to the fore, with Alf relegated to stagehand as he ran around after his brother.

As the years went by, after countless successful performances, the press began referring to 'Douglas and Alf' as simply 'Douglas!' – including the exclamation mark. Little did they know that while Douglas was out celebrating after every show, Alf was working tirelessly backstage, perfecting the mechanical devices used in their routines, making sure that everything was set up for the next performance.

One morning Douglas stormed into Alf's bedroom (at a quaint little inn just outside Kettering), still in a drunken stupor from the previous night, waving a letter and laughing manically.

Alf read the letter, written on thick parchment, with an impressive seal above the heading. It was an invitation for Douglas – and Douglas alone – to become a member of the Inner Magic Circle and to top the bill at the unveiling of the society's new Grand Theatre.

'Finally!' shouted Douglas. '*Finally* I get the recognition I deserve!'

He sneered at Alf, who'd been hoping to catch a mention of himself. 'It's like you don't even exist any more!' he said, enjoying the crestfallen look on his younger brother's face.

The two argued well into the night, Alf desperate for his brother to see how self-aggrandizing he'd become, pleading for him to see reason. But Douglas would not be swayed.

The day of the opening arrived. Ever the professional, Alf checked and rechecked the apparatus, determined that his brother should shine.

Douglas paced around backstage, taking swigs from his hip flask, Alf's words echoing inside his head. Who was his brother to tell him how to behave? What did *he* know about being a magician? A mere assistant, a shadow . . . He took another swig, preparing for the performance of his life, eyes blurry, sweating profusely, the doves inside his waistcoat damp.

The curtain rose and the packed auditorium fell silent, the spectators eager to see the famous Douglas!

Douglas walked forward into the spotlight, looking out into the sea of faces and . . .

Stumbled.

At first the audience thought it was part of the act – a joke; an affectation, perhaps. But they soon realized that this was a man who was currently one part magician to nineteen parts gin.

Douglas staggered on as Alf stood wincing in the wings, the Magic Circle members becoming increasingly restless.

'We can see how you're doing it!' heckled a bespectacled young lad called Ernest in the back of the stalls.

'Go back to the bar!' shouted one angry lady, furious not only with the cack-handed display on stage, but with the guy who'd dragged her out on this 'date' in the first place.

'You're a nobody!' shouted another mysterious figure in box five.

Alf watched, helpless, as his brother pushed on, fumbling card flourishes, teetering around, eventually dropping the rabbit that had been stowed in his top hat.

All of a sudden Douglas turned to look at his brother in the wings – the crowd now jeering at him savagely, calling him to get off in an amalgamation of boos and shrieks. Douglas threw down the handkerchief he'd been stuffing into his fist, along with the egg he'd been hiding, which had been specially hollowed out to secretly contain the handkerchief once inside the hand but which wouldn't usually be handled in such a clumsy way.

He stumbled over to the wings, his legs criss-crossing wildly as he approached his brother, his bloodshot eyes full of hate, a touch of regret perhaps, either way with a suitably gin-infused glaze. Grabbing Alf by the collar, he dragged him out on to the stage into the light, the crowd now frantic, appalled to see someone they had once revered so highly self-destruct in such a brazen, exhaustingly pitiful way.

Alf tried to resist, but his brother was too strong. 'My wondsssserful baby brotherrr!' Douglas slurred.

'Leave him alone!' cried the audience.

'Bring the curtain down!' someone bayed from the gods.

'Oi, you – the brother – show us a trick!' shouted the bespectacled youth at the back of the stalls.

How or why this particular comment got Douglas's attention amid everything else that was going on, Alf never knew, but before he knew it, Douglas had plonked him centre stage, his arms open wide, in a mocking pose. 'Be my guest!' spat Douglas snidely, goading Alf. 'It's been a long time, hasn't it, little brother!'

The audience fell silent, all eyes now on the diminutive figure of Alf Rattlebag.

He peered out, blinded by the spotlights – though he could sense the eyes on him, watching, waiting. There was an electric hum in the air, an anticipation . . . Could this possibly be the moment he'd been waiting for all his life? A chance to shine? But how had it come to this?

He blinked, trying to quell his doubts.

Slowly, deliberately, Alf picked up the handkerchief and the egg. He placed the egg in his left fist, and slowly began to push the handkerchief inside the hollowed-out middle. He clicked his fingers, opening his hand – and a dove flew out over the audience, cooing. Everyone remained silent as the bird flew into the upper gallery.

Keep going – keep going, Alf!

He moved to the table and picked up some cards hidden under the mess Douglas had left. Fanning out the cards with one hand, he made a swift upward gesture – the fan vanishing instantly. The audience breathed in. Slowly, one at a time, cards started appearing in Alf's other hand, creating a new fan, until finally all the cards had swapped over. The audience breathed out, applauding. Instantly Alf crushed the new fan between his palms, the cards falling to the floor, transforming mid-air into a flurry of red rose petals. The audience cheered.

Keep going!

Alf picked up the top hat. He waved Douglas's wand deftly through the air and produced one, two, three rabbits, a fox, a heron, a stream of multi-coloured silks and – finally – a twelve-foot ladder. The audience had never seen anything like it!

More! More!

Douglas couldn't bear it. He edged towards the wings, a knot of pain growing in his temples. It was ... It was like he didn't *exist*. No one was watching; no one cared about him any more. His brother was now producing live goldfish from the end of a cane and placing them kindly in a fish bowl. Everyone was on their feet, whooping and cheering. *Where has this guy been hiding?* they screamed.

Alf placed a silk scarf over the fish bowl and closed his eyes. Steadily the bowl began to rise up, floating high above the stage and taking on a life of its own, pulling Alf from side to side as he held on to the ends of the scarf. With a final swish, he whipped away the cloth – the bowl had vanished!

He stood there motionless, spent, his eyes filling with tears as the crowd chanted out his name – 'Alf! Alf! Alf!' It was thunderous. It was like nothing he'd ever experienced. It was the greatest moment of his life.

Alf took a step back as the curtain began to cascade down from the flies. It touched the floorboards, and for a brief period the chanting was muffled – though it hadn't stopped.

The curtain rose, and once more Alf basked in the cheers. He watched as the giant piece of cloth dropped once more.

Still the crowd cheered from behind the thick fabric, waiting for another curtain call.

Suddenly, from behind, Douglas's warm hands groped around Alf's neck, fingers digging into the flesh, squeezing his windpipe. Alf tried to turn, clawing at the tentacles around his neck, but his older brother had always been stronger.

Tighter and tighter, Alf could feel Douglas's nails scratching deep inside his skin, burning the lining of his throat. He tried to grab hold of the curtain, to get help, but the audience cheered on from the other side, completely oblivious.

Douglas could feel the pathetic man's insides begin to squirm as his unyielding grip intensified, Alf's heart begging for more oxygen, a final attempt at resistance. But his brother's hold was unrelenting – until, with a pop,

Alf's neck snapped, the sound ringing in his ears . . . and then . . . nothing.

The curtain began to rise once again. The audience fell silent at the sight of Alf sprawled across the floor, his head at an impossible angle, eyes bulging.

From the back of the room, the angry lady who was on the date screamed and fainted – her beau catching her in his arms just in time, resulting in their early marriage the following year. Only to lead to a horrific, phenomenally unamicable and spectacularly drawn-out divorce.

And that is the story of Douglas and Alf.

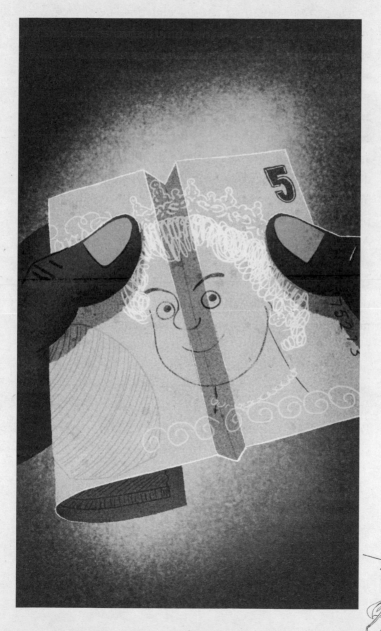

4. DAVENPORT'S MAGIC STUDIO

So. Davenport's. Lovely place. Little magic shop located beneath Charing Cross Station which has been open for about a hundred years (not continuously, mind!!!! *laughs so hard is actually physically sick*). It deals in magic tricks and books, and would be idyllic if it weren't for the constant smell of – there's no nice way to put this – *urine* around the place. Fortunately the shop has a thick, airtight door and so – providing no magician deliberately empties his or her bladder mid-shop – the ammonia-rich gas mostly remains outside. Apart from when the door opens, that is. Anyway, Davenport's is a family-run business. The youngest member (Alton) is a sort of half-magician/half-salesman hybrid, always hovering behind the counter trying to sell you his latest wares (if he can find them) but not quite proficient enough to show them off. It's fun to pop in and ask Alton for a demonstration of the latest piece of fiddly paraphernalia – to see his jaw drop. In fact, popping in to annoy Alton is arguably a rite of passage for any young magician. So why not pay Alton a visit! DISCLAIMER: Please don't *ever* pay Alton a visit – he's wholly fictitious! The shop, however, is real.

5. ANY CARD AT ANY NUMBER (ACAAN)

Let's examine this perplexing piece of card magic by imagining it is a question in a GCSE maths paper. WHY NOT?

A magician – let's call him David Berglas – opens a deck of playing cards and places them on the table. He turns to the person on his left – let's call her Sharon Baron – and asks her to name any playing card. Sharon names the five of diamonds.

Mr Berglas then turns to his right and asks a stout gentleman to name any number between 1 and 52. The man, who we shall refer to as Tadaaki Ogunyinka, chooses the number 29.

David then counts openly, slowly and fairly to the 29th card in the deck – which has been in full view of Sharon and Tadaaki all the time. He rotates his wrist gradually, revealing that the card in the 29th position is indeed the five of diamonds. Tadaaki bangs his forehead in disbelief as Sharon exclaims in amazement.

David Berglas exits the room, pleased, leaving the cards to be fully examined.

This effect is called Any Card At Any Number (ACAAN) and is arguably the Holy Grail of card magic, mainly because of its limiting *conditions*. David Berglas insisted that only a normal deck of cards was used, that there were no stooges (so Sharon and Tadaaki are both completely normal) and that their choices of both playing card and position in the deck were completely free – no forces of any kind. And no spurious or fiddly moves – natch!

Of course, it could just be down to pure chance: Mr Berglas could just have got lucky that evening. Even then, the statistics are deceptive. It's easy to assume that, given there are two independent variables at play (namely the choice of playing card *and* the choice of position in the deck), this isn't merely a 1 in 52 problem. That by giving part of the decision to Sharon and then part to Tadaaki, we're complicating the effect further, making this a 1 in 52 problem multiplied by a 1 in 52 problem (a 1 in 2,704 problem in fact).

However, the truth is that regardless of Sharon and Tadaaki, the five of diamonds can still only lie in 1 of 52 positions in the deck – just as the likelihood of shuffling a deck of cards into an order that goes ace through to king across the suits (making it look rather pretty) is just the same as that of shuffling it into any other specific order.

It's wholly counter-intuitive, though – and David would often play up (or, more correctly speaking, play *down*) the fact that this was actually just a 1 in 52 dilemma which – statistically at least – can actually work 1 in 52 times. Which isn't bad if – like David – you gig a lot. Though hardly failsafe.

Still, there must be a way of increasing the odds, because – somehow – David managed to succeed *every single time he performed the effect* – which still stumps magicians to this day. How do you meet fair conditions while staying true to the effect? There's no compromise, there's no real room for improvement, it's too pure and straightforward an idea. It's almost *too* impossible ... Of course countless magicians have since tried to recreate the effect, but none as openly fair as David's. Perhaps it's just a thing of myth.

Acknowledgements

Huge, huge thanks to the children's fiction department at Penguin Random House who have somehow made it possible for me to pass as a children's author (I hope!).

Extra-special thanks to Ruth Knowles, Mainga Bhima, Annie Eaton, Dominica Clements, Rosamund Hutchison and Wendy Shakespeare. It's fair to say that this book wouldn't have been realized (nor delivered on time!) without their constant enthusiasm, good humour and advice. Thank you, all of you. It's been so much fun – and apologies once again for the ever-shifting deadlines! We're there though now, right? RIGHT?!

I owe a huge amount to Glenn Thomas who has taken the strange descriptions of things in my head and made them into something infinitely more plausible and enjoyable on the page!

To my agent Robert Kirby at United Agents for making it all so seamless. And to Kitty, Carly and Hannah B too for their endless support.

To my family and friends who have had to endure the refrain 'pick a card' for the past thousand years!

To those at the Northern Magic Circle and Bradford Magic Circle who have nurtured and inspired me – I think you all know who you are. Some of you are no longer with us, which might make reading this somewhat tricky, but I'm convinced you of all people will find a way! THANK YOU.

And finally to B, b, F and PD who are my absolute everything.

HOUDINI'S 21-CARD TRICK

DID YOU KNOW...

... in 1904 Houdini escaped from a Washington D.C. prison? Not only that but on his way out he managed to shuffle several other prisoners around so that they were all in different cells by the end! To celebrate this piece of mystifying and MAGICAL mayhem, here is HOUDINI'S 21-CARD TRICK!

♣ The year is 1904 and Houdini finds himself in a Washington D.C. prison, along with 20 other inmates. To start, take 21 cards from your deck – we'll be using those.

♥ Shuffle the 21 cards and then deal them into three columns of seven cards. That's three cells, seven inmates per cell. You need to ensure that you lay out the cards row by row – across then down, not down then across!

♠ Ask one of your avid audience members to mentally choose which card they wish to represent Houdini and to let you know in which 'cell' he is currently being held.

♣ Stack the 'cells' into three piles, then place them into a single stack (making sure Houdini's 'cell' goes in the middle). Deal them out into three columns of seven cards again.

♥ Ask the audience member in which of the 'cells' Houdini now resides. Is it a different cell? That Houdini is a tricky customer! If it's not a different cell then maybe Houdini is finding it more difficult to escape than usual!

♠ Repeat steps 4, 5 and 6 one last time, just to see if you can catch Houdini out!

♣ Aha! No one could contain the great Harry Houdini! Count out the cards – dealing a card for each letter – using the one word that describes all of Houdini's escapes: I-M-P-O-S-S-I-B-L-E! The next card after the letter E will be the card your audience member selected to represent Houdini.

♥ **HE'S ESCAPED!**

THE **YOUNG**
MAGICIANS
AND THE
THIEVES' ALMANAC

WHICH YOUNG MAGICIAN ARE YOU?

Take this quiz to find out which character you are most like!

Your preferred form of magic is . . .

A. Card tricks – they're logical, satisfying and you don't have to look anyone in the eye . . .

B. Vanishing tricks – you're one of the best pickpockets in London (but always put things back).

C. Mentalism – you have the niftiest hypnosis skills around.

D. You're still getting the hang of it, but you love combining magic with science – all you need is a glass jar filled with water and a box of matchsticks . . .

If you weren't a magician, you would be . . .

A. Doing something solitary that doesn't involve talking to many people . . . Perhaps in an office . . .

B. In musical theatre. You're a natural showman and can do a pretty mean rendition of *Les Misérables*.

C. Nonsense! You couldn't imagine not being a magician.

D. A mad scientist!

On a Saturday afternoon, where are you most likely to be found?

A. In your bedroom, worrying about how to perfect your latest trick.

B. Pretending to be practising the clarinet but actually learning how to make it vanish entirely.

C. Walking through the Lake District, making a mental note of the name, circumference and depth of each and every lake.

D. Hanging out with your granddad, trying to glean as much magical wisdom from him as possible.

What is your most prized possession?

A. Your well-thumbed edition of *Expert Card Technique* – perfect for learning new skills AND keeping your face hidden in social situations.

B. Your watch – sneaking around and uncovering secrets requires excellent time-keeping.

C. Material possessions don't carry much weight with you. Your mind is all you need!

D. Your rucksack, crammed full of magical and scientific apparatus.

Your hidden skill is . . .

A. You can pick a lock more quickly than most people can say 'Abracadabra'.

B. Your logical thinking can solve even the most perplexing of mind puzzles.

C. Lip-reading. You once caught every word of a private conversation while wearing headphones and listening to a particularly loud rendition of Beethoven's Ninth Symphony . . .

D. You're a maths whizz and understand angles well enough to create a zip-line from the Magic Circle all the way to Buckingham Palace (hypothetically, of course).

Mostly A:

You are Alex – you don't say much and are scared of pretty much everything, but you have fantastic attention to detail and are always there to help a friend in need.

Mostly B:

You are Zack – you're confident and outgoing, a quick thinker and can divert people's attention like no other.

Mostly C:

You are Sophie – you're fiercely intelligent and fearless and have the power to bend even the most resistant of minds.

Mostly D:

You are Jonny – you're relatively inexperienced (not to mention reckless!) when it comes to mixing magic and science, but your creativity can lead to some spectacular results.

Your story starts here . . .

Do you **love books** and
discovering new stories?
Then **www.puffin.co.uk**
is the place for you . . .

- Thrilling adventures, fantastic fiction
  and laugh-out-loud fun

- Brilliant videos featuring your favourite authors
  and characters

- Exciting competitions, news, activities,
  the Puffin blog and SO MUCH more . . .

It all started with a Scarecrow

Puffin is over seventy years old.
Sounds ancient, doesn't it? But Puffin has never been
so lively. We're always on the lookout for the next big
idea, which is how it began all those years ago.

Penguin Books was a big idea from the mind of
a man called Allen Lane, who in 1935 invented
the quality paperback and changed the world.
**And from great Penguins, great Puffins grew,
changing the face of children's books forever.**

The first four Puffin Picture Books were hatched in 1940 and the
first Puffin story book featured a man with broomstick arms called
Worzel Gummidge. In 1967 Kaye Webb, Puffin Editor, started the
Puffin Club, promising to **'make children into readers'**.
She kept that promise and over 200,000 children became devoted
Puffineers through their quarterly instalments of *Puffin Post*.

Many years from now, we hope you'll look back and
remember Puffin with a smile. **No matter what your age
or what you're into, there's a Puffin for everyone.**
The possibilities are endless, but one thing is for sure:
whether it's a picture book or a paperback, a sticker book
or a hardback, **if it's got that little Puffin
on it – it's bound to be good.**

www.puffin.co.uk